BEAUTIFUL JOE

AN AUTOBIOGRAPHY

By MARSHALL SAUNDERS

Author of

"For the Other Boy's Sake, and Other Stories,"
"The Girl from Vermont," "My Pets,"
"The House of Armour," etc.

WITH AN INTRODUCTION

By HEZEKIAH BUTTERWORTH

Of "Youth's Companion"

PHILADELPHIA

THE JUDSON PRESS

BOSTON   CHICAGO   LOS ANGELES
KANSAS CITY   SEATTLE   TORONTO

PRINTED IN U. S. A.

TO

George Thorndike Angell

PRESIDENT OF THE AMERICAN HUMANE EDUCATION
SOCIETY, THE MASSACHUSETTS SOCIETY FOR THE PRE-
VENTION OF CRUELTY TO ANIMALS, AND THE PARENT
AMERICAN BAND OF MERCY, 19 MILK STREET, BOSTON
THIS BOOK IS RESPECTFULLY DEDICATED
BY THE AUTHOR

PREFACE

Beautiful Joe was a real dog, and "Beautiful Joe" was his real name. He belonged during the first part of his life to a cruel master, who mutilated him in the manner described in the story. He was rescued from him, and lived for many years in a happy home with pleasant surroundings, where he enjoyed a wide local celebrity.

The character of Laura is drawn from life, and to the smallest detail is truthfully depicted. The Morris family has its counterparts in real life, and nearly all of the incidents of the story are founded on fact.

THE AUTHOR.

INTRODUCTION

The wonderfully successful book, entitled " Black Beauty," came like a living voice out of the animal kingdom. But it spake for the horse, and made other books necessary; it led the way. After the ready welcome that it received, and the good it has accomplished and is doing, it followed naturally that some one should be inspired to write a book to interpret the life of a dog to the humane feeling of the world. Such a story we have in " Beautiful Joe."

The story speaks not for the dog alone, but for the whole animal kingdom. Through it we enter the animal world, and are made to see as animals see, and to feel as animals feel. The sympathetic sight of the author, in this interpretation, is ethically the strong feature of the book.

Such a book as this is one of the needs of our progressive system of education. The day-school, the Sunday school, and all libraries for the young, demand the influence that shall *teach* the reader *how* to live in sympathy with the animal world; how to understand the languages of the creatures that we have long been accustomed to call " dumb," and the sign-language of the lower order of these dependent beings. The church owes it to her

mission to preach and to teach the enforcement
of the "bird's-nest commandment"; the principle
recognized by Moses in the Hebrew world, and
echoed by Cowper in English poetry, and Burns
in the "Meadow Mouse," and by our own Longfel-
low in songs of many keys.

Kindness to the animal kingdom is the first, or
a first, principle in the growth of true philanthropy.
Young Lincoln once waded across a half-frozen
river to rescue a dog, and stopped in a walk with
a statesman to put back a bird that had fallen out
of its nest. Such a heart was trained to be a leader
of men, and to be crucified for a cause. The
conscience that runs to the call of an animal
in distress is girding itself with power to do
manly work in the world.

The story of "Beautiful Joe" awakens an intense interest, and sustains it through a series of
vivid incidents and episodes, each of which is
a lesson. The story merits the widest circulation,
and the universal reading and response accorded
to "Black Beauty." To circulate it is to do good;
to help the human heart as well as the creatures
of quick feelings and simple language.

When, as one of the committee to examine the
manuscripts offered for prizes to the Humane Society, I read the story, I felt that the writer had
a higher motive than to compete for a prize; that
the story was a stream of sympathy that flowed
from the heart; that it was genuine; that it only
needed a publisher who should be able to com-

mand a wide influence, to make its merits known, to give it a strong educational mission.

I am pleased that the manuscript has found such a publisher, and am sure that the issue of the story will honor the Publication Society. In the development of the book, I believe that the humane cause has stood above any speculative thought or interest. The book comes because it is called for; the times demand it. I think that the publishers have a right to ask for a little un-selfish service on the part of the public in helping to give it a circulation commensurate with its opportunity, need, and influence.

HEZEKIAH BUTTERWORTH.

(One of the committee of readers of the prize stories offered to the Humane Society.)

BOSTON, MASS., December, 1893.

CONTENTS

BEAUTIFUL JOE

CHAPTER I

ONLY A CUR

Y name is Beautiful Joe, and I am a brown dog of medium size. I am called Beautiful Joe, but not because I am a beauty. Mr. Morris, the clergyman, in whose family I have lived for the last twelve years, says that he thinks I must be called Beautiful Joe for the same reason that his grandfather, down South, called a very ugly colored slave lad Cupid, and his mother Venus.

I do not know what he means by that, but when he says it, people always look at me and smile. I know that I am not beautiful, and I know that I am not well-bred. I am only a cur.

When my mistress went every year to register me and pay my tax, and the man in the office asked what breed I was, she said part fox-terrier and part bull-terrier; but he always put me down a cur. I don't think she liked having him call me a cur; still, I have heard her say that she preferred curs, for they have more character than well-bred dogs. Her father said that she liked ugly dogs for the same reason that a nobleman at the court of a certain king did—namely, that no one else would.

I am an old dog now, and am writing, or rather getting a friend to write, the story of my life. I have seen my mistress laughing and crying over a little book that she says is a story of a horse's life, and sometimes she puts the book down close to my nose to let me see the pictures.

I love my dear mistress; I can say no more than that; I love her better than any one else in the world; and I think it will please her if I write the story of a dog's life. She loves dumb animals, and it always grieves her to see them treated cruelly.

I have heard her say that if all the boys and girls in the world were to rise up and say that there should be no more cruelty to animals, they could put a stop to it. Perhaps it will help a little if I tell a story. I am fond of boys and girls, and though I have seen many cruel men and women, I have seen few cruel children. I think the more stories there are written about dumb animals, the better it will be for us.

In telling my story, I think I had better begin at the first and come right on to the end. I was born in a stable on the outskirts of a small town in Maine called Fairport. The first thing I remember was lying close to my mother and being very snug and warm. The next thing I remember was being always hungry. I had a number of brothers and sisters—six in all—and my mother never had enough milk for us. She was always half starved herself, so she could not feed us properly.

I am very unwilling to say much about my early life. I have lived so long in a family where there is never a harsh word spoken, and where no one thinks of ill-treating anybody or anything, that it seems almost wrong even to think or speak of such a matter as hurting a poor dumb beast.

The man that owned my mother was a milk-man. He kept one horse and three cows, and he had a shaky old cart in which he used to put his milk-cans. I don't think there can be a worse man in the world than that milkman. It makes me shudder to think of him. His name was Jenkins, and I am glad to think that he is getting punished now for his cruelty to poor dumb animals and to human beings. If you think it is wrong that I am glad, you must remember that I am only a dog.

The first notice that he took of me when I was a little puppy, just able to stagger about, was to give me a kick that sent me into a corner of the stable. He used to beat and starve my mother. I have seen him use his heavy whip to punish her till her body was covered with blood. When I got older I asked her why she did not run away. She said she did not wish to but I soon found

out that the reason she did not run away was
because she loved Jenkins. Cruel and savage as
he was, she yet loved him, and I believe she
would have laid down her life for him.

Now that I am old, I know that there are more
men in the world like Jenkins. They are not
crazy, they are not drunkards; they simply seem
to be possessed with a spirit of wickedness. There
are well-to-do people, yes, and rich people, who
will treat animals, and even little children, with
such terrible cruelty, that one cannot even mention the things of which they are guilty.

One reason for Jenkins' cruelty was his idleness.
After he went his rounds in the morning with his
milk-cans, he had nothing to do till late in the
afternoon but take care of his stable and yard. If
he had kept them neat, and groomed his horse,
and cleaned the cows, and dug up the garden, it
would have taken up all his time; but he never
tidied the place at all, till his yard and stable got
so littered up with things he threw down, that he
could not make his way about.

His house and stable stood in the middle of a
large field, and they were at some distance from
the road. Passers-by could not see how untidy
the place was. Occasionally a man came to look
at the premises and see that they were in good
order, but Jenkins always knew when to expect
him and had things cleaned up a little.

I used to wish that some of the people that took
milk from him would come and look at his cows.

In the spring and summer he drove them out to pasture, but during the winter they stood all the time in the dirty dark stable where the chinks in the wall were so big that the snow swept through almost in drifts. The ground was always muddy and wet; there was only one small window on the north side, where the sun shone in for a short time in the afternoon.

They were very unhappy cows, but they stood patiently and never complained, though sometimes I knew they must have nearly frozen in the bitter winds that blew through the stable on winter nights. They were lean and poor, and were never in good health. Besides being cold they were fed on very poor food.

Jenkins used to come home nearly every afternoon with a great tub in the back of his cart that was full of what he called "peelings." It was kitchen stuff that he asked the cooks at the different houses where he delivered milk to save for him. They threw decayed vegetables, fruit parings, and scraps from the table into a tub, and gave them to him at the end of a few days. A sour, nasty mess it always was, and not fit to give any creature.

Sometimes, when he had not many "peelings," he would go to town and get a load of old vegetables, that grocers were glad to have taken off their hands.

This food, together with poor hay, made the cows give very poor milk, and Jenkins used to pur some white powder in it, to give it "body," as he said.

Once a very sad thing happened about the milk that no one knew of but Jenkins and his wife. She was a poor, unhappy creature, very frightened of her husband, and not daring to speak much to him. She was not a clean woman, and I never saw a worse-looking house than she kept.

She used to do very queer things, that I know now housekeepers should not do. I have seen her catch up the broom to pound potatoes in the pot. She pounded with the handle, and the broom would fly up and down in the air. dropping dust into the pot where the potatoes were. Her pan of soft-mixed bread she often left uncovered in the kitchen, and sometimes the hens walked in and sat in it.

The children used to play in mud-puddles about the door. It was the youngest of them that sickened with some kind of fever early in the spring, before Jenkins began driving the cows out to pasture. The child was very ill, and Mrs. Jenkins wanted to send for a doctor, but her husband would not let her. They made a bed in the kitchen, close to the stove, and Mrs. Jenkins nursed the child as best she could. She did all her work near-by, and I saw her several times wiping the child's face with the cloth that she used for washing her milk-pans.

Nobody knew outside the family that the little girl was ill. Jenkins had such a bad name, that none of his neighbors would visit them. By and by the child got well, and a week or two later Jenkins came home with quite a frightened face, and told his wife that the husband of one of his customers was very ill with typhoid fever.

After a time the gentleman died, and the cook told Jenkins that the doctor wondered how he could have taken the fever, for there was not a case in town.

There was a widow left with three orphans, and they never knew that they had to blame a dirty, careless milkman for taking a kind husband and father from them.

CHAPTER II

I HAVE said that Jenkins spent most of his days in idleness. He had to start out very early in the morning, in order to supply his customers with milk for breakfast. Oh, how ugly he always was, when he came into the stable on cold winter mornings, before the sun was up.

He would hang his lantern on a hook, and get his milking-stool, and if the cows did not step aside just to suit him, he would seize a broom or fork, and beat them cruelly.

My mother and I slept on a heap of straw in the corner of the stable, and when she heard his step in the morning she always roused me, so that we could run out as soon as he opened the stable-door. He always aimed a kick at us as we passed, but my mother taught me how to dodge him.

After he finished milking, he took the pails of milk up to the house for Mrs. Jenkins to strain and put in the cans, and he came back and harnessed his horse to the cart. His horse was called Toby, and a poor, miserable, broken-down creature he was. He was weak in the knees, and weak in the back, and weak all over, and Jenkins had to beat him all the time to make him go. He had been a cab-horse, and his mouth had been jerked, and twisted, and sawed at, till one would think there could be no feeling left in it; still I have seen him wince and curl up his lip when Jenkins thrust in the frosty bit on a winter's morning.

Poor old Toby! I used to lie on my straw sometimes and wonder he did not cry out with pain. Cold and half-starved he always was in the wintertime, and often with raw sores on his body that Jenkins would try to hide by putting bits of cloth under the harness. But Toby never murmured, and he never tried to kick and bite, and he minded the least word from Jenkins, and if he swore at him, Toby would start back, or step up quickly; he was so anxious to please him.

After Jenkins had put him in the cart, and lifted in the cans, he would set out on his rounds. My mother, whose name was Jess, always went with him. I used to ask her why she followed such a brute of a man, and she would hang her head, and say that sometimes she got a bone from the different houses they stopped at. But that was not the whole reason. She liked Jenkins so much that she wanted to be with him.

I had not her sweet and patient disposition, and I would not go with her. I watched her out of sight, and then ran up to the house to see if Mrs. Jenkins had any scraps for me. I nearly always got something, for she pitied me, and often gave me a kind word or look with the bits of food that she threw to me.

When Jenkins came home, I often coaxed mother to run about and see some of the neighbors' dogs with me. But she never would, and I would not leave her. So, from morning to night we had to sneak about, keeping out of Jenkins' way as much as we could, and yet trying to keep him in sight. He always sauntered around with a pipe in his mouth, and his hands in his pockets, growling first at his wife and children, and then at his dumb creatures.

I have not told what became of my brothers and sisters. One rainy day, when we were eight weeks old, Jenkins, followed by two or three of his ragged, dirty children, came into the stable and looked at us. Then he began to swear because we were so ugly, and said if we had been good-looking, he might have sold some of us. Mother watched him anxiously, and fearing that some danger threatened her puppies, ran and jumped in the middle of us, and looked pleadingly up at him.

It only made him swear the more. He took one pup after another, and right there, before his children and my poor distracted mother, put an end to their lives. It was very terrible. My mother ran up and down the stable screaming with pain, and I lay weak and trembling, and expecting every instant that my turn would come next. I don't know why he spared me. I was the only one left.

His children cried, and he sent them out of the stable and went out himself. Mother picked up all the puppies and brought them to our bed in the straw and licked them, and tried to bring them back to life, but it was of no use. They were quite dead. We had them in our corner of the stable for some days, till Jenkins discovered them, and swearing horribly at us, he took his stable-fork and threw them out in the yard, and put some earth over them.

My mother never seemed the same after this. She was weak and miserable, and though she was only four years old, she seemed like an old dog. This was on account of the poor food that had been fed to her. She could not run after Jenkins, and she lay on our heap of straw, only turning over with her nose the scraps of food I brought her to eat. One day she licked me gently, wagged her tail, and died.

As I sat by her, feeling lonely and miserable, Jenkins came into the stable. I could not bear to look at him. He had killed my mother. There she lay, a little, gaunt, scarred creature, starved and worried to death by him. Her mouth was half open, her eyes were staring. She would never again look kindly at me, or curl up to me at night to keep me warm. Oh, how I hated her murderer! But I sat quietly, even when he went up and turned her over with his foot to see if she

was really dead. I think he was a little sorry, for
he turned scornfully toward me and said: "She
was worth two of you; why didn't you go instead?"

Still I kept quiet till he walked up to me and
kicked at me. My heart was nearly broken and I
could stand no more. I flew at him and gave him
a savage bite on the ankle.

"Oho," he said, "so you are going to be a
fighter, are you? I'll fix you for that." His face
was red and furious. He seized me by the back
of the neck and carried me out to the yard where
a log lay on the ground. "Bill," he called to one
of his children, "bring me the hatchet."

He laid my head on the log and pressed one
hand on my struggling body. I was now a year
old and a full-sized dog. There was a quick,
dreadful pain, and he had cut off my ear, not in
the way they cut puppies' ears, but close to my
head, so close that he cut off some of the skin
beyond it. Then he cut off the other ear, and
turning me swiftly round, although I struggled
desperately, cut off my tail close to my body.

Then he let me go, and stood looking at me as
I rolled on the ground and yelped in agony. He
was in such a passion that he did not realize that
people passing by on the road might hear me.

CHAPTER III

HERE was a young man going by on a bicycle. He heard my screams, and springing off his wheel, came hurrying up the path, and stood among us before Jenkins caught sight of him.

In the midst of my pain, I heard him say fiercely, "What have you been doing to that dog?"

"I've been cuttin' his ears for fightin', my young gentleman," said Jenkins. "There's no law to prevent that, is there?"

"And there is no law to prevent my giving you a thrashing," said the young man angrily. In a trice, he had seized Jenkins by the throat, and was pounding him with all his might. Mrs. Jenkins came and stood at the house door, crying, but she made no effort to help her husband.

"Bring me a towel," the young man cried to her, after he had stretched Jenkins, bruised and frightened, on the ground. She snatched off her apron, and ran down with it, and the young man wrapped me in it, and taking me carefully in his arms, walked down the path to the gate. There were some little boys standing there watching

25

him, their mouths wide open with astonishment. "Sonny," he said to the largest of them, "if you will come behind and carry this dog, I will give you a quarter."

The boy took me, and we set out. I was all smothered up in the apron and moaning with pain, but still I looked out occasionally to see which way we were going. We took the road to the town, and stopped in front of a house on Washington Street. The young man leaned his bicycle up against the house, took a quarter from his pocket, and put it in the boy's hand. Then he lifted me gently in his arms and went up a lane leading to the back of the house.

There was a small stable there. He went into it, put me down on the floor, and uncovered my body. Some boys were playing about the stable, and I heard them say in horrified tones, "Oh! Cousin Harry, what is the matter with that dog?"

"Hush," he said. "Don't make a fuss. You, Jack, go down to the kitchen and ask Mary for a basin of warm water and a sponge, and don't let your mother or Laura hear you."

A few minutes later, the young man had bathed my bleeding ears and tail, and had rubbed something on them that was cool and pleasant, and had bandaged them firmly with strips of cotton. I felt much better, and was able to look about me.

I was in a small stable, that was evidently not used for a stable, but more for a play-room. There were various kinds of toys scattered about,

and a swing and bar, such as boys love to twist
about on, were in two of the corners. In a box
against the wall was a guinea-pig, which looked at
me in an interested way. This guinea-pig's name
was Jeff, and he and I became good friends. A
long-haired French rabbit was hopping about, and
a tame white rat was perched on the shoulder
of one of the boys, and kept his foothold there, no
matter how suddenly the boy moved. There were
so many boys, and the stable was so small, that
I suppose he was afraid he would get stepped on
if he went on the floor. He stared hard at me with
his little red eyes, and never even glanced at a
queer-looking gray cat that was watching me
from her bed in the back of the vacant horse-
stall. Out in the sunny yard, some pigeons were
pecking at grain and a spaniel lay asleep by
the fence.

I had never seen anything like this before, and
my wonder at it almost drove the pain away.
Mother and I always chased rats and birds, and
once we killed a kitten. While I was puzzling
over it, one of the boys cried out, " Here comes
Laura ! "

" Take that rag out of the way," said Mr. Harry,
kicking aside the old apron I had been wrapped
in, and that was stained with my blood. One of
the boys stuffed it into a barrel, and then they all
looked toward the house.

A young girl, holding up one hand to shade her
eyes from the sun, was coming up the walk that

led from the house to the stable. I thought then, that I never had seen such a beautiful girl, and I think so still. She was tall and slender, and had lovely brown eyes and brown hair, and a sweet smile, and just to look at her was enough to make one love her. I stood in the stable-door, staring at her with all my might.

"Why, what a funny dog," she said, and stopped short to look at me. Up to this, I had not thought what a queer-looking sight I must be. Now I twisted around my head, saw the white bandage on my tail, and knowing I was not a fit spectacle for a pretty young lady like that, I slunk into a corner.

"Poor doggie, have I hurt your feelings?" she said, and with a sweet smile at the boys, she passed by them, and came up to the guinea-pig's box, behind which I had taken refuge. "What is the matter with your head, good dog?" she said curiously, as she stooped over me.

"He has a cold in it," said one of the boys with a laugh, "so we put a nightcap on." She drew back, and turned very pale. "Cousin Harry, there are drops of blood on this cotton. Who has hurt this dog?"

"Dear Laura," and the young man coming up, laid his hand on her shoulder, "he got hurt, and I have been bandaging him."

"Who hurt him?"

"I would rather not tell you."

"But I wish to know." Her voice was as gentle

as ever, but she spoke so decidedly that the young man was obliged to tell her everything. All the time he was speaking, she kept touching me gently with her fingers. When he had finished his account of rescuing me from Jenkins, she said quietly, " You will have the man punished, won't you? "

" What is the use? That won't stop him from being cruel."

" It will put a check on his cruelty."

" I don't think it would do any good," said the young man doggedly.

" Cousin Harry!" and the young girl stood up very straight and tall, her brown eyes flashing, and one hand pointing at me, " will you let that pass? That animal has been wronged, it looks to you to right it. The coward who has maimed it for life should be punished. A child has a voice to tell its wrongs—a poor, dumb creature must suffer in silence; in bitter, bitter silence. And," eagerly, as the young man tried to interrupt her, " you are doing the man himself an injustice. If he is bad enough to ill-treat his dog, he will ill-treat his wife and children. If he is checked and punished now for his cruelty, he may reform. And even if his wicked heart is not changed, he will be obliged to treat them with outward kindness, through fear of punishment."

The young man looked convinced, and almost as ashamed as if he had been the one to crop my ears. " What do you want me to do? " he said, slowly, looking sheepishly at the boys who were staring open-mouthed at him and the young girl.

The girl pulled a little watch from her belt. " I want you to report that man immediately. It is now five o'clock. I will go down to the police station with you, if you like."

" Very well," he said, his face brightening. And together they went off to the house.

CHAPTER IV

THE MORRIS BOYS ADD TO MY NAME

HE boys watched them out of sight, then one of them, whose name I afterward learned was Jack, and who came next to Miss Laura in age, gave a low whistle and said: "Doesn't the old lady come out strong when any one or anything gets abused? I'll never forget the day she found me setting Jim on that black cat of the Wilsons'. She scolded me, and then she cried, till I didn't know where to look. Plague on it, how was I going to know he'd kill the old cat? I only wanted to drive it out of the yard. Come on, let's look at the dog."

They all came and bent over me, as I lay on the floor in my corner. I wasn't much used to boys, and I didn't know how they would treat me. But I soon found by the way they handled me and talked to me that they knew a good deal about dogs, and were accustomed to treat them kindly. It seemed very strange to have them pat me and call me "good dog." No one had ever said that to me before today.

"He's not much of a beauty, is he?" said one of the boys, whom they called Tom.

"Not by a long shot," said Jack Morris, with

a laugh. "Not any nearer the beauty mark than yourself, Tom."

Tom flew at him, and they had a scuffle. The other boys paid no attention to them, but went on looking at me. One of them, a little boy with eyes like Miss Laura's, said, "What did Cousin Harry say the dog's name was?"

"Joe," answered another boy. "The little chap that carried him home, told him."

"We might call him 'Ugly Joe,' then," said a lad with a round, fat face and laughing eyes. I wondered very much who this boy was, and, later on, I found out that he was another of Miss Laura's brothers, and his name was Ned. There seemed to be no end to the Morris boys.

"I don't think Laura would like that," said Jack Morris, suddenly coming up behind him. He was very hot, and was breathing fast, but his manner was as cool as if he had never left the group about me. He had beaten Tom, who was sitting on a box ruefully surveying a hole in his jacket. "You see," he went on gaspingly, "if you call him 'Ugly Joe' her ladyship will say that you are wounding the dear dog's feelings. 'Beautiful Joe' would be more to her liking."

A shout went up from the boys. I didn't wonder that they laughed. Plain-looking, I naturally was, but hideous in those bandages.

"'Beautiful Joe,' then let it be!" they cried. "Let us go and tell mother, and ask her to give us something for our beauty to eat."

They all trooped out of the stable, and I was very sorry, for when they were with me I did not mind so much the tingling in my ears and the terrible pain in my back. They soon brought me some nice food, but I could not touch it; so they went away to their play, while I lay in my box, trembling with pain and wishing that the pretty young lady was there to stroke me with her gentle fingers.

By and by it got dark. The boys finished their play and went into the house, and I saw lights twinkling in the windows. I felt lonely and miserable in this strange place. I would not have gone back to Jenkins for the world, still it was the only home I had known, and though I felt that I should be happy here, I had not yet become used to the change. Then the pain all through my body was dreadful. My head seemed to be on fire, and there were sharp, darting pains up and down my back-bone. I did not dare to howl, lest I should make the big dog, Jim, angry. He was sleeping in a kennel out in the yard.

The stable was very quiet. Up in the loft above, some rabbits, that I had heard running about, had now gone to sleep. The guinea-pig was nestling in the corner of his box, and the cat and the tame rat had scampered into the house long ago.

At last I could bear the pain no longer. I sat up in my box and looked about me. I felt as if I was going to die, and, though I was very weak, there was something inside me that made me feel

c

as if I wanted to crawl away somewhere out of sight. I slunk out into the yard and along the stable wall, where there was a thick clump of raspberry bushes. I crept in among them and lay down on the damp earth. I tried to scratch off my bandages, but they were fastened on too firmly, and I could not do it. I thought about my poor mother, and wished she was here to lick my sore ears. Though she was so unhappy herself, she never wanted to see me suffer. If I had not disobeyed her I would not now be suffering so much pain. She had told me again and again not to snap at Jenkins, for it made him worse.

In the midst of my trouble I heard a soft voice calling, "Joe! Joe!" It was Miss Laura's voice, but I felt as if there were weights on my paws, and I could not go to her.

"Joe! Joe!" she said again. She was going up the walk to the stable, holding up a lighted lamp in her hand. She had on a white dress, and I watched her till she disappeared in the stable. She did not stay long in there. She came out and stood on the gravel. "Joe, Joe, Beautiful Joe, where are you? You are hiding somewhere, but I shall find you." Then she came right to the spot where I was. "Poor doggie," she said, stooping down and patting me. "Are you very miserable, and did you crawl away to die? I have had dogs do that before, but I am not going to let you die, Joe." And she set her lamp on the ground and took me in her arms.

I was very thin then, not nearly so fat as I am now, still I was quite an armful for her. But she did not seem to find me heavy. She took me right into the house, through the back door, and down a long flight of steps, across a hall, and into a snug kitchen.

"For the land sakes, Miss Laura," said a woman who was bending over a stove, "what have you got there?"

"A poor, sick dog, Mary," said Miss Laura, seating herself on a chair. "Will you please warm a little milk for him? And have you a box or a basket down here that he can lie in?"

"I guess so," said the woman; "but he's awful dirty; you're not going to let him sleep in the house, are you?"

"Only for tonight. He is **very** ill. A dreadful thing happened to him, Mary," and Miss Laura went on to tell her how my ears had been cut off.

"Oh, that's the dog the boys were talking about," said the woman. "Poor creature, he's welcome to all I can do for him." She opened a closet door and brought out a box, and folded a piece of blanket for me to lie on. Then she heated some milk in a saucepan and poured it in a saucer, and watched me while Miss Laura went up-stairs to get a little bottle of something that would make me sleep. They poured a few drops of this medicine into the milk and offered it to me. I lapped a little, but I could not finish it, even though Miss Laura coaxed me very gently to do so. She dipped her finger in the milk and held it out to me, and though I did not want it, I could not be ungrateful enough to refuse to lick her finger as often as she offered it to me. After the milk was gone, Mary lifted up my box and carried me into the washroom that was off the kitchen.

I soon fell sound asleep, and could not rouse myself through the night, though Miss Laura came to see me once or twice. Whenever there was a sick animal in the house, no matter if it was only the tame rat, she would get up two or three times in the night to see if there was anything she could do to make it more comfortable.

CHAPTER V

MY NEW HOME AND A SELFISH LADY

DON'T believe that a dog could fall into a happier home than I have had. In a week, thanks to good nursing, good food, and kind words, I was almost well. Mr. Harry washed and dressed my sore ears and tail every day till he went home, and one day he and the boys gave me a bath out in the stable. They carried out a tub of warm water and stood me in it. I had never been washed before in my life, and it felt very queer. Miss Laura stood by laughing and encouraging me not to mind the streams of water trickling all over me. I couldn't help wondering what Jenkins would have said if he could have seen me in that tub.

That reminds me to say that two days after I arrived, Jack, followed by all the other boys, came running into the stable. He had a newspaper in his hand, and with a great deal of laughing and joking read this to me:

"*Fairport Daily News,* June 3d. In the police court this morning, James Jenkins, for cruelly torturing and mutilating a dog, fined ten dollars and costs."

Then he said, "What do you think of that, Joe?

Five dollars apiece for your ears and your tail thrown in. That's all they're worth in the eyes of the law. Jenkins has had his fun and you'll go through life worth about three-quarters of a dog. I'd lash rascals like that. Tie them up and flog them till they were scarred and mutilated a little bit themselves. Just wait till I'm president; but there's some more, old fellow. Listen: 'Our reporter visited the house of the above-mentioned Jenkins and found a most deplorable state of affairs. The house, yard, and stable were indescribably filthy. His horse bears the marks of ill usage and is in an emaciated condition. His cows are plastered up with mud and filth, and are covered with vermin. Where is our health inspector, that he does not exercise a more watchful supervision over establishments of this kind? To allow milk from an unclean place like this to be sold in the town is endangering the health of its inhabitants. Upon inquiry it was found that the man Jenkins bears a very bad character. Steps are being taken to have his wife and children removed from him.'"

Jack threw the paper into my box, and he and the other boys gave three cheers for the *Fairport Daily News* and then ran away. How glad I was! It did not matter so much for me, for I had escaped him, but now that it had been found out what a cruel man he was, there would be a restraint upon him, and poor Toby and the cows would have a happier time.

I was going to tell about the Morris family. There were Mr. Morris, who was a clergyman and preached in a church in Fairport; Mrs. Morris, his wife; Miss Laura, who was the eldest of the family; then Jack, Ned, Carl, and Willie. I think one reason why they were such a good family was because Mrs. Morris was such a good woman. She loved her husband and children, and did everything she could to make them happy.

Mr. Morris was a very busy man and rarely interfered in household affairs. Mrs. Morris was the one who said what was to be done and what was not to be done. Even then, when I was a young dog, I used to think that she was very wise. There was never any noise or confusion in the house, and though there was a great deal of work to be done, everything went on smoothly and pleasantly, and no one ever got angry and scolded as they did in the Jenkins family.

Mrs. Morris was very particular about money matters. Whenever the boys came to her for money to get such things as candy and ice-cream, expensive toys and other things that boys often crave, she asked them why they wanted them. If it was for some selfish reason, she said firmly: " No, children, we are not rich people, and we must save our money for your education. I cannot buy you foolish things."

If they asked her for money for books or something to make their pet animals more comfortable, or for their outdoor games, she gave it to them willingly. Her ideas about the bringing up of children I cannot explain as clearly as she can herself, so I will give part of a conversation that she had with a lady who was calling on her shortly after I came to Washington Street.

I happened to be in the house at the time. Indeed, I used to spend the greater part of my time in the house. Jack one day looked at me and exclaimed, "Why does that dog stalk about, first after one and then after another, looking at us with such solemn eyes?"

I wished that I could speak to tell him that I had so long been used to seeing animals kicked about and trodden upon, that I could not get used to the change. It seemed too good to be true. I could scarcely believe that dumb animals had rights, but while it lasted, and human beings were so kind to me, I wanted to be with them all the time. Miss Laura understood. She drew my head up to her lap, and put her face down to me: "You like to be with us, don't you, Joe? Stay in the house as much as you like. Jack doesn't mind, though he speaks so sharply. When you get tired of us go out in the garden and have a romp with Jim."

But I must return to the conversation to which I have referred. It was one fine June day, and Mrs. Morris was sewing in a rocking-chair by the window. I was beside her, sitting on a hassock, so that I could look out into the street. Dogs love variety and excitement, and like to see what is going on out-of-doors, as well as human beings. A carriage drove up to the house, and a finely dressed lady got out and came up the steps.

Mrs. Morris seemed glad to see her, and called her Mrs. Montague. I was pleased with her, for she had some kind of perfume about her that I liked to smell, so I went and sat on the hearth-rug quite near her.

They had a little talk about things I did not understand, and then the lady's eyes fell on me. She looked at me through a bit of glass that was hanging by a chain from her neck, and pulled away her beautiful dress lest I should touch it.

I did not care any longer for the perfume, and went away and sat very straight and stiff at Mrs. Morris' feet. The lady's eyes still followed me.

"I beg your pardon, Mrs. Morris," she said; "but that is a very queer-looking dog you have there."

"Yes," said Mrs. Morris quietly, "he is not a handsome dog."

"And he is a new one, isn't he?" said Mrs. Montague.

"Yes."

"And that makes——"

"Two dogs, a cat, fifteen or twenty rabbits, a rat, about a dozen canaries, and two dozen gold-fish, I don't know how many pigeons, a few bantams, a guinea-pig, and—well, I don't think there are any more."

They both laughed, and Mrs. Montague said:

"You have quite a menagerie. My father would never allow one of his children to keep a pet animal. He said it would make his girls rough and noisy to romp about the house with cats, and his boys would look like rowdies if they went about with dogs at their heels."

"I have never found that it made my children rough to play with their pets," said Mrs. Morris.

"No, I should think not," said the lady languidly. "Your boys are the most gentlemanly lads in Fairport, and as for Laura, she is a perfect little lady. I like so much to have them come and see Charlie. They wake him up, and yet don't make him naughty."

"They enjoyed their last visit very much," said Mrs. Morris. "By the way, I have heard them talking about getting Charlie a dog."

"Oh," cried the lady, with a little shudder, "beg them not to. I cannot sanction that. I hate dogs."

"Why do you hate them?" asked Mrs. Morris gently.

"They are such dirty things, they always smell and have vermin on them."

"A dog," said Mrs. Morris, "is something like a child. If you want it clean and pleasant, you must keep it so. This dog's skin is as clean as yours or mine. Hold still, Joe," and she brushed the hair on my back the wrong way, and showed Mrs. Montague how pink and clean my skin was.

Mrs. Montague looked at me more kindly, and

even held out the tips of her fingers to me. I did not lick them. I only smelled them, and she drew her hand back again.

"You have never been brought in contact with the lower creation as I have," said Mrs. Morris; "just let me tell you, in a few words, what a help dumb animals have been to me in the upbringing of my children—my boys, especially. When I was a young married woman, going about the slums of New York with my husband, I used to come home and look at my two babies as they lay in their little cots, and say to him, 'What are we going to do to keep these children from selfishness —the curse of the world?'

"'Get them to do something for somebody besides themselves,' he always said. And I have tried to act on that principle. Laura is naturally unselfish. With her tiny, baby fingers, she would take food from her own mouth and put it into Jack's, if we did not watch her. I have never had any trouble with her. But the boys were born selfish, tiresomely, disgustingly selfish. They were good boys in many ways. As they grew older, they were respectful, obedient, they were not untidy, and not particularly rough, but their one thought was for themselves, and they used to quarrel with each other in regard to their rights. While we were in New York, we had only a small backyard. When we came here, I said, 'I am going to try an experiment.' We bought this house because it had a large garden, and a stable that would do for the

boys to play in. Then I got them together, and
said I was not pleased with the way in which
they were living. They did nothing for any one
but themselves from morning to night. If I
wanted them to do an errand for me, it was done
unwillingly. I asked them if they thought they
were going to make real, manly Christian boys at
this rate, and they said no. Then I proposed a
series of tasks. They all agreed to this, and told
me to allot the tasks. If I could have afforded it,
I would have bought a horse and cow, but I could
not do that, so I invested in a pair of rabbits for
Jack, a pair of canaries for Carl, pigeons for Ned,
and bantams for Willie. I brought these creatures
home, and told them to provide for them. They
were delighted with my choice, and it was very
amusing to see them scurrying about to provide
food and shelter for their pets, and hear their
consultations with other boys. The end of it all
is, that my boys, in caring for these dumb creatures, have become unselfish and thoughtful. They
would rather go to school without their own breakfast than have the inmates of the stable go hungry,
They are getting a heart education, added to the
intellectual education of their schools. Then it
keeps them at home. I used to be worried with
the lingering about the street corners, the dawdling
around with other boys, and the idle, often worse
than idle talk, indulged in. Now they are mer.
of business. They are always hammering at boxes
and partitions out there in the stable, or cleaning

up, and if they are sent out on an errand they do it and come right home. I don't mean to say that we have deprived them of liberty. They have their days for baseball, and football, and excursions to the woods, but they have so much to do at home that they won't go away unless for a specific purpose."

While Mrs. Morris was talking, her visitor leaned forward in her chair and listened attentively. When she finished, Mrs. Montague said quietly: "Thank you, I am glad that you told me this. I shall get Charlie a dog."

"I am pleased to hear you say that," replied Mrs. Morris. "It will be a good thing for your little boy. A child can learn many a lesson from a dog. This one," pointing to me, "might be held up as an example to many a human being. He is patient, quiet, and obedient. My husband says that he reminds him of three words in the Bible—'through much tribulation.'"

"Why does he say that?" asked Mrs. Montague curiously.

"Because he came to us from a very unhappy home," and Mrs. Morris went on to tell her friend what she knew of my early days.

When she stopped, Mrs. Montague's face was shocked and pained. "How dreadful to think that there are such creatures as that man Jenkins in the world. And you say that he has a wife and children. Mrs. Morris, tell me plainly, are there many such unhappy homes in Fairport?"

Mrs. Morris hesitated for a minute, then she said earnestly, "My dear friend, if you could see all the wickedness, and cruelty, and vileness that is practised in this little town of ours in one night you could not rest in your bed."

Mrs. Montague looked dazed. "I did not dream that it was as bad as that," she said. "Are we worse than other towns?"

"No, not worse, but bad enough. Over and over again the saying is true, one half the world does not know how the other half lives. How can all this misery touch you? You live in your lovely house out of the town. When you come in, you drive about, do your shopping, make calls, and go home again. You never visit the poorer streets. The people from them never come to you."

"But that is not right," said the lady. "I read a great deal in the papers about the misery of the lower classes, and I think we richer ones ought to do something to help them. Mrs. Morris, what can I do?"

The tears came in Mrs. Morris' eyes. She looked at the little, frail woman, and said: "Dear Mrs. Montague, I think the root of the whole matter lies in this. The Lord made us all one family. We are all brothers and sisters. The lowest woman is your sister and my sister. The man lying in the gutter is our brother. What should we do to help these members of our common family, who are not as well off as we are? We should share our last crust with them. You and

I, but for God's grace, might be in their places. I think it is criminal neglect in us to ignore this."

"It is, it is," cried Mrs. Montague, in a despairing voice. "I can't help feeling it. Tell me something I can do to help some one."

Mrs. Morris sank back in her chair, her face very sad, and yet with something like pleasure in her eyes, as she looked at her caller. "Your washerwoman," she said, "has a drunken husband and a cripple boy. I have often seen her standing over her tub, washing your delicate muslins and laces, and dropping tears into the water."

"I will never send her anything more—she shall not be troubled," said Mrs. Montague hastily.

Mrs. Morris could not help smiling. "It is not the washing that troubles her, it is her husband who beats her, and her boy who worries her. If you and I take our work from her she will have that much less money to depend upon, and will suffer in consequence. She is a hard-working and capable woman, and makes a fair living. I should not advise you to give her money, for her husband would take it from her. It is sympathy that she wants. If you could visit her occasionally and show that you are interested in her, by talking or reading to her poor, foolish boy or showing him a picture-book, you have no idea how grateful she would be to you, and how it would cheer her on her dreary way."

"I will go to see her tomorrow," said Mrs.

Montague. "Can you think of any one else I could visit?"

"A great many," said Mrs. Morris, "but I don't think you had better undertake too much at once. I will give you the addresses of three or four poor families, where an occasional visit would do untold good, if you treat them as you do your richer friends. Don't give them too much money, or too many presents, till you find out what they need. Find out their ways of living, and what they are doing with their children, and help them to get situations for them if you can. Be sure to remember that poverty does not always take away one's self-respect."

"I will, I will," said Mrs. Montague eagerly. "When can you give me these addresses?"

Mrs. Morris smiled again, and, taking a piece of paper and a pencil from her work-basket, wrote a few lines and handed them to Mrs. Montague.

The lady got up to take her leave. "And in regard to the dog," said Mrs. Morris, following her to the door, "if you decide to allow Charlie to have one, you had better let him come in and have a talk with my boys about it. They seem to know all the dogs that are for sale in the town."

"Thank you, I shall be most happy to do so. He shall have his dog. When can you have him?"

"Tomorrow, the next day, any day at all. It makes no difference to me. Let him spend an afternoon and evening with the boys, if you do not object."

"It will give me much pleasure," and the little lady bowed and smiled, and after stooping down to pat me, tripped down the steps and got into her carriage and drove away.

Mrs. Morris stood looking after her with a beaming face, and I began to think that I should like Mrs. Montague, too, if I knew her long enough. Two days later I was quite sure I should, for I had a proof that she really liked me. When her little boy Charlie came to the house he brought something for me done up in white paper. Mrs. Morris opened it, and there was a handsome, nickel-plated collar, with my name on it—*Beautiful Joe*. Wasn't I pleased! They took off the little shabby leather strap that the boys had given me when I came, and fastened on my new collar, and then Mrs. Morris held me up to a glass to look at myself. I felt so happy. Up to this time I had been a little ashamed of my cropped ears and docked tail, but now that I had a fine new collar I could hold up my head with any dog.

"Dear old Joe," said Mrs. Morris, pressing my head tightly between her hands. "You did a good thing the other day in helping me to start that little woman out of her selfish way of living."

I did not know about that, but I knew that I felt very grateful to Mrs. Montague for my new collar, and ever afterward, when I met her in the street, I paused and looked at her. Sometimes she saw me and stopped her carriage to speak to me; but I always wagged my tail, or rather my

D

body, for I had no tail to wag, whenever I saw her, whether she saw me or not.

Her son got a beautiful Irish setter, called "Brisk." He had a silky coat and soft brown eyes, and his young master seemed very fond of him.

CHAPTER VI

THE FOX-TERRIER BILLY

HEN I came to the Morris family, I knew nothing about the proper way of bringing up a puppy. I once heard of a little boy whose sister beat him so much that he said he was brought up by hand; so I think as Jenkins kicked me so much, I may say that I was brought up by foot.

Shortly after my arrival in my new home I had a chance of seeing how one should bring up a little puppy.

One day I was sitting beside Miss Laura in the parlor, when the door opened, and Jack came in. One of his hands was laid over the other, and he said to his sister, " Guess what I've got here? "

" A bird," she said.

" No."

" A rat."

" No."

" A mouse."

" No—a pup."

"O Jack," she said reprovingly; for she thought he was telling a story.

He opened his hands, and there lay the tiniest morsel of a fox-terrier puppy that I ever saw.

He was white, with black and tan markings. His body was pure white, his tail black, with a dash of tan; his ears black, and his face evenly marked with black and tan. We could not tell the color of his eyes, as they were not open. Later on, they turned out to be a pretty brown. His nose was pale pink, and when he got older it became jet black.

"Why Jack!" exclaimed Miss Laura, "his eyes aren't open; why did you take him from his mother?"

"She's dead," said Jack. "Poisoned—left her pups to run about the yard for a little exercise. Some brute had thrown over a piece of poisoned meat, and she ate it. Four of the pups died. This is the only one left. Mr. Robinson says his man doesn't understand raising pups without their mothers, and as he's going away, he wants us to have it, for we always had such luck in nursing sick animals."

Mr. Robinson I knew was a friend of the Morrises, and a gentleman who was fond of fancy stock, and imported a great deal of it from England. If this puppy came from him, it was sure to be a good one.

Miss Laura took the tiny creature and went upstairs very thoughtfully. I followed her, and watched her get a little basket and line it with cotton wool. She put the puppy in it, and looked at him. Though it was midsummer, and the house seemed very warm to me, the little creature was shivering, and making a low, murmuring noise. She pulled the wool all over him, and put the window down, and set his basket in the sun.

Then she went to the kitchen and got some warm milk. She dipped her finger in it, and offered it to the puppy, but he went nosing about in a stupid way, and wouldn't touch it. "Too young," Miss Laura said. She got a little piece of muslin, put some bread in it, tied a string around it, and dipped it in the milk. When she put this to the puppy's mouth, he sucked it greedily. He acted as if he was starving, but Miss Laura let him have only a little.

Every few hours, for the rest of the day, she gave him some more milk, and I heard the boys say that for many nights she got up once or twice and heated milk over a lamp for him. One night the milk got cold before he took it, and he became so ill that Miss Laura had to get some hot water in which to plunge him. That made him well again, and no one seemed to think it was a great trouble to take for a creature that was nothing but a dog.

He fully repaid them for all this care, for he turned out to be one of the prettiest and most lovable dogs that I ever saw. They called him Billy, and the two events of his early life were the opening of his eyes and the swallowing of his muslin rag. The rag did not seem to hurt him; but Miss Laura said that, as he had got so strong and so greedy, he must learn to eat like other dogs.

He was very amusing when he was a puppy.
He was full of tricks, and he crept about in a mischievous way when one did not know he was
near. He was a very small puppy, and used to
climb inside Miss Laura's jersey sleeve up to her
shoulder when he was six weeks old. One day,
when the whole family was in the parlor, Mr.
Morris suddenly flung aside his newspaper and
began jumping up and down. Mrs. Morris was
very much alarmed, and cried out, "My dear
William, what is the matter?"

"There's a rat up my leg," he said, shaking it
violently. Just then little Billy fell out on the
floor and lay on his back looking up at Mr. Morris
with a surprised face. He had felt cold and
thought it would be warm inside Mr. Morris's
trousers' leg.

However, Billy never did any real mischief,
thanks to Miss Laura's training. She began to
punish him just as soon as he began to tear and
worry things. The first thing he attacked was
Mr. Morris' felt hat. The wind blew it down the
hall one day, and Billy came along and began to
try it with his teeth. I dare say it felt good to
them, for a puppy is very like a baby and loves
something to bite.

Miss Laura found him, and he rolled his eyes
at her quite innocently, not knowing that he was
doing wrong. She took the hat away, and pointing from it to him, said, "Bad Billy." Then she
gave him two or three slaps with a bootlace. She

never struck a little dog with her hand or a stick. She said sticks were for big dogs and switches for little dogs, if one had to use them. The best way was to scold them, for a good dog feels a severe scolding as much as a whipping.

Billy was very much ashamed of himself. Nothing would induce him even to look at a hat again. But he thought it was no harm to worry other things. He attacked one thing after another, the rugs on the floor, curtains, anything flying or fluttering, and Miss Laura patiently scolded him for each one, till at last it dawned upon him that he must not worry anything but a bone. Then he got to be a very good dog.

There was one thing that Miss Laura was very particular about, and that was to have him fed regularly. We both had three meals a day. We were never allowed to go into the dining-room, and while the family was at the table we lay in the hall outside and watched what was going on.

Dogs take a great interest in what any one gets to eat. It was quite exciting to see the Morrises passing each other different dishes, and to smell the nice, hot food. Billy often wished that he could get up on the table. He said that he would make things fly. When he was growing, he hardly ever got enough to eat. I used to tell him that he would kill himself if he ate all he wanted.

As soon as meals were over, Billy and I scampered after Miss Laura to the kitchen. Each one had his own plate for food. Mary, the cook, often laughed at Miss Laura, because she would not let her dogs "dish" together. Miss Laura said that if she did, the larger one would get more than his share, and the little one would starve.

It was quite a sight to see Billy eat. He spread his legs apart to steady himself, and gobbled at his food like a duck. When he finished he always looked up for more, and Miss Laura would shake her head and say: "No, Billy, better longing than loathing. I believe that a great many little dogs are killed by overfeeding."

I often heard the Morrises speak of the foolish way in which some people stuff their pets with food, and either kill them by it or keep them in continual ill health. A case occurred in our neighborhood while Billy was a puppy. Some people, called Dobson, who lived only a few doors from us, had a fine bay mare and a little colt called Sam. They were very proud of this colt, and Mr. Dobson had promised it to his son James. One day Mr. Dobson asked Mr. Morris to come in and see the colt, and I went too. I watched Mr. Morris while he examined it. It was a pretty little creature, and I did not wonder that they thought so much of it.

When Mr. Morris went home, his wife asked him what he thought of it.

"I think," he said, "that it won't live long."

"Why, papa!" exclaimed Jack, who overheard the remark, "it is as fat as a seal."

"It would have a better chance for its life if it

were lean and scrawny," said Mr. Morris. "They are overfeeding it, and I told Mr. Dobson so; but he wasn't inclined to believe me."

Now, Mr. Morris had been brought up in the country, and knew a great deal about animals, so I was inclined to think he was right. And sure enough, in a few days we heard that the colt was dead.

Poor James Dobson felt very badly. A number of the neighbors' boys went in to see him, and there he stood gazing at the dead colt, and looking as if he wanted to cry. Jack was there and I was at his heels, and though he said nothing for a time, I knew he was angry with the Dobsons for sacrificing the colt's life. Presently he said, "You won't need to have that colt stuffed now he's dead, Dobson."

"What do you mean? Why do you say that?" asked the boy peevishly.

"Because you stuffed him while he was alive," said Jack saucily.

Then we had to run for all we were worth, for the Dobson boy was after us, and as he was a big fellow he would have whipped Jack soundly.

I must not forget to say that Billy was washed regularly—once a week with nice-smelling soap, and once a month with strong-smelling, disagreeable, carbolic soap. He had his own towels and wash-cloths, and after being rubbed and scrubbed he was rolled in a blanket and put by the fire to dry. Miss Laura said that a little dog that has

been petted and kept in the house, and has become
tender, should never be washed and allowed to
run about with a wet coat, unless the weather is
very warm, for he would be sure to take cold.

Jim and I were more hardy than Billy, and we
took our baths in the sea. Every few days the
boys took us down to the shore, and we went in
swimming with them.

CHAPTER VII

TRAINING A PUPPY

ED, dear," said Miss Laura one day, "I wish you would train Billy to follow and retrieve. He is four months old now, and I shall soon want to take him out on the street."

"Very well, sister," said mischievous Ned; and catching up a stick he said, "Come out into the garden, dogs."

Though he was brandishing his stick very fiercely, I was not at all afraid of him; and as for Billy, he loved Ned.

The Morris garden was really not a garden, but a large piece of ground with the grass worn bare in many places, a few trees scattered about, and some raspberry and currant bushes along the fence. A lady who knew that Mr. Morris had not a large salary, said one day when she was looking out of the dining-room window: "My dear Mrs. Morris, why don't you have this garden dug up? You could raise your own vegetables. It would be so much cheaper than buying them."

Mrs. Morris laughed in great amusement. "Think of the hens, and cats, and dogs, and rabbits, and, above all, the boys that I have. What sort of a garden would there be, and do you think

59

it would be fair to take their playground from them?"

The lady said, no, she did not think it would be fair.

I am sure I don't know what the boys would have done without this strip of ground. Many a frolic and game they had there. In the present case, Ned walked around and around it, with his stick on his shoulder, Billy and I strolling after him. Presently Billy made a dash aside to get a bone. Ned turned around and said firmly, "To heel."

Billy looked at him innocently, not knowing what he meant. "To heel!" exclaimed Ned again. Billy thought he wanted to play, and putting his head on his paws he began to bark. Ned laughed, still he kept saying, "To heel." He would not say another word. He knew if he said, "Come here," or "Follow," or "Go behind," it would confuse Billy.

Finally, as Ned kept saying the words over and over, and pointing to me, it seemed to dawn upon Billy that he wanted him to follow him. So he came beside me, and together we followed Ned around the garden, again and again.

Ned often looked behind with a pleased face, and I felt so proud to think I was doing well; but suddenly I got dreadfully confused when he turned around and said, "Hie out!"

The Morrises all used the same words in training their dogs, and I had heard Miss Laura say this, but I had forgotten what it meant. "Good Joe," said Ned, patting me, "you have forgotten. I wonder where Jim is? He would help us."

He put his fingers in his mouth and blew a shrill whistle, and soon Jim came trotting up the lane from the street. He looked at us with his large, intelligent eyes, and wagged his tail slowly, as if to say, "Well, what do you want of me?"

"Come and give me a hand at this training business, old Sobersides," said Ned with a laugh. "It's too slow to do it alone. Now, young gentlemen, attention! To heel!" He began to march around the garden again, and Jim and I followed closely at his heels, while little Billy, seeing that he could not get us to play with him, came lagging behind.

Soon Ned turned around and said, "Hie out!" Old Jim sprang ahead and ran off in front as if he was after something. Now I remembered what "Hie out" meant. We were to have a lovely race wherever we liked. Little Billy loved this. We ran and scampered hither and thither, and Ned watched us, laughing at our antics.

After tea he called us out in the garden again, and said he had something else to teach us. He turned up a tub on the wooden platform at the back door and sat on it, and then called Jim to him.

He took a small leather strap from his pocket. It had a nice, strong smell. We all licked it, and each dog wished to have it. "No, Joe and Billy," said Ned, holding us both by our collars, "you wait a minute. Here, Jim."

Jim watched him very earnestly, and Ned threw the strap half-way across the garden and said, "Fetch it."

Jim never moved till he heard the words, "Fetch it." Then he ran swiftly, brought the strap, and dropped it in Ned's hand. Ned sent him after it two or three times, then he said to Jim, "Lie down," and turned to me. "Here, Joe, it is your turn."

He threw the strap under the raspberry bushes, then looked at me and said, "Fetch it." I knew quite well what he meant, and ran joyfully after it. I soon found it by the strong smell, but the queerest thing happened when I got it in my mouth. I began to gnaw it and play with it, and when Ned called out, "Fetch it," I dropped it and ran toward him. I was not obstinate, but stupid.

Ned pointed to the place where it was, and spread out his empty hands. That helped me, and I ran quickly and got it. He made me get it for him several times. Sometimes I could not find it, and sometimes I dropped it; but he never stirred. He sat still till I brought it to him.

After a while he tried Billy, but it soon got dark, and we could not see, so he took Billy and went into the house.

I stayed out with Jim for a while, and he asked me if I knew why Ned had thrown a strap for us, instead of a bone or something hard.

Of course I did not know, so Jim told me it was on his account. He was a bird-dog, and was never allowed to carry anything hard in his mouth, because it would make him hard-mouthed, and he would be apt to bite the birds when he was bringing them back to any person who was shooting with him.

I said to him: "Jim, how is it you never go out shooting? I have always heard you were a dog for that, and yet you never leave home."

He hung his head a little, and said he did not wish to go, and then, for he was an honest dog, he gave me the true reason.

CHAPTER VIII

A RUINED DOG

"I WAS a sporting dog," he said bitterly, "for the first three years of my life. I belonged to a man who keeps a livery stable here in Fairport, and he used to hire me out to shooting parties.

"I was a favorite with all the gentlemen. I was crazy with delight when I saw the guns brought out, and would jump up and bite at them. I loved to chase birds and rabbits, and even now, when the pigeons come near me, I tremble all over and have to turn away lest I should seize them. I used often to be in the woods from morning till night. I liked to have a hard search for a bird after it had been shot, and to be praised for bringing it out without biting or injuring it in any way.

"I never got lost, for I am one of those dogs that can always tell where human beings are. I did not smell them. I would be too far away for that, but if my master was standing in some place and I took a long round through the woods, I knew exactly where he was, and could make a short cut back to him without doubling on my tracks.

64

"But I must tell you about my trouble. One Saturday afternoon a party of young men came to get me. They had a dog with them, a cocker spaniel called Bob, but they wanted another. For some reason or other, my master was very unwilling to have me go. However, he at last consented, and they put me in the back of the wagon with Bob and the lunch-baskets, and we drove off into the country. This Bob was a happy, merry-looking dog, and as we went along he told me of the fine time we should have the next day. The young men would shoot a little, then they would get out their baskets and have something to eat and drink, and would play cards and go to sleep under the trees, and we should be able to help ourselves to legs and wings of chickens, and anything we liked from the baskets.

"I did not like this at all. I was used to working hard through the week, and I preferred to spend my Sundays quietly at home. However, I said nothing.

"That night we slept at a country hotel, and drove the next morning to the banks of a small lake where the young men were told there would be plenty of wild ducks. They were in no hurry to begin their sport. They sat down in the sun on some flat rocks at the water's edge, and said they would have something to drink before setting to work. They got out some of the bottles from the wagon and began to take long drinks from them. Then they got quarrelsome and mischievous, and

E

seemed to forget all about their shooting. One of them proposed to have some fun with the dogs. They tied us both to a tree, and throwing a stick in the water told us to get it. Of course, we struggled and tried to get free, and chafed our necks with the rope.

"After a time one of them began to swear at me, and say that he believed I was gun-shy. He staggered to the wagon and got out his fowling-piece, and said he was going to try me.

"He loaded it, went to a little distance, and was going to fire, when the young man who owned Bob said he wasn't going to have his dog's legs shot off, and coming up he unfastened him and took him away. You can imagine my feelings, as I stood there tied to the tree, with that stranger pointing his gun directly at me. He fired close to me a number of times—over my head and under my body. The earth was cut up all around me. I was terribly frightened, and howled and begged to be freed.

"The other young men, who were sitting laughing at me, thought it such good fun that they got their guns too. I never wish to spend such a terrible hour again. I was sure they would kill me. I dare say they would have done so, for they were all quite drunk by this time, if something had not happened.

"Poor Bob, who was almost as frightened as I was, and who lay shivering under the wagon, was killed by a shot fired by his own master, whose hand was the most unsteady of all. He gave one loud howl, kicked convulsively, then turned over on his side, and lay still. It sobered them all. They ran up to him, but he was quite dead. They sat for a while very silent, then they threw the rest of the bottles into the lake, dug a shallow grave for Bob, and putting me in the wagon drove slowly back to town. They were not bad young men. I don't think they meant to hurt me, or to kill Bob. It was the nasty stuff in the bottles that took away their reason.

"I was never the same dog again. I was quite deaf in my right ear, and though I strove against it, I was so terribly afraid of even the sight of a gun that I would run and hide myself whenever one was shown to me. My master was very angry with those young men, and it seemed as if he could not bear the sight of me. One day he took me very kindly and brought me here, and asked Mr. Morris if he did not want a good-natured dog to play with the children.

"I have a happy home here, and I love the Morris boys; but I often wish that I could keep from putting my tail between my legs and running home as fast as I can every time I hear the sound of a gun."

"Never mind that, Jim," I said. "You should not fret over a thing for which you are not to blame. I am sure you must be glad for one reason that you have left your old life."

"What is that?" he said.

"On account of the birds. You know Miss Laura thinks it is wrong to kill the pretty creatures that fly about the fields."

"So it is," he said, "unless one kills them at once. I have often felt angry with men for only half killing a bird. I hated to pick up the little, warm body, and see the bright eye looking so reproachfully at me, and feel the flutter of life. We animals kill mercifully. It is only human beings who butcher their prey, and seem, some of them, to rejoice in their agony. I used to be eager to kill birds and rabbits, but I did not want to keep them before me long after they were dead. I often stop in the street and look up at fine ladies' hats, and wonder how they can wear dead birds in such dreadful positions. Some of them have their heads twisted under their wings and over their shoulders, and looking toward their tails, and their eyes are so horrible that I wish I could take those ladies into the woods and let them see how graceful and pretty a live bird is, and how unlike the stuffed creatures they wear. Have you ever had a good run in the woods, Joe?"

"No, never," I said.

"Some day I will take you, but now it is late and I must go to bed. Are you going to sleep in the kennel with me, or in the stable?"

"I think I shall sleep with you, Jim. Dogs like company, you know, as well as human beings." I curled up in the straw beside him, and soon we were fast asleep.

I have known a good many dogs, but I don't think I ever saw such a good one as Jim. He was gentle and kind, and so sensitive that a hard word hurt him more than a blow. He was a great pet with Mrs. Morris, and as he had been so well trained, he made himself very useful to her.

When she went shopping, he often carried a parcel in his mouth for her. He would never leave it anywhere. One day she dropped her purse, and Jim picked it up, and brought it home in his mouth. She did not notice him, for he always walked behind her. When she got to her own door, she missed the purse, and turning around saw it in Jim's mouth.

Another day, a lady gave Jack Morris a canary cage as a present for Carl. He was bringing it home, when one of the little seed-boxes fell out. Jim picked it up and carried it a long way before Jack discovered it.

CHAPTER IX

THE PARROT BELLA

I OFTEN used to hear the Morrises speak about vessels that ran between Fairport and a place called the West Indies, carrying cargoes of lumber and fish, and bringing home molasses, spices, fruit, and other things. On one of these vessels was a cabin-boy, who was a friend of the Morris boys, and often brought them presents.

One day, after I had been at the Morrises' for some months, this boy arrived at the house with a bunch of green bananas in his arms and a parrot on his shoulder. The boys were delighted with the parrot, and called their mother to see what a pretty bird she was.

Mrs. Morris seemed very much touched by the boy's thoughtfulness in bringing a present such a long distance, and thanked him warmly. The cabin-boy became very shy, and all he could say was, "Go way!" over and over again, in a very awkward manner.

Mrs. Morris smiled, and left him with the boys. I think that she thought he would be more comfortable with them; and indeed he did talk quite freely as soon as she had gone.

Jack put me up on the table to look at the parrot. The boys held her by a string tied around one of her legs. She was a gray parrot with a few red feathers in her tail, and she had bright eyes, and a very knowing air.

The boy said he had been careful to buy a young one that could not speak, for he knew the Morris boys would not want one chattering foreign gibberish, nor yet one that would swear. He had kept her in his bunk in the ship, and had spent all his leisure time in teaching her to talk. Then he looked at her anxiously, and said, "Show off now, can't ye?"

I didn't know what he meant by all this, until afterward. I had never heard of such a thing as birds talking. I stood on the table staring hard at her, and she stared hard at me. I was just thinking that I would not like to have her sharp little beak fastened in my skin, when I heard some one say, "Beautiful Joe." The voice seemed to come from the room, but I knew all the voices there, and this was one I had never heard before, so I thought I must be mistaken, and it was some one in the hall. I struggled to get away from Jack, to run and see who it was. But he held me fast, and laughed with all his might. I looked at the other boys and they were laughing too. Presently, I heard again, "Beau-ti-ful Joe, Beau-ti-ful Joe." The sound was close by, and yet it did not come from the cabin-boy, for he was all doubled up laughing, his face as red as a beet.

"It's the parrot, Joe," said Ned. "Look at her, you gaby. Her eyes are on the cabin-boy's. He's spent hours in teaching her to say things about this family. She doesn't recognize any of us."

I did look at her, and with her head on one side, and the sauciest air in the world, she was saying, "Beau-ti-ful Joe, Beau-ti-ful Joe!"

I had never heard a bird talk before, and I felt so sheepish that I tried to get down and hide myself under the table. Then she began to laugh at me. "Ha, ha, ha, good dog—sic 'em, boy. Rats, rats! Beau-ti-ful Joe, Beau-ti-ful Joe," she cried, rattling off the words as fast as she could.

I never felt so queer before in my life, and the boys were just roaring with delight at my puzzled face. Then the parrot began calling for Jim: "Where's Jim, where's good old Jim? Poor old dog. Give him a bone."

The boys brought Jim in, and when he heard her funny little cracked voice calling him, he nearly went crazy: 'Jimmy, Jimmy, James Augustus!" she said, which was Jim's long name.

He made a dash out of the room, and the boys screamed so that Mr. Morris came down from his study to see what the noise meant. As soon as the parrot saw him, she would not utter another word. The boys told him, though, what she had been saying, and he seemed much amused to think that the cabin-boy should have remembered so many of his boys' expressions, and taught them to the parrot. "Clever Polly," he said, kindly; "Good Polly."

The cabin-boy looked at him shyly, and Jack, who was a very sharp lad, said quickly, "Is not that what you call her, Henry?"

"No," said the boy, "I call her Bell, short for Bellzebub."

"I beg your pardon," said Jack, very politely.

"Bell—short for Bellzebub," repeated the boy. "Ye see, I thought ye'd like a name from the Bible, bein' a minister's sons. I hadn't my Bible with me on this cruise, savin' yer presence, an' I couldn't think of any girls' names out of it, but Eve or Queen of Sheba, an' they didn't seem very fit, so I asks one of me mates, an' he says, for his part he guessed Bellzebub was as pretty a girl's name as any, so I guv her that. 'Twould 'a been better to let you name her, but ye see 'twouldn't 'a been handy not to call her somethin', where I was teachin' her every day."

Jack turned away and walked to the window, his face a deep scarlet. I heard him mutter, "Beelzebub, prince of devils," so I suppose the cabin-boy had given his bird a bad name.

Mr. Morris looked kindly at the cabin-boy. "Do you ever call the parrot by her whole name?"

"No, sir," he replied, "I always give her Bell, but she calls herself Bella."

"'Bella,'" repeated Mr. Morris, "that is a very pretty name. If you keep her, boys, I think you had better stick to that."

"Yes, father," they all said; and then Mr. Morris started to go back to his study. On the doorsill he paused to ask the cabin-boy when his ship sailed. Finding that it was to be in a few days, he took out his pocket-book and wrote something in it. The next day he asked Jack to go to town with him, and when they came home, Jack said that his father had bought an oil-skin coat for Henry Smith, and a handsome Bible in which they were all to write their names.

After Mr. Morris left the room, the door opened, and Miss Laura came in. She knew nothing about the parrot, and was very much surprised to see it. Seating herself at the table, she held out her hands to it. She was so fond of pets of all kinds, that she never thought of being afraid of them. At the same time, she never laid her hand suddenly on any animal. She held out her fingers and talked gently, so that if it wished to come to her it could. She looked at the parrot as if she loved it, and the queer little thing walked right up, and nestled its head against the lace in the front of her dress. "Pretty lady," she said, in a cracked whisper, "give Bella a kiss."

The boys were so pleased with this, and set up such a shout, that their mother came into the room and said they had better take the parrot out to the stable. Bella seemed to enjoy the fun. "Come on, boys," she screamed as Henry Smith lifted her on his finger. "Ha, ha, ha—come on, let's have some fun. Where's the guinea-pig?

Where's Davy the rat? Where's Pussy? Pussy, pussy, come here. Pussy, pussy, dear, pretty puss."

Her voice was shrill and distinct, and very like the voice of an old woman who came to the house for rags and bones. I followed her out to the stable, and stayed there until she screamed out: "Ha, Joe, Beautiful Joe! Where's your tail? Who cut your ears off?"

I don't think it was kind in the cabin-boy to teach her this, and I think she knew it teased me, for she said it over and over again, and laughed and chuckled with delight. I left her, and did not see her till the next day, when the boys had got a fine, large cage for her.

The place for her cage was by one of the hall windows; but everybody in the house got so fond of her that she was moved about from one room to another.

She hated her cage, and used to put her head close to the bars and plead: "Let Bella out; Bella will be a good girl. Bella won't run away."

After a time, the Morrises did let her out, and she kept her word and never tried to get away. Jack put a little handle on her cage door so that she could open and shut it herself, and it was very amusing to hear her say in the morning, "Clear the track, children! Bella's going to take a walk," and see her turn the handle with her claw and come out into the room. She was a very clever bird, and I have never seen any creature but a human being that could reason as she did. She

was so petted and talked to that she got to know
a great many words, and on one occasion she
saved the Morrises from being robbed.

It was in the wintertime. The family was having tea in the dining-room at the back of the
house, and Billy and I were lying in the hall
watching what was going on. There was no one
in the front of the house. The hall lamp was
lighted, and the hall-door closed, but not locked.
Some sneak thieves, who had been doing a great
deal of mischief in Fairport, crept up the steps
and into the house, and, opening the door of the
hall closet, laid their hands on the boys' winter
overcoats.

They thought no one saw them, but they were
mistaken. Bella had been having a nap up-stairs,
and had not come down when the tea-bell rang.
Now she was hopping down on her way to the
dining-room, and hearing the slight noise below,
stopped and looked through the railing. Any pet
creature that lived in this nice family knew what
happened when beggar boys came to call.

"Company's coming!" she screamed loudly.
"Get out the tea. Bring some cake! Quick,
quick!"

Billy and I sprang up and pushed open the door
leading to the front hall. We had smelt the thieves,
who, in a terrible fright, were just rushing down
the outside steps. One of them got away, but the
other fell, and I caught him by the coat, till
Mr. Morris ran and put his hand on his shoulder.

He was a young fellow about Jack's age, but not one-half so manly, and he was sniffling and scolding about "that pesky parrot." Mr. Morris made him come back into the house, and had a talk with him. He found out that he was a poor, ignorant lad, half starved by a drunken father. He and his brother stole clothes, and sent them to his sister in Boston, who sold them and returned part of the money.

Mr. Morris asked him if he would not like to get his living in an honest way, and he said he had tried to, but no one would employ him. Mr. Morris told him to go home and take leave of his father and get his brother and bring him to Washington Street the next day. He told him plainly that if he did not he would send a policeman after him.

The boy begged Mr. Morris not to do that, and early the next morning he appeared with his brother. Mrs. Morris gave them a good breakfast and fitted them out with clothes. Then they were sent off in the train to one of her brothers, who was a kind farmer in the country, and who had been telegraphed to that these boys were coming, and wanted situations where they would have a chance to make honest men of themselves.

CHAPTER X

HEN Billy was five months old, he had his first walk in the street. Miss Laura knew that he had been well trained, so she did not hesitate to take him into the town. She was not the kind of a young girl to go into the street with a dog that would not behave himself, and she was never willing to attract attention to herself by calling out orders to any of her pets when she had them with her away from the house.

As soon as we got down the front steps, she said quietly to Billy, "To heel." It was very hard for little, playful Billy to keep close to her, when he saw so many new and wonderful things about him. He had become acquainted with everything in the house and garden, but this outside world was full of things he wanted to look at and smell, and he was fairly crazy to play with some of the pretty dogs he saw running about. But he did just as he was told.

Soon we came to a shop, and Miss Laura went in to buy some ribbons. She said to me, "Stay out," but Billy she took in with her. I watched them through the glass door, and saw her go to a counter and sit down. Billy stood behind her till she said, "Lie down." Then he curled himself at her feet.

He lay quietly, even when she left him and went to another counter. But he eyed her very anxiously till she came back and said "Up" to him. Then he sprang up and followed her out to the street.

She stood in the shop door, and looked lovingly down on us as we fawned on her. "Good dogs," she said softly, "you shall have a present." We went behind her again, and she took us to a shop where we both lay beside the counter. When we heard her ask the clerk for solid rubber balls, we could scarcely keep still. We both knew what "ball" meant.

Taking the parcel in her hand, she came out into the street. She did not do any more shopping, but turned her face toward the sea. She was going to give us a nice walk along the beach, although it was a dark, disagreeable, cloudy day, when most young girls would have stayed in the house. The Morris children never minded the weather. Even in the pouring rain the boys would put on rubber boots and coats and go out to play. Miss Laura walked along, the high wind blowing her cloak and dress about, and when we got past the houses, she had a little run with us. We jumped, and frisked, and barked, till we were tired; and then we walked quietly along.

A little distance ahead of us were some boys throwing sticks in the water for two Newfoundland dogs. Suddenly a quarrel sprang up between the dogs. They were both powerful creatures, and fairly matched as regarded size. It was terrible to hear their fierce growling, and to see the way in which they tore at each other's throats. I looked at Miss Laura. If she had said a word, I would have run in and helped the dog that was getting the worst of it. But she told me to keep back, and ran on herself.

The boys were throwing water on the dogs, and pulling their tails, and hurling stones at them, but they could not separate them. Their heads seemed locked together, and they went back and forth over the stones, the boys crowding around them, shouting, and beating, and kicking at them.

"Stand back, boys," said Miss Laura, "I'll stop them." She pulled a little parcel from her purse, bent over the dogs, scattered a powder on their noses, and the next instant the dogs were yards apart, nearly sneezing their heads off.

"I say, Missis, what did you do? What's that stuff—whew, it's pepper!" the boys exclaimed.

Miss Laura sat down on a flat rock, and looked at them with a very pale face. "Oh boys," she said, "why did you make those dogs fight? It is so cruel. They were playing happily till you set them on each other. Just see how they have torn their handsome coats, and how the blood is dripping from them."

"'Tain't my fault," said one of the lads sullenly. "Jim Jones there said his dog could lick my dog, and I said he couldn't—and he couldn't, nuther."

"Yes, he could," cried the other boy, "and if you say he couldn't, I'll smash your face."

The two boys began sidling up to each other with clenched fists, and a third boy, who had a mischievous face, seized the paper that had had the pepper in it, and running up to them shook it in their faces.

There was enough left to put all thoughts of fighting out of their heads. They began to cough, and choke, and splutter, and finally found themselves beside the dogs, where the four of them had a lively time.

The other boys yelled with delight, and pointed their fingers at them. "A sneezing concert. Thank you, gentlemen. *Angcore, angcore!*"

Miss Laura laughed too, she could not help it, and even Billy and I curled up our lips. After a while they sobered down, and then finding that the boys hadn't a handkerchief between them, Miss Laura took her own soft one, and dipping it in a spring of fresh water near-by, wiped the red eyes of the sneezers.

Their ill humor had gone, and when she turned to leave them and said coaxingly, "You won't make those dogs fight any more, will you?" they said, "No, siree, Bob."

Miss Laura went slowly home, and ever afterward when she met any of those boys, they called her "Miss Pepper."

F

When we got home we found Willie curled up by the window in the hall, reading a book. He was too fond of reading, and his mother often told him to put away his book and run about with the other boys. This afternoon Miss Laura laid her hand on his shoulder and said, " I was going to give the dogs a little game of ball, but I'm rather tired."

" Gammon and spinach," he replied, shaking off her hand, " you're always tired."

She sat down in a hall chair and looked at him. Then she began to tell him about the dog fight. He was much interested, and the book slipped to the floor. When she finished he said: " You're a daisy every day. Go now and rest yourself." Then snatching the balls from her, he called us and ran down to the basement. He was not quick enough, though, to escape her arm. She caught him to her and kissed him repeatedly. He was the baby and pet of the family, and he loved her dearly, though he spoke impatiently to her oftener than any of the other boys.

We had a grand game with Willie. Miss Laura had trained us to do all kinds of things with balls—jumping for them, playing hide-and-seek, and catching them.

Billy could do more things than I could. One of his games I thought was very clever. He played ball by himself. He was so crazy about ball play that he could never get enough of it. Miss Laura played all she could with him, but she had to help her mother with the sewing and the housework, and do lessons with her father, for she was only seventeen years old, and had not left off studying. So Billy would take his ball and go off by himself. Sometimes he rolled it over the floor, and sometimes he threw it in the air and pushed it through the staircase railings to the hall below. He always listened till he heard it drop, then he ran down and brought it back and pushed it through again. He did this till he was tired, and then he brought the ball and laid it at Miss Laura's feet.

We both had been taught a number of tricks. We could sneeze and cough, and be dead dogs, and say our prayers, and stand on our heads, and mount a ladder and say the alphabet—this was the hardest of all, and it took Miss Laura a long time to teach us. We never began till a book was laid before us. Then we stared at it, and Miss Laura said, " Begin, Joe and Billy—say A."

For A, we gave a little squeal. B was louder. C was louder still. We barked for some letters, and growled for others. We always turned a somersault for S. When we got to Z, we gave the book a push, and had a frolic around the room.

When any one came in, and Miss Laura made us show off any of our tricks, the remark always was : " What clever dogs. They are not like other dogs."

That was a mistake. Billy and I were not any

brighter than many a miserable cur that skulked
about the streets of Fairport. It was kindness
and patience that did it all. When I was with
Jenkins he thought I was a very stupid dog. He
would have laughed at the idea of any one teaching me anything. But I was only sullen and obstinate because I was kicked about so much. If
he had been kind to me, I would have done anything for him.

I loved to wait on Miss Laura and Mrs. Morris,
and they taught both Billy and me to make ourselves useful about the house. Mrs. Morris didn't
like going up and down the three long staircases,
and sometimes we just raced up and down, waiting on her.

How often I have heard her go into the hall
and say: "Please send me down a clean duster,
Laura. Joe, you get it." I would run gaily up
the steps, and then would come Billy's turn.
"Billy, I have forgotten my keys. Go get them."

After a time we began to know the names of
different articles, and where they were kept, and
could get them ourselves. On sweeping days we
worked very hard, and enjoyed the fun. If Mrs.
Morris was too far away to call to Mary for what
she wanted, she wrote the name on a piece of
paper, and told us to take it to her.

Billy always took the letters from the postman,
and carried the morning paper up to Mr. Morris'
study, and I always put away the clean clothes.
After they were mended, Mrs. Morris folded each

article and gave it to me, mentioning the name of the owner, so that I could lay it on his bed. There was no need for her to tell me the names. I knew by the smell. All human beings have a strong smell to a dog, even though they mayn't notice it themselves. Mrs. Morris never knew how she bothered me by giving away Miss Laura's clothes to poor people. Once, I followed her track all through town, and found it was only a pair of her boots on a ragged child in the gutter.

I must say a word about Billy's tail before I close this chapter. It is the custom to cut the ends of fox-terriers' tails, but leave their ears untouched. Billy came to Miss Laura so young that his tail had not been cut off, and she would not have it done.

One day Mr. Robinson came in to see him, and he said, "You have made a fine-looking dog of him, but his appearance is ruined by the length of his tail."

"Mr. Robinson," said Mrs. Morris, patting little Billy, who lay on her lap, "don't you think that this little dog has a beautifully proportioned body?"

"Yes, I do," said the gentleman.

"But," she said, "if our Creator made that beautiful little body, don't you think He was wise enough to know what length of tail would be in proportion to it?"

Mr. Robinson laughed, and said that he thought she and Miss Laura were both "cranks."

CHAPTER XI

GOLDFISH AND CANARIES

THE Morris boys were all different. Jack was bright and clever, Ned was a wag, Willie was a bookworm, and Carl was a born trader.

He was always exchanging toys and books with his schoolmates, and they never got the better of him in a bargain. He said that when he grew up he was going to be a merchant, and he had already begun to carry on a trade in canaries and goldfish. He was very fond of what he called "his yellow pets," yet he never kept a pair of birds or a goldfish, if he had a good offer for them.

He slept alone in a large, sunny room at the top of the house. By his own request, it was barely furnished, and there he raised his canaries and 1 t his goldfish.

He was not fond of having visitors coming to his room, because, he said, they frightened the canaries. After Mrs. Morris made his bed in the morning, the door was closed, and no one was supposed to go in till he came from school. Once Billy and I followed him up-stairs without his knowing it, but as soon as he saw us he sent us down in a great hurry.

One day Bella walked into his room to inspect the canaries. She was quite a spoiled bird by this time, and I heard Carl telling the family afterward that it was as good as a play to see Miss Bella strutting in with her breast stuck out, and her little, conceited air, and hear her say shrilly: "Good morning, birds, good morning! How do you do, Carl? Glad to see you, boy."

"Well, I'm not so glad to see you," he said decidedly, "and don't you ever come up here again. You'd frighten my canaries to death." And he sent her flying down-stairs.

How cross she was! She came shrieking to Miss Laura. "Bad boy! Poor Bella!"

Miss Laura petted and smoothed her, telling her to go find Davy, and he would play with her. Bella and the rat were great friends. It was very funny to see them going about the house together. From the very first she had liked him, and coaxed him into her cage, where he soon became quite at home—so much so that he always slept there. About nine o'clock every evening, if he was not with her, she went all over the house, crying: "Davy! Davy! time to go to bed. Come sleep in Bella's cage."

He was very fond of the nice sweet cakes she got to eat, but she never could get him to eat coffee-grounds—the food she liked best.

Miss Laura spoke to Carl about Bella, and told him he had hurt her feelings, so he petted her a little to make up for it. Then his mother told him that she thought he was making a mistake in keeping his canaries so much to themselves. They had become so timid, that when she went into the room they were uneasy till she left it. She told him that petted birds or animals are sociable and like company, unless they are kept by themselves, when they become shy. She advised him to let the other boys go into the room, and occasionally to bring some of his pretty songsters down-stairs, where all the family could enjoy seeing and hearing them, and where they would get used to other people besides himself.

Carl looked thoughtful, and his mother went on to say that there was no one in the house, not even the cat, that would harm his birds.

"You might even charge admission for a day or two," said Jack gravely, "and introduce us to them, and make a little money."

Carl was rather annoyed at this, but his mother calmed him by showing him a letter she had just received from one of her brothers, asking her to let one of her boys spend his Christmas holidays in the country with him.

"I want you to go, Carl," she said.

He was very much pleased, but looked sober when he thought of his pets. "Laura and I will take care of them," said his mother, "and start the new way of treating them."

"Very well," said Carl, "I will go then; I've no young ones now, so you will not find them much trouble."

I thought it was a great deal of trouble to take care of them. The first morning after Carl left, Billy, and Bella, and Davy, and I followed Miss Laura up-stairs. She made us sit in a row by the door, lest we should startle the canaries. She had a great many things to do. First, the canaries had their baths. They had to get them at the same time every morning. Miss Laura filled the little white dishes with water and put them in the cages, and then came and sat on a stool by the door. Bella, and Billy, and Davy climbed into her lap, and I stood close by her. It was so funny to watch those canaries. They put their heads on one side and looked first at their little baths and then at us. Finally, as we were all very quiet, they got into the water; and what a good time they had, fluttering their wings and splashing, and cleaning themselves so nicely.

Then they got up on their perches and sat in the sun, shaking themselves and picking at their feathers.

Miss Laura cleaned each cage, and gave each bird some mixed rape- and canary-seed. I heard Carl tell her before he left not to give them much hemp-seed, for that was too fattening. He was very careful about their food. During the summer I had often seen him taking up nice green things to them: celery, chickweed, tender cabbage, peaches, apples, pears, bananas; and now at Christmastime, he had green stuff growing in pots on the window ledge.

Besides that, he gave them crumbs of coarse bread, crackers, lumps of sugar, cuttle-fish to peck at, and a number of other things. Miss Laura did everything just as he told her, but I think she talked to the birds more than he did. She was very particular about their drinking-water, and carefully washed out the little glass cups that held it.

After the canaries were clean and comfortable, Miss Laura set their cages in the sun, and turned to the goldfish. They were in large glass globes on the window-seat. She took a long-handled tin cup, and dipped out the fish from one into a basin of water. Then she washed the globe thoroughly and put the fish back, and scattered wafers of fish food on the top. The fish came up and snapped at it, and acted as if they were glad to get it. She did each globe, and then her work was over for one morning.

She went away for a while, but every few hours through the day she ran up to Carl's room to see how the fish and canaries were getting on. If the room was too chilly she turned on more heat, but she did not keep it too warm, for that would make the birds tender.

After a time the canaries got to know her, and hopped gaily around their cages, and chirped and sang whenever they saw her coming. Then she began to take some of them down-stairs, and to let them out of their cages for an hour or two every day. They were very happy little creatures, and chased each other about the room, and flew on Miss Laura's head, and pecked saucily at her face as she sat sewing and watching them. They were not at all afraid of me or of Billy, and it was quite a sight to see them hopping up to Bella. She looked so large beside them.

One little bird became ill while Carl was away, and Miss Laura had to give it a great deal of attention. She gave it plenty of hemp-seed to make it fat, and very often the yolk of a hard-boiled egg, and kept a nail in its drinking-water, and gave it a few drops of alcohol in its bath every morning to keep it from taking cold. The moment the bird finished taking its bath, Miss Laura took the dish from the cage, for the alcohol made the water poisonous. Then vermin came on it, and she had to write to Carl to ask him what to do. He told her to hang a muslin bag full of sulphur over the swing, so that the bird would dust it down on its feathers. That cured the little thing, and when Carl came home, he found it quite well again.

One day, just after he got back, Mrs. Montague drove up to the house with a canary cage carefully done up in a shawl. She said that a bad-tempered housemaid, in cleaning the cage that morning, had become angry with the bird and struck it, breaking its leg. She was very much annoyed with the girl, and had dismissed her, and now she wanted Carl to take her bird and nurse it, as she knew nothing about canaries.

Carl had just come in from school. He threw down his books, took the shawl from the cage and looked in. The poor little canary was sitting in a corner. Its eyes were half shut, one leg hung loose, and it was making faint chirps of distress.

Carl was very much interested in it. He got Mrs. Montague to help him, and together they split matches, tore up strips of muslin, and bandaged the broken leg. He put the little bird back in the cage, and it seemed more comfortable. " I think he will do now," he said to Mrs. Montague, " but hadn't you better leave him with me for a few days?"

She gladly agreed to this and went away, after telling him that the bird's name was Dick.

The next morning at the breakfast-table, I heard Carl telling his mother that as soon as he woke up he sprang out of bed and went to see how the canary was. During the night, poor, foolish Dick had picked off the splints from his leg, and now it was as bad as ever. " I shall have to perform a surgical operation," he said.

I did not know what he meant, so I watched him when, after breakfast, he brought the bird down to his mother's room. She held it while he took a pair of sharp scissors, and cut its leg right off a little way above the broken place. Then he put some vaseline on the tiny stump, bound it up, and left Dick in his mother's care. All the morning, as she sat sewing, she watched him to see that he did not pick the bandage away.

When Carl came home, Dick was so much better that he had managed to fly up on his perch, and was eating seeds quite gaily. "Poor Dick!" said Carl, "a leg and a stump!" Dick imitated him in a few little chirps, "A leg and a stump!"

"Why, he is saying it too," exclaimed Carl, and burst out laughing.

Dick seemed cheerful enough, but it was very pitiful to see him dragging his poor little stump around the cage, and resting it against the perch to keep him from falling. When Mrs. Montague came the next day, she could not bear to look at him. "Oh, dear!" she exclaimed, "I cannot take that disfigured bird home."

I could not help thinking how different she was from Miss Laura, who loved any creature all the more for having some blemish about it. "What shall I do?" said Mrs. Montague. "I miss my little bird so much. I shall have to get a new one. Carl, will you sell me one?"

"I will *give* you one, Mrs. Montague," said the boy eagerly. "I should like to do so."

Mrs. Morris looked pleased to hear Carl say this. She used to fear sometimes that, in his love for making money, he would become selfish.

Mrs. Montague was very kind to the Morris family, and Carl seemed quite pleased to do her a favor. He took her up to his room, and let her choose the bird she liked best. She took a handsome yellow one, called Barry. He was a good singer, and a great favorite of Carl's. The boy put him in the cage, wrapped it up well, for it was a cold, snowy day, and carried it out to Mrs. Montague's sleigh.

She gave him a pleasant smile, drove away, and Carl ran up the steps into the house. "It's all right, mother," he said, giving Mrs. Morris a hearty, boyish kiss, as she stood waiting for him. "I don't mind letting her have it."

"But you expected to sell that one, didn't you?" she asked.

"Mrs. Smith said maybe she'd take it when she came home from Boston, but I dare say she'd change her mind and get one there."

"How much were you going to ask for him?"

"Well, I wouldn't sell Barry for less than ten dollars, or rather, I wouldn't have sold him," and he ran out to the stable.

Mrs. Morris sat on the hall chair, patting me in an absent-minded way as I rubbed against her. Then she got up and went into her husband's study, and told him what Carl had done.

Mr. Morris seemed very pleased to hear about it, but when his wife asked him to do something to make up the loss to the boy, he said: "I would rather not do that. To encourage a child in a kind action, and then to reward him for it, is not always a sound principle to go upon."

But Carl did not go without his reward. That evening, Mrs. Montague's coachman brought a note to the house addressed to Master Carl Morris. He read it aloud to the family.

My Dear Carl: I am charmed with my little bird, and he has whispered to me one of the secrets of your room. You want fifteen dollars very much to buy something for it. I am sure you won't be offended with an old friend for supplying you with the means to get this something.

ADA MONTAGUE.

"Just the thing for my stationary tank for the goldfish," exclaimed Carl. "I've wanted it for a long time, it isn't good to keep them in globes; but how in the world did she find out? I've never told any one."

Mrs. Morris smiled, and said, "Barry must have told her," as she took the money from Carl to put away for him.

Mrs. Montague got to be very fond of her new pet. She took care of him herself, and I have heard her tell Mrs. Morris most wonderful stories about him—stories so wonderful that I should say they were not true if I did not know how intelligent dumb creatures get to be under kind treatment.

She kept him in his cage only at night, and when she began looking for him at bedtime to put him there, he always hid himself. She would search a short time, and then sit down, and he always came out of his hiding-place, chirping in a saucy way to make her look at him.

She said that he seemed to take delight in teasing her. Once when he was in the drawing-room with her, she was called away to speak to some one at the telephone. When she came back, she found that one of the servants had come into the room and left the door open leading to a veranda. The trees outside were full of yellow birds, and she was in despair, thinking that Barry had flown out with them. She looked out, but could not see him. Then, lest he had not left the room, she got a chair and carried it about, standing on it to examine the walls, and see if Barry was hidden among the pictures and bric-à-brac. But no Barry was there. She at last sank down exhausted on a sofa. She heard a wicked little peep, and looking up, saw Barry sitting on one of the rounds of the chair that she had been carrying about to look for him. He had been there all the time. She was so glad to see him, that she never thought of scolding him.

He was never allowed to fly about the dining-room during meals, and the table maid drove him out before she set the table. It always annoyed him, and he perched on the staircase, watching the door through the railings. If it was left open for an instant, he flew in. One evening, before tea, he did this. There was a chocolate cake on the sideboard, and he liked the look of it so much, that he began to peck at it. Mrs. Montague happened to come in, and at once drove him back to the hall.

While she was having tea that evening, with her husband and little boy, Barry flew into the room again. Mrs. Montague told Charlie to send him out, but her husband said, "Wait, he is looking for something."

He was on the sideboard, peering into every dish, and trying to look under the covers. "He is after the chocolate cake," exclaimed Mrs. Montague. "Here, Charlie, put this on the staircase for him."

She cut off a little scrap, and when Charlie took it to the hall, Barry flew after him, and ate it up.

As for poor little lame Dick, Carl never sold him, and he became a family pet. His cage hung in the parlor, and from morning till night his cheerful voice was heard, chirping and singing as if he had not a trouble in the world. They took great care of him. He was never allowed to be too hot or too cold. Everybody gave him a cheerful word in passing his cage, and if his singing was too loud, they gave him a little mirror. He loved this mirror, and often stood before it for an hour at a time.

G

CHAPTER XII

MALTA, THE CAT

HE first time I had a good look at the Morris cat, I thought she was the queerest-looking animal I had ever seen. She was dark-gray—just the color of a mouse. Her eyes were a yellowish-green, and for the first few days, she looked very unkindly at me. Then she got over her dislike, and we became very good friends. She was a beautiful cat, and so gentle and affectionate that the whole family loved her.

She was three years old, and she had come to Fairport in a vessel with some sailors, who had brought her from a far-away place. Her name was Malta, and she was called a Maltese cat.

I have seen a great many cats, but I never saw one as kind as Malta. Once she had some little kittens and they all died. It almost broke her heart. She cried and cried about the house till it made one feel sad to hear her. Then she ran away to the woods. She came back with a little squirrel in her mouth, and putting it in her basket, she nursed it like a mother, till it grew old enough to run away from her.

She was a very knowing cat, and always came when she was called. Miss Laura used to wear a little silver whistle that she blew when she wanted any of her pets. It was a shrill whistle, and we could hear it a long way from home. I have seen her standing at the back door whistling for Malta, and the pretty creature's head would appear somewhere—always high up, for she was a great climber, and she would come running along the top of the fence, saying, "Meow, meow," in a funny, short way.

Miss Laura would pet her, or give her something to eat, or walk around the garden carrying her on her shoulder. Malta was a most affectionate cat, and if Miss Laura would not let her lick her face, she licked her hair with her little, rough tongue. Often Malta lay by the fire, licking my coat or little Billy's, in order to show her affection for us.

Mary, the cook, was very fond of cats, and used to keep Malta in the kitchen as much as she could, but nothing would make her stay down there if there was any music going on up-stairs. The Morris pets were all fond of music. As soon as Miss Laura sat down at the piano to sing or play, we came from all parts of the house. Malta cried to get up-stairs, Davy scampered through the hall, and Bella hurried after him. If I was outside I ran into the house, and Jim got on a box and looked through the window.

Davy's place was on Miss Laura's shoulder, his pink nose run in the curls at the back of her neck. I sat under the piano beside Malta and Bella, and we never stirred till the music was over; then we went quietly away.

Malta was a beautiful cat—there was no doubt about it. While I was with Jenkins I thought cats were vermin, like rats, and I chased them every chance I got. Mrs. Jenkins had a cat, a gaunt, long-legged, yellow creature, that ran whenever we looked at it.

Malta had been so kindly treated that she never ran from any one, except from strange dogs. She knew they would be likely to hurt her. If they came upon her suddenly, she faced them, and she was a pretty good fighter when she was forced to it. I once saw her having a brush with a big mastiff that lived a few blocks from us, and giving him a good fright, which just served him right.

I was shut up in the parlor. Some one had closed the door, and I could not get out. I was watching Malta from the window, as she daintily picked her way across the muddy street. She was such a soft, pretty, amiable-looking cat. She didn't look that way, though, when the mastiff rushed out of the alleyway at her.

She sprang back and glared at him like a fierce little tiger. Her tail was enormous. Her eyes were like balls of fire, and she was spitting and snarling, as if to say, "If you touch me, I'll tear you to pieces!"

The dog, big as he was, did not dare attack her. He walked around and around, like a great, clumsy elephant, and she turned her small body as he turned his, and kept up a dreadful hissing and spitting. Suddenly, I saw a Spitz dog hurrying down the street. He was going to help the mastiff, and Malta would be badly hurt. I had barked, and no one had come to let me out, so I sprang through the window.

Just then there was a change. Malta had seen the second dog, and knew she must get rid of the mastiff. With an agile bound, she sprang on his back, dug her sharp claws in, till he put his tail between his legs and ran up the street, howling with pain. She rode a little way, then jumped off, and ran up the lane to the stable.

I was very angry, and wanted to fight something, so I pitched into the Spitz dog. He was a snarly, cross-grained creature, no friend to Jim and me, and he would have been only too glad of a chance to help kill Malta.

I gave him one of the worst beatings he ever had. I don't suppose it was quite right for me to do it, for Miss Laura says dogs should never fight; but he had worried Malta before, and he had no business to do it. She belonged to our family. Jim and I never worried *his* cat. I had been longing to give him a shaking for some time, and now I felt for his throat through his thick hair, and dragged him all around the street. Then I let him go, and he was a civil dog ever afterward.

Malta was very grateful, and licked a little place where the Spitz had bitten me. I did not get

scolded for the broken window. Mary had seen
me from the kitchen, and told Mrs. Morris that
I had gone to help Malta.

Malta was a very wise cat. She knew quite
well that she must not harm the parrot nor the
canaries, and she never tried to catch them, even
though she was left alone in the room with them.

I have seen her lying in the sun, blinking sleep-
ily, and listening with great pleasure to Dick's
singing. Miss Laura taught her not to hunt even
the birds outside.

For a long time she had tried to get it into
Malta's head, that it was cruel to catch the little
sparrows that came about the door, and just after
I arrived, she succeeded in doing so.

Malta was so fond of Miss Laura, that whenever she caught a bird, she came and laid it at
her feet. Miss Laura always picked up the dead
little creature, pitied it and stroked it, and scolded
Malta till she crept into a corner. Then Miss
Laura put the bird on the limb of a tree, and
Malta watched her attentively.

One day Miss Laura stood at the window, looking out into the garden. Malta was lying on the
platform, staring at the sparrows that were picking up crumbs from the ground. She trembled,
and half rose every few minutes, as if to go after
them. Then she lay down again. She was trying
very hard not to creep on them. Presently a
neighbor's cat came stealing along the fence, keeping one eye on Malta and the other on the spar-

rows. Malta was so angry! She sprang up and chased her away, and then came back to the platform, where she lay down again and waited for the sparrows to come back. For a long time she stayed there, and never once tried to catch them.

Miss Laura was so pleased. She went to the door, and said softly, " Come here, Malta."

The cat put up her tail, and, meowing gently, came into the house. Miss Laura took her up in her arms, and going down to the kitchen, asked Mary to give her a saucer of her very sweetest milk for the best cat in the United States of America.

Malta got great praise for this, and I never knew of her catching a bird afterward. She was well fed in the house, and had no need to hurt such harmless creatures.

She was very fond of her home, and never went far away, as Jim and I did. Once, when Willie was going to spend a few weeks with a little friend who lived fifty miles from Fairport, he took it into his head that Malta should go with him. His mother told him that cats did not like to go away from home, but he said he would be good to her, and begged so hard to take her, that at last his mother consented.

He had been a few days in this place, when he wrote home to say that Malta had disappeared. She had seemed very uneasy, and though he had kept her with him all the time, she had acted as if she wanted to get away.

When the letter was read to Mr. Morris, he said: "Malta is coming back. Cats have a wonderful cleverness in finding their way to their own dwelling. She will be very tired. Let us go out and meet her."

Willie had gone to this place in a coach. Mr. Morris got a buggy and took Miss Laura and me with him, and we started out. We went slowly along the road. Every little while Miss Laura blew her whistle, and called, "Malta, Malta," and I barked as loudly as I could. Mr. Morris drove for several hours, then we stopped at a house, had dinner, and set out again. We were going through a thick wood, where there was a pretty straight road, when I saw a small, dark creature away ahead, trotting toward us. It was Malta. I gave a joyful bark, but she did not know me, and plunged into the wood.

I ran in after her, barking and yelping, and Miss Laura blew her whistle as loudly as she could. Soon there was a little gray head peeping at us from the bushes, and Malta bounded out, gave me a look of surprise, and then leaped into the buggy on Miss Laura's lap.

What a happy cat she was! She purred with delight, and licked Miss Laura's gloves over and over again. Then she ate the food they had brought, and went sound asleep. She was very thin, and for several days after getting home she slept most of the time.

Malta did not like dogs, but she was very good

to cats. One day, when there was no one about and the garden was very quiet, I saw her go stealing into the stable, and come out again, followed by a sore-eyed, starved-looking cat, that had been deserted by some people that lived in the next street. She led this cat up to her catnip bed, and watched her kindly, while she rolled and rubbed herself in it. Then Malta had a roll in it herself, and they both went back to the stable.

Catnip is a favorite plant with cats, and Miss Laura always kept some of it growing for Malta.

For a long time this sick cat had a home in the stable. Malta carried food to her every day, and after a while Miss Laura found out about her, and did what she could to make her well. In time she grew to be a strong, sturdy-looking cat, and Miss Laura found a home for her with an invalid lad

It was nothing new for the Morrises to feed deserted cats. Some summers, Mrs. Morris had a dozen to take care of. Careless people would go away for the summer, shutting up their houses, and making no provision for the poor cats that had been allowed to sit snugly by the fire all winter. At last, Mrs. Morris got into the habit of putting a little notice in the Fairport paper, asking people who were going away for the summer to provide for their cats during their absence.

CHAPTER XIII

THE BEGINNING OF AN ADVENTURE

HE first winter I was with the Morrises, I had an adventure. It was a week before Christmas, and we were having cold, frosty weather. Not much snow had fallen, but there was plenty of skating, and the boys were off every day with their skates on a little lake near Fairport.

Jim and I often went with them, and we had great fun scampering over the ice after them, and slipping at every step.

On this Saturday night we had just come home. It was quite dark outside, and there was a cold wind blowing, so when we came in the front door, and saw the red light from the big hall stove and the blazing fire in the parlor, they looked very cheerful.

I was quite sorry for Jim that he had to go out to his kennel. However, he said he didn't mind. The boys got a plate of nice, warm meat for him and a bowl of milk, and carried them out, and afterward he went to sleep. Jim's kennel was a very snug one. Being a spaniel, he was not a very large dog, but his kennel was roomy enough for a great Dane. He told me that Mr. Morris and the boys made it, and he liked it very much, because he could get up in the night and stretch himself, whenever he got tired of lying in one position.

It was raised a little from the ground, and it had a thick layer of straw over the floor. Above was a broad shelf, wide enough for him to lie on, and covered with an old catskin sleigh-robe. Jim always slept here in cold weather, because it was farther away from the ground.

To return to this December evening. I can remember yet how hungry I was. I could scarcely lie still till Miss Laura finished her tea. Mrs. Morris, knowing that her boys would be very hungry, had requested Mary to broil some beef-steak and roast some potatoes for them, and didn't they smell good!

They ate all the steak and potatoes. It didn't matter to me, for I wouldn't have been given any if they had been left. Mrs. Morris could not afford to feed to the dogs good meat that she had bought for her children, so she used to get the butcher to send her liver, and bones, and tough meat, and Mary cooked them, and made soup, and mixed porridge with them for us.

We never got meat three times a day. Miss Laura said that it was all very well to feed hunting-dogs on meat, but dogs that are kept about a house get ill if they are fed too well. So we had meat only once a day, and bread and milk, porridge, or dog-biscuits, for our other meals.

I make a dreadful noise when I am eating.
Ever since Jenkins cut my ears off, I have had
trouble in breathing. The flaps kept the wind
and dust from the inside of my ears. Now that
they are gone my head is stuffed up all the
time. The cold weather makes me worse, and
sometimes I have such trouble to get my breath
that it seems as if I should choke. If I opened
my mouth, and breathed through it, as I have seen
some people doing, I should be more comfortable,
but dogs always like to breathe through their
noses.

"You have taken more cold," said Miss Laura,
this night, as she put my plate of food on the floor
for me. "Finish your meat, and then come and
sit by the fire with me. What! do you want
more?"

I gave a little bark, so she filled my plate for
the second time. Miss Laura never allowed any
one to meddle with us when we were eating. One
day she found Willie teasing me by snatching at
a bone that I was gnawing. "Willie," she said,
"what would you do if you were sitting down
to the table feeling very hungry, and just as you
began to eat your meat and potatoes, I should
come along and snatch the plate from you?"

"I don't know what I'd *do*," he said laughingly;
"but I'd *want* to wallop you."

"Well," she said, "I'm afraid that Joe will
'wallop' you some day if you worry him about
his food, for even a gentle dog will sometimes

snap at any one who disturbs him at his meals; so you had better not try his patience too far."

Willie never teased me after that, and I was very glad, for two or three times I had been tempted to snarl at him.

After I finished my tea, I followed Miss Laura up-stairs. She took up a book and sat in a low chair, and I lay down on the hearth-rug beside her.

"Do you know, Joe," she said with a smile, "why you scratch with your paws, as if to make a hollow bed, and turn around a great many times before you lie down?"

Of course I did not know, so I only stared at her. "Years and years ago," she went on, gazing down at me, "there weren't any dogs living in people's houses, as you are, Joe. They were all wild creatures running about the woods. They always scratched among the leaves to make a comfortable bed for themselves, and the habit has come down to you, Joe, for you are descended from them."

This sounded very interesting, and I think she was going to tell me some more about my wild forefathers, but just then the rest of the family came in.

I always thought that this was the snuggest time of the day—when the family all sat around the fire—Mrs. Morris sewing, the boys reading or studying, and Mr. Morris with his head buried in in a newspaper, and Billy and I on the floor at their feet.

This evening I was feeling very drowsy, and had almost dropped asleep, when Ned gave me a push with his foot. He was a great tease, and he delighted in getting me to make a simpleton of myself. I tried to keep my eyes on the fire, but I could not, and just had to turn and look at him.

He was holding his book up between himself and his mother, and was opening his mouth as wide as he could and throwing back his head, pretending to howl.

For the life of me I could not help giving a loud howl. Mrs. Morris looked up and said, " Bad Joe, keep still."

The boys were all laughing behind their books, for they knew what Ned was doing. Presently he started off again, and I was just beginning another howl that might have made Mrs. Morris send me out of the room, when the door opened, and a young girl called Bessie Drury came in.

She had a cap on and a shawl thrown over her shoulders, and she had just run across the street from her father's house. " Oh! Mrs. Morris," she said, " will you let Laura come over and stay with me to-night? Mamma has just had a telegram from Bangor, saying that her aunt is very ill, and she wants to see her, and papa is going to take her there by tonight's train, and she is afraid I shall be lonely if I don't have Laura."

" Can you not come and spend the night here? " asked Mrs. Morris.

"No, thank you; I think mamma would rather have me stay in our house."

"Very well," said Mrs. Morris, "I think Laura would like to go."

"Yes, indeed," said Miss Laura, smiling at her friend. "I will come over in half an hour."

"Thank you so much," said Miss Bessie. And she hurried away.

After she left, Mr. Morris looked up from his paper. "There will be some one in the house besides those two girls?"

"Oh, yes," said Mrs. Morris; "Mrs. Drury has her old nurse, who has been with her for twenty years, and there are two maids besides, and Donald, the coachman, who sleeps over the stable. So they are well protected."

"Very good," said Mr. Morris. And he went back to his paper.

Of course dumb animals do not understand all that they hear spoken; but I think human beings would be astonished if they knew how much we can gather from their looks and voices. I knew that Mr. Morris did not quite like the idea of having his daughter go to the Drurys' when the master and mistress of the house were away, so I made up my mind that I would go with her.

When she came down-stairs with her little satchel on her arm, I got up and stood near her. "Dear old Joe," she said, "you must not come."

I pushed myself out the door beside her after

she had kissed her mother and father and the boys. " Go back, Joe," she said firmly.

I had to step back then, but I cried and whined, and she looked at me in astonishment. " I shall be back in the morning, Joe," she said gently; " don't squeal in that way." Then she shut the door and went out.

I felt dreadfully. I walked up and down the floor and ran to the window, and howled without having to look at Ned. Mrs. Morris peered over her glasses at me in utter surprise. " Boys," she said, " did you ever see Joe act in that way before? "

" No, mother," they all replied.

Mr. Morris was looking at me very intently. He had always taken more notice of me than any other creature about the house, and I was very fond of him. Now I ran up and put my paws on his knees.

" Mother," he said, turning to his wife, " let the dog go."

" Very well," she said in a puzzled way. " Jack, just run over with him, and tell Mrs. Drury how he is acting, and that I shall be very much obliged if she will let him stay all night with Laura."

Jack sprang up, seized his cap, and raced down the front steps, across the street, through the gate, and up the graveled walk, where the little stones were all hard and fast in the frost.

The Drurys lived in a large, white house, with trees all around it, and a garden at the back.

They were rich people and had a great deal of company. Through the summer I had often seen carriages at the door, and ladies and gentlemen in light clothes walking over the lawn, and sometimes I smelled nice things they were having to eat. They did not keep any dogs, or pets of any kind, so Jim and I never had an excuse to call there.

Jack and I were soon at the front door, and he rang the bell and gave me in charge of the maid who opened it. The girl listened to his message for Mrs. Drury, then she walked up-stairs, smiling and looking at me over her shoulder.

There was a trunk in the upper hall, and an elderly woman was putting clothes in it. A lady stood watching her, and when she saw me, she gave a little scream: "Oh! nurse! look at that horrid dog! Where did he come from? Put him out, Susan."

I stood quite still, and the girl who had brought me up-stairs gave her Jack's message.

"Certainly, certainly," said the lady, when the maid finished speaking. "If he is one of the Morris dogs, he is sure to be a well-behaved one. Tell the little boy to thank his mamma for letting Laura come over, and say that we shall keep the dog with pleasure. Now, nurse, we must hurry; the cab will be here in five minutes."

I walked softly into a front room, and there I found my dear Miss Laura. Miss Bessie was with her, and they were cramming things into a port-

H

manteau. They both ran out to ask how I got there, and just then a gentleman came hurriedly up-stairs, and said the cab had come.

There was a scene of great confusion and hurry, but in a few minutes it was all over. The cab had rolled away, and the house was quiet.

"Nurse, you must be tired, you had better go to bed," said Miss Bessie, turning to the elderly woman, as we all stood in the hall. "Susan, will you bring some supper to the dining-room for Miss Morris and me? What will you have, Laura?"

"What are you going to have?" asked Miss Laura with a smile.

"Hot chocolate and tea-biscuits."

"Then I will have the same."

"Bring some cake too, Susan," said Miss Bessie, "and something for the dog. I dare say he would like some of that turkey left from dinner."

If I had had any ears, I would have pricked them up at this, for I was very fond of fowl, and I never got any from the Morrises, unless it might be a stray bone or two.

What fun we had over our supper! The two girls sat at the big dining-table, and sipped their chocolate, and laughed and talked, and I had the skeleton of a whole turkey on a newspaper that Susan spread on the carpet.

I was very careful not to drag it about, and Miss Bessie laughed at me till the tears came in her eyes. "That dog is a gentleman," she said; "see how he holds the bones on the paper with

his paws, and strips the meat off with his teeth.
Oh Joe, Joe, you are a funny dog! And you are
having a funny supper. I have heard of quail on
toast, but I never heard of turkey on newspaper."

" Hadn't we better go to bed?" said Miss Laura,
when the hall-clock struck eleven.

" Yes, I suppose we had," said Miss Bessie.
" Where is this animal to sleep?"

" I don't know," said Miss Laura; " he sleeps in
the stable at home, or in the kennel with Jim."

" Suppose Susan makes him a nice bed by the
kitchen stove?" said Miss Bessie.

Susan made the bed, but I was not willing to
sleep in it. I barked so loudly when they shut
me up alone, that they had to let me go up-stairs
with them.

Miss Laura was almost angry with me, but I
could not help it. I had come to protect her, and
I wasn't going to leave her, if I could help it.

Miss Bessie had a handsomely furnished room,
with a soft carpet on the floor, and pretty curtains
at the windows. There were two single beds in
it, and the girls dragged them close together, so
that they could talk after they got in bed.

Before Miss Bessie put out the light, she told
Miss Laura not to be alarmed if she heard any
one walking about in the night, for the nurse was
sleeping across the hall from them, and she would
probably come in once or twice to see if they were
sleeping comfortably.

The two girls talked for a long time, and then

they fell asleep. Just before Miss Laura dropped off she forgave me, and put down her hand for me to lick as I lay on a fur rug close by her bed.

I was very tired and as I had a soft and pleasant bed, I soon fell into a heavy sleep; but I waked up at the slightest noise. Once Miss Laura turned in bed, and another time Miss Bessie laughed in her sleep, and again, there were queer crackling noises in the frosty limbs of the trees outside, that made me start up quickly out of my sleep.

There was a big clock in the hall, and every time it struck I waked up. Once, just after it had struck some hour, I jumped up out of a sound nap. I had been dreaming about my early home. Jenkins was after me with a whip, and my limbs were quivering and trembling as if I had been trying to get away from him.

I sprang up and shook myself. Then I took a turn around the room. The two girls were breathing gently; I could scarcely hear them. I walked to the door and looked out into the hall. There was a dim light burning there. The door of the nurse's room stood open. I went quietly to it and looked in. She was breathing heavily and muttering in her sleep.

I went back to my rug and tried to go to sleep, but I could not. Such an uneasy feeling was upon me that I had to keep walking about. I went out into the hall again and stood at the head of the staircase. I thought I would take a walk through the lower hall, and then go to bed again.

The Drurys' carpets were all like velvet, and my paws did not make a rattling on them as they did on the oil-cloth in the Morris house. I crept down the stairs like a cat, and walked along the lower hall, smelling under all the doors, listening as I went. There was no night-light burning down here, and it was quite dark; but if there had been any strange person about I should have smelled him.

I was surprised when I got near the farther end of the hall, to see a tiny gleam of light shine for an instant from under the dining-room door. Then it went away again. The dining-room was the place to eat. Surely none of the people in the house would be there after the supper we had.

I went and sniffed under the door. There was a smell there; a strong smell like beggars and poor people. It smelled like Jenkins. It *was* Jenkins.

CHAPTER XIV

HOW WE CAUGHT THE BURGLAR

WHAT was the wretch doing in the house with my dear Miss Laura? I thought I should go crazy. I scratched at the door, and barked and yelped. I sprang upon it, and though I was quite a heavy dog by this time, I felt as light as a feather.

It seemed to me that I should go mad if I could not get that door open. Every few seconds I stopped and put my head down to the door-sill to listen. There was a rushing about inside the room, and a chair fell over, and some one seemed to be getting out of the window.

This made me worse than ever. I did not stop to think that I was only a medium-sized dog, and that Jenkins would probably kill me, if he got his hands on me. I was so furious that I thought only of getting hold of him.

In the midst of the noise that I made, there was a screaming and a rushing to and fro up-stairs. I ran up and down the hall, and half-way up the steps and back again. I did not want Miss Laura to come down, but how was I to make her understand? There she was, in her white gown, leaning over the railing and holding back her long

118

hair, making no outcry, but her face a picture of surprise and alarm.

"The dog has gone mad," screamed Miss Bessie. "Nurse, pour a pitcher of water on him."

The nurse was more sensible. She ran downstairs, her night-cap flying, and a blanket that she had seized from her bed trailing behind her. "There are thieves in the house," she shouted at the top of her voice, "and the dog has found it out."

She did not go near the dining-room door, but threw open the front one, crying, "Policeman, policeman, help, help, thieves, murder!"

Such a screaming as that old woman made! She was worse than I was. I dashed by her, out through the hall door, and away down to the gate, where I heard some one running. I gave a few loud yelps to call Jim, and leaped the gate as the man before me had done.

There was something savage in me that night. I think it must have been the smell of Jenkins. I felt as if I could tear him to pieces. I have never felt so wicked since. I was hunting him, as he had hunted me and my mother, and the thought gave me pleasure.

Old Jim soon caught up with me, and I gave him a push with my nose, to let him know I was glad he had come. We rushed swiftly on, and at the corner caught up with the miserable man who was running away from us.

I gave an angry growl, and jumping up, bit at

his leg. He turned around, and though it was not a very bright night, there was light enough for me to see the ugly face of my old master.

He seemed so angry to think that Jim and I dared to snap at him. He caught up a handful of stones, and with some bad words threw them at us. Just then, away in front of us, was a queer whistle, and then another one like it behind us. Jenkins made a strange noise in his throat, and started to run down a side street, away from the direction of the two whistles.

I was afraid that he was going to get away, and though I could not hold him, I kept springing up on him, and once I tripped him up. Oh, how furious he was! He kicked me against the side of a wall, and gave me two or three hard blows with a stick that he caught up.

I would not give in, though I could scarcely see him for the blood that was running over my eyes. Old Jim got so angry whenever Jenkins touched me, that he ran up behind and nipped his calves, to make him turn on him.

Soon Jenkins came to a high wall, where he stopped, and with a hurried look behind, began to climb over it. The wall was too high for me to jump. He was going to escape. What should I do? I barked as loudly as I could for some one to come, and then sprang up and held him by the leg as he was getting over.

I had such a grip, that I went over the wall with him, and left Jim on the other side. Jenkins fell on his face in the earth. Then he got up, and with a look of deadly hatred on his face pounced upon me. If help had not come, I think he would have dashed out my brains against the wall, as he dashed out my poor little brothers' against the horse's stall. But just then there was a running sound. Two men came down the street and sprang upon the wall, just where Jim was leaping up and down and barking in distress.

I saw at once by their uniform and the clubs in their hands, that they were policemen. In one short instant they had hold of Jenkins. He gave up then, but he stood snarling at me like an ugly dog. "If it hadn't been for that cur, I'd never a been caught. Why——" and he staggered back and uttered a bad word, "it's me own dog."

"More shame to you," said one of the policemen sternly; "what have you been up to at this time of night, to have your own dog and a quiet minister's spaniel dog a-chasing you through the street?"

Jenkins began to swear and would not tell anything. There was a house in the garden, and just at this minute some one in an upper room opened a window and called out, "Hallo, there, what are you doing?"

"We're catching a thief, sir," said one of the policemen, "leastwise I think that's what he's been up to. Could you throw us down a bit of rope? We've no handcuffs here, and one of us has to go to the lock-up and the other to Washington Street, where there's a woman yelling blue murder; hurry up, please, sir."

The gentleman threw down a rope, and in two minutes Jenkin's wrists were tied together, and he was walked through the gate, saying bad words as fast as he could to the policeman who was leading him. " Good dogs," said the other police-man to Jim and me. Then he ran up the street and we followed him.

As we hurried along Washington Street, and came near our house, we saw lights gleaming through the darkness, and heard people running to and fro. The nurse's shrieking had alarmed the neighborhood. The Morris boys were all out in the street only half clad and shivering with cold, and the Drurys' coachman, with no hat on, and his hair sticking up all over his head, was running about with a lantern.

The neighbors' houses were all lighted up, and a good many people were hanging out of their windows and opening their doors, and calling to each other to know what all this noise meant.

When the policeman appeared with Jim and me at his heels, quite a crowd gathered around him to hear his part of the story. Jim and I dropped on the ground panting as hard as we could, and with little streams of water running from our tongues. We were both pretty well used up. Jim's back was bleeding in several places from the stones that Jenkins had thrown at him, and I was a mass of bruises.

Presently we were discovered, and then what a fuss was made over us. "Brave dogs! noble dogs!" everybody said, and patted and praised us. We were very proud and happy, and stood up and wagged our tails, at least Jim did, and I wagged what I could. Then they found what a state we were in. Mrs. Morris cried, and catching me up in her arms, ran into the house with me, and Jack followed with old Jim.

We all went into the parlor. There was a good fire there, and Miss Laura and Miss Bessie were sitting over it. They sprang up when they saw us, and right there in the parlor washed our wounds, and made us lie down by the fire.

"You saved our silver, brave Joe," said Miss Bessie; "just wait till my papa and mamma come home, and see what they will say. Well, Jack, what is the latest?" as the Morris boys came trooping into the room.

"The policeman has been questioning your nurse, and examining the dining-room, and has gone down to the station to make his report, and do you know what he has found out?" said Jack excitedly.

"No—what?" asked Miss Bessie.

"Why that villain was going to burn your house."

Miss Bessie gave a little shriek. "Why, what do you mean?"

"Well," said Jack, "they think by what they have discovered, that he planned to pack his bag with silver, and carry it off; but just before he did so he meant to pour oil around the room, and set fire to it, so that people would not find out that he had been robbing you."

"Why we might have all been burned to death," said Miss Bessie. "He couldn't burn the dining-room without setting fire to the rest of the house."

"Certainly not," said Jack, "that shows what a villain he is."

"Do they know this for certain, Jack?" asked Miss Laura.

"Well, they suppose so; they found some bottles of oil along with the bag he had for the silver."

"How horrible! You darling old Joe, perhaps you saved our lives," and pretty Miss Bessie kissed my ugly, swollen head. I could do nothing but lick her little hand, but always after that I thought a great deal of her.

It is now some years since all this happened, and I might as well tell the end of it: The next day the Drurys came home, and everything was found out about Jenkins. The night they left Fairport he had been hanging about the station. He knew just who were left in the house, for he had once supplied them with milk, and knew all about their family. He had no customers at this time, for after Mr. Harry rescued me, and that piece came out in the paper about him, he found that no one would take milk from him. His wife died, and some kind people put his children in a home, and he was obliged to sell Toby and the cows. Instead of learning a lesson from all this, and leading a better life, he kept sinking lower and lower.

He was, therefore, ready for any kind of mischief that turned up, and when he saw the Drurys going away in the train, he thought he would steal a bag of silver from their sideboard, then set fire to the house, and run away and hide the silver. After a time he would take it to some city and sell it.

He was made to confess all this. Then for his wickedness he was sent to prison for ten years, where I hope he will learn to be a better man.

I was sore and stiff for a long time, and one day Mrs. Drury came over to see me. She did not love dogs as the Morrises did. She tried to, but she could not.

Dogs can see fun in things as well as human beings can, and I buried my muzzle in the hearth-rug, so that she would not see how I was curling up my lip and smiling at her.

"You—are—a—good—dog," she said slowly. "You are"—then she stopped, and could not think of anything else to say to me. I got up and stood in front of her, for a well-bred dog should not lie down when a lady speaks to him. I wagged my body a little, and I would gladly have said something to help her out of her difficulty, but I couldn't. If she had stroked me it might have helped her, but she didn't want to touch me, and I knew she didn't want me to touch her, so I just stood looking at her.

" Mrs. Morris," she said, turning from me with a puzzled face, " I don't like animals, and I can't pretend to, for they always find me out; but can't you let that dog know that I shall feel eternally grateful to him for saving not only our property, for that is a trifle, but my darling daughter from fright and annoyance, and a possible injury or loss of life?"

" I think he understands," said Mrs. Morris. " He is a very wise dog." And smiling in great amusement, she called me to her and put my paws on her lap. " Look at that lady, Joe. She is pleased with you for driving Jenkins away from her house. You remember Jenkins?"

I barked angrily and limped to the window.

" How intelligent he is," said Mrs. Drury. " My husband has sent to New York for a watch-dog, and he says that from this on our house shall never be without one. Now I must go. Your dog is happy, Mrs. Morris, and I can do nothing for him, except to say that I shall never forget him, and I wish he would come over occasionally to see us. Perhaps when we get our dog he will. I shall tell my cook whenever she sees him to give him something to eat. This is a souvenir for Laura of that dreadful night. I feel under a deep obligation to you, so I am sure you will allow her to accept it." Then she gave Mrs. Morris a little box and went away.

When Miss Laura came in, she opened the box, and found in it a handsome diamond ring. On the inside was engraved: "Laura, in memory of December 20th, 18—. From her grateful friend, Bessie."

The diamond was worth hundreds of dollars, and Mrs. Morris told Miss Laura that she would rather she did not wear it then, while she was a young girl. It was not suitable for her, and she knew Mrs. Drury did not expect her to do so. She wished to give her a valuable present, and this would always be worth a great deal of money.

CHAPTER XV

VERY other summer, the Morris children
were sent to some place in the country, so
that they could have a change of air, and
see what country life was like. As there were so
many of them, they usually went different ways.

The summer after I came to them, Jack and
Carl were sent to an uncle in Vermont, Miss Laura
visited another in New Hampshire, and Ned and
Willie spent their holidays with a maiden aunt who
lived in the White Mountains.

Mr. and Mrs. Morris stayed at home. Fairport
was a lovely place in summer, and many people
came there to visit.

The children took some of their pets with them,
and the others they left at home for their mother
to care for. She never allowed them to take a
a bird or an animal anywhere, unless she knew it
would be perfectly welcome. "Don't let your pets
be a worry to other people," she often said to
them, "or they will dislike them and you too."

Miss Laura went away earlier than the others,
for she had not been well through the spring, and
was pale and thin. One day, early in June, we
set out. I say "we," for after my adventure with
128

Jenkins, Miss Laura said that I should never be parted from her. If any one invited her to come and see them, and didn't want me, she would stay at home.

The whole family went to the station to see us off. They put a chain on my collar, and took me to the baggage-office, and got two tickets for me. One was tied to my collar, and the other Miss Laura put in her purse. Then I was put in a baggage-car, and chained in a corner. I heard Mr. Morris say that as we were only going a short distance, it was not worth while to get an express ticket for me.

There was a dreadful noise and bustle at the station. Whistles were blowing, and people were rushing up and down the platform. Some men were tumbling baggage so fast into the car where I was, that I was afraid some of it would fall on me.

For a few minutes Miss Laura stood by the door and looked in, but soon the men had piled up so many boxes and trunks that she could not see me. Then she went away. Mr. Morris asked one of the men to see that I did not get hurt, and I heard some money rattle. Then he too went away.

It was the beginning of June, and the weather had suddenly become very hot. We had had a long, cold spring, and not being used to the heat, it seemed very hard to bear.

Before the train started, the doors of the baggage-car were closed, and it became quite dark

I

inside. The darkness, and the heat, and the close smell, and the noise, as we went rushing along, made me fell sick and frightened.

I did not dare to lie down, but sat up trembling and wishing that we might soon come to Riverdale Station. But we did not get there for some time, and I was to have a great fright.

I was thinking of all the stories that I knew of animals traveling. In February, the Drurys' Newfoundland watch-dog Pluto had arrived from New York, and he told Jim and me that he had had a miserable journey.

A friend of Mr. Drury's had brought him from New York. He saw him chained up in his car, then went into his Pullman, first tipping the baggage-master handsomely to look after him. Pluto said that the baggage-master had a very red nose, and he was always getting drinks for himself when they stopped at a station, but he never once gave him a drink or anything to eat, from the time they left New York till they got to Fairport. When the train stopped there, and Pluto's chain was unfastened, he sprang out on the platform, and nearly knocked Mr. Drury down. He saw some snow that had sifted through the station roof, and he was so thirsty that he began to lick it up. When the snow was all gone he jumped up and licked the frost on the windows.

Mr. Drury's friend was very angry. He found the baggage-master, and said to him: "What did you mean, by coming into my car every few hours, to tell me that the dog was fed, and watered, and comfortable? I shall report you."

He went into the office at the station, and complained of the man, and was told that he was a drinking man, and was going to be dismissed.

I was not afraid of suffering like Pluto, because it was going to take us only a few hours to get to Riverdale. I found that we always went slowly before we came in to a station, and one time when we began to slacken speed I thought that surely we must be at our journey's end. However, it was not Riverdale. The car gave a jump, then there was a crashing sound ahead, and we stopped.

I heard men shouting and running up and down, and I wondered what had happened. It was all dark and still in the car, and nobody came in, but the noise kept up outside, and I knew something had gone wrong with the train. Perhaps Miss Laura had got hurt. Something must have happened to her or she would come to me.

I barked and pulled at my chain till my neck was sore, but for a long, long time I was there alone. The men running about outside must have heard me. If ever I hear a man in trouble and crying for help I go to him and see what he wants.

After such a long time that it seemed to me it must be the middle of the night, the door at the end of the car opened, and a man looked in. "This is all through baggage for New York, miss," I heard him say, "they wouldn't put your dog in here."

"Yes, they did—I am sure this is the car," I heard in the voice I knew so well, "and will you get him out, please? He must be terribly frightened."

The man found me, stooped down, and unfastened my chain, grumbling to himself because I had not been put in another car. "Some folks tumble a dog round as if he was a junk of coal," he said, patting me kindly.

I was nearly wild with delight to get with Miss Laura again, but I had barked so much, and pressed my neck so hard with my collar that my voice was all gone. I fawned on her, and wagged myself about, and opened and shut my mouth, but no sound came out of it.

It made Miss Laura nervous. She tried to laugh and cry at the same time, and then bit her lip hard, and said, "Oh Joe, don't."

"He's lost his bark, hasn't he?" said the man, looking at me curiously.

"It is a wicked thing to confine an animal in a dark and closed car," said Miss Laura, trying to see her way down the steps through her tears.

The man put out his hand and helped her. "He's not suffered much, miss," he said, "don't you distress yourself. Now if you'd been a brakeman on a train, as I was a few years ago and seen the animals run in for the stockyards, you might talk about cruelty. Cars that ought to hold a certain number of pigs, or sheep, or cattle, jammed full with twice as many, and half of 'em thrown out choked and smothered to death. I've seen a man running up and down, raging and swearing because the railway people hadn't let him get in to tend to his pigs on the road."

Miss Laura turned and looked at the man with a very white face. "Is it like that now?"

"No, no," he said hastily. "It's better now. They've got new regulations about taking care of the stock, but mind you, miss, the cruelty to animals isn't all done on the railways. There's a great lot of dumb creatures suffering all round everywhere, and if they could speak, 'twould be a hard showing for some other people besides the railway men."

He lifted his cap and hurried down the platform, and Miss Laura, her face very much troubled, picked her way among the bits of coal and wood scattered about the platform, and went into the waiting-room of the little station.

She took me up to the filter and let some water run in her hand, and gave it to me to lap. Then she sat down and I leaned my head against her knees, and she stroked my throat gently.

There were some people sitting about the room, and from their talk, I found out what had taken place. There had been a freight-train on a side-track at this station, waiting for us to pass it. The switchman had carelessly left the switch open after this train went by, and when we came along afterward, our train, instead of running in by the platform, went crashing into the freight-train.

If we had been going fast, great damage might have been done. As it was, our engine was smashed so badly that it could not take us on; the passengers were frightened; and we were having a tedious time waiting for another engine to come and take us to Riverdale.

After the accident, the trainmen were so busy that Miss Laura could get no one to release me.

While I sat by her, I noticed an old gentleman staring at us. He was such a queer-looking old gentleman. He looked like a poodle. He had bright brown eyes, and a pointed face, and a shock of white hair that he shook every few minutes. He sat with his hands clasped on the top of his cane, and he scarcely took his eyes from Miss Laura's face. Suddenly he jumped up and came and sat down beside her.

"An ugly dog, that," he said, pointing to me.

Most young girls would have resented this, but Miss Laura looked only amused. "He seems beautiful to me," she said gently.

"H'm, because he's your dog," said the old man, darting a sharp look at me. "What's the matter with him?"

"This is his first journey by rail and he's a little frightened."

"No wonder. The Lord only knows the suffering of animals in transportation," said the old gentleman. "My dear young lady, if you could see what I have seen, you'd never eat another bit of meat all the days of your life."

Miss Laura wrinkled her forehead. "I know—I have heard," she faltered. "It must be terrible."

"Terrible—it's awful," said the gentleman. "Think of the cattle on the Western plains. Choked with thirst in summer and starved and frozen in winter. Dehorned and goaded on to trains and steamers. Tossed about and wounded and suffering on voyages. Many of them dying and being thrown into the sea. Others landed sick and frightened. Some of them slaughtered on docks and wharves to keep them from dropping dead in their tracks. What kind of food does their flesh make? It's rank poison. Three of my family have died of cancer. I never eat meat."

The strange old gentleman darted from his seat, and began to pace up and down the room. I was very glad he had gone, for Miss Laura hated to hear of cruelty of any kind, and her tears were dropping thick and fast on my brown coat.

The gentleman had spoken very loudly, and every one in the room had listened to what he said. Among them, was a very young man, with a cold, handsome face. He looked as if he was annoyed that the older man should have made Miss Laura cry.

"Don't you think, sir," he said, as the old gentleman passed near him, "that there is a great deal of mock sentiment about this business of taking care of the dumb creation? They were made for us. They've got to suffer and be killed to supply our wants. The cattle and sheep, and other animals would overrun the earth, if we didn't kill them."

"Granted," said the old man, stopping right in front of him. "Granted, young man, if you take out that word suffer. The Lord made the sheep, and the cattle, and the pigs. They are his creatures just as much as we are. We can kill them, but we've no right to make them suffer."

"But we can't help it, sir."

"Yes, we can, my young man. It's a possible thing to raise healthy stock, treat it kindly, kill it mercifully, eat it decently. When men do that, I, for one, will cease to be a vegetarian. You're only a lad. You haven't traveled as I have. I've been from one end of this country to the other. Up North, down South, and out West, I've seen sights that made me shudder, and I tell you the Lord will punish this great American nation if it doesn't change its treatment of the dumb animals committed to its care."

The young man looked thoughtful, and did not reply. A very sweet-faced old lady sitting near him, answered the old gentleman. I don't think I have ever seen such a fine-looking old lady as she was. Her hair was snowy white, and her face was deeply wrinkled, yet she was tall and stately, and her expression was as pleasing as my dear Miss Laura's.

"I do not think we are a wicked nation," she said softly. "We are a younger nation than many

on the earth, and I think that many of our sins
arise from ignorance and thoughtlessness."

"Yes, madam," said the fiery old gentleman,
staring hard at her. "I agree with you there."

She smiled pleasantly at him, and went on. "I
too have been a traveler, and I have talked to
a great many wise and good people on the subject
of the cruel treatment of animals, and I find that
many of them have never thought about it. They
themselves, never knowingly ill-treat a dumb creature, and when they are told stories of inhuman
conduct, they say in surprise, 'Why, these things
surely can't exist!' You see they have never
been brought in contact with them. As soon as
they learn about them, they begin to agitate and
say: 'We must have this thing stopped. Where
is the remedy?'"

"And what is it, what is it, madam, in your
opinion?" he said, pawing the floor with impatience.

"Just the remedy that I would propose for the
great evil of intemperance," said the old lady.
"Legislation for the old and hardened and education for the young and tender. I would tell the
schoolboys and schoolgirls that alcohol will destroy the framework of their beautiful bodies, and
that cruelty to any of God's living creatures will
blight and destroy their innocent young souls."

The young man spoke again. "Don't you think,"
he said, "that you temperance and humane people lay too much stress upon the education of our

youth in all lofty and noble sentiments? The human heart will always be wicked. Your Bible tells you that, doesn't it? You can't educate all the badness out of children."

We don't expect to do that," said the old lady, turning her pleasant face toward him; "but even the human heart is desperately wicked, shouldn't that make us much more eager to try to educate, to ennoble, and restrain? However, as far as my experience goes, and I have lived in this wicked world for seventy-five years, I find that the human heart, though wicked and cruel as you say, has yet some soft and tender spots, and the impressions made upon it in youth are never effaced. Do you not remember better than anything else, standing at your mother's knee—the pressure of her hand, her kiss on your forehead?"

By this time our engine had arrived. A whistle was blowing, and nearly every one was rushing from the room, the impatient old gentleman among the first. Miss Laura was hurriedly trying to do up her shawl-strap, and I was standing by, wishing that I could help her. The old lady and the young man were the only other people in the room, and we could not help hearing what they said.

"Yes, I do," he said in a thick voice, and his face got very red. "She is dead now—I have no mother."

"Poor boy!" and the old lady laid her hand on his shoulder. They were standing up, and she was taller than he was. "May God bless you. I

know you have a kind heart. I have four stalwart
boys, and you remind me of the youngest. If you
are ever in Washington, come to see me." She
gave him some name, and he lifted his hat and
looked as if he was astonished to find out who she
was. Then he too went away, and she turned to
Miss Laura. "Shall I help you, my dear?"

"If you please," said my young mistress. "I
can't fasten this strap."

In a few seconds the bundle was done up, and
we were joyfully hastening to the train. It was
only a few miles to Riverdale, so the conductor
let me stay in the car with Miss Laura. She
spread her coat out on the seat in front of her,
and I sat on it and looked out of the car-window
as we sped along through a lovely country, all
green and fresh in the June sunlight. How light
and pleasant this car was—so different from the
baggage-car. What frightens an animal most of
all, is not to see where it is going, not to know
what is going to happen to it. I think that they
are very like human beings in this respect.

The lady had taken a seat beside Miss Laura,
and as we went along, she too looked out of the
window and quoted in a low voice:

"What is so rare as a day in June,
    Then, if ever, come perfect days."

"That is very true," said Miss Laura, "how
sad that the autumn must come and the cold
winter."

"No, my dear, not sad. It is but a preparation for another summer."

"Yes, I suppose it is," said Miss Laura. Then she continued a little shyly, as her companion leaned over to stroke my cropped ears, "You seem very fond of animals."

"I am, my dear. I have four horses, two cows, a tame squirrel, three dogs, and a cat."

"You should be a happy woman," said Miss Laura with a smile.

"I think I am. I must not forget my horned toad, Diego, that I got in California. I keep him in the greenhouse, and he is very happy catching flies and holding his horny head to be scratched whenever any one comes near."

"I don't see how any one can be unkind to animals," said Miss Laura thoughtfully.

"Nor I, my dear child. It has always caused me intense pain to witness the torture of dumb animals. Over sixty years ago, when I was a little girl walking the streets of Boston, I would tremble and grow faint at the cruelty of drivers to overloaded horses. I was timid and did not dare to speak to them. Very often, I ran home and flung myself in my mother's arms with a burst of tears, and asked her if nothing could be done to help the poor animals. With mistaken motherly kindness, she tried to put the subject out of my thoughts. But the animals went on suffering just the same, and when I became a woman, I agitated the matter among my friends, and was able to assist in the formation of several societies for the prevention of cruelty to animals. Oh! if people would only understand that their unkind deeds will recoil upon their own heads with tenfold force—but, my dear child, I am fancying that I am addressing a drawing-room meeting—and here we are at your station. Good-bye; keep your happy face and gentle ways. I hope that we may meet again some day." She pressed Miss Laura's hand, gave me a farewell pat, and the next minute we were outside on the platform, and she was smiling through the window at us.

CHAPTER XVI

DINGLEY FARM

Y dear niece," and a stout, middle-aged woman, with a red, lively face, threw both her arms around Miss Laura. "How glad I am to see you, and this is the dog. Good Joe, I have a bone waiting for you. Here is Uncle John."

A tall, good-looking man stepped up and put out a big hand, in which my mistress' little fingers were quite swallowed up. "I am glad to see you, Laura. Well, Joe, how d'ye do, old boy? I've heard about you."

It made me feel very welcome to have them both notice me, and I was so glad to be out of the train that I frisked for joy around their feet as we went to the wagon. It was a big double one, with an awning over it for shelter from the sun's rays, and the horses were drawn up in the shade of a spreading tree. They were two powerful black horses, and as they had no blinders on, they could see us coming. Their faces lighted up, and they moved their ears and pawed the ground, and whinnied when Mr. Wood went up to them. They tried to rub their heads against him, and I saw plainly that they loved him. "Steady there, Cleve

142

and Pacer," he said; "now back, back up." And they were quick to obey.

By this time Mrs. Wood, Miss Laura, and I were in the wagon. Then Mr. Wood jumped in, took up the reins, and off we went. How the two black horses did spin along! I sat on the seat beside Mr. Wood, and sniffed the delicious air with its lovely smell of flowers and grass. How glad I was to be in the country! What long races I should have in the green fields. I wished that I had another dog to run with me, and wondered very much whether Mr. Wood kept one. I knew I should soon find out, for whenever Miss Laura went to a place she wanted to know what animals there were about.

We drove a little more than a mile along a country road where there were occasional houses. Miss Laura answered questions about her family, and asked questions about Mr. Harry, who was away at college and hadn't got home. I don't think I have said before that Mr. Harry was Mrs. Wood's son. She was a widow with one son when she married Mr. Wood, so that Mr. Harry, though the Morrises called him cousin, was not really their cousin.

I was very glad to hear them say that he was soon coming back, for I had not forgotten that but for him I should never have found my pleasant home, or known Miss Laura.

By and by I heard Miss Laura say, "Uncle John, have you a dog?"

"Yes, Laura," he said, "I have one today, but I sha'n't have one to-morrow."

"Oh uncle, what do you mean?" she asked.

"Well, Laura," he replied, "you know animals are pretty much like people. There are some good ones and some bad ones. Now, this dog is a snarling, cross-grained, cantankerous beast, and when I heard Joe was coming I said, 'Now we'll have a good dog about the place, and here's an end to the bad one.' So I tied Bruno up, and to-morrow I shall shoot him. Something's got to be done or he'll be biting some one."

"Uncle," said Miss Laura, "people don't always die when they are bitten by dogs, do they?"

"No, certainly not," replied Mr. Wood. "In my humble opinion there's a great lot of nonsense talked about the poison of a dog's bite and people dying of hydrophobia. Ever since I was born I've had dogs snap at me and stick their teeth in my flesh, and I've never had a symptom of hydrophobia and never intend to have. I believe half the people that are bitten by dogs frighten themselves into thinking they are fatally poisoned. I was reading the other day about the policemen in a big city in England that have to catch stray dogs, and dogs supposed to be mad, and they get bitten over and over again, and never think anything about it. But let a lady or gentleman walking along the street have a dog bite them, and they worry themselves till their blood is in a fever, and they have to hurry across to France to get

Pasteur to cure them. They imagine they've got hydrophobia, and they have it because they think they have it. I believe if I fixed my attention on that right thumb of mine, and thought I had a sore there, and picked at it and worried it, in a short time a sore would come, and I'd be off to the doctor to have it cured. At the same time, dogs have no business to bite, and I don't recommend any one to get bitten."

"But, uncle," said Miss Laura, "isn't there such a thing as hydrophobia?"

"Oh, yes, I dare say there is. I believe that a careful examination of the records of deaths reported in Boston from hydrophobia for the space of thirty-two years, shows that two people actually died from it. Dogs are like all other animals. They're liable to sickness, and they've got to be watched. I think my horses would go mad if I starved them, or overfed them, or overworked them, or let them stand in laziness, or kept them dirty, or didn't give them water enough. They'd get some disease, anyway. If a person owns an animal, let him take care of it, and it's all right. If it shows signs of sickness, shut it up and watch it. If the sickness is incurable, kill it. Here's a sure way to prevent hydrophobia. Kill off all ownerless and vicious dogs. If you can't do that, have plenty of water where they can get at it. A dog that has all the water he wants will never go mad.

"This dog of mine has not one single thing

K

the matter with him but pure ·ugliness. Yet, if I let him loose, and he ran through the village with his tongue out, I'll warrant you there'd be a cry of ' mad dog.' However, I'm going to kill him. I've no use for a bad dog.

" Have plenty of animals, I say, and treat them kindly, but if there's a vicious one among them, put it out of the way, for it is a constant danger to man and beast. It's queer how unreasonable some people are about their dogs. They'll keep them, no matter how they worry other people, and even when they're snatching the bread out of their neighbors' mouths. But I say that it is not the fault of the four-legged dog. A human dog is the worst of all.

" There's a band of sheep-killing dogs here in Riverdale, that their owners can't or won't keep out of mischief. Meek-looking fellows some of them are. The owners go to bed at night, and the dogs pretend to go too, but when the house is quiet, and the family asleep, off goes Rover or Fido to worry poor, defenseless creatures that can't defend themselves. Their taste for sheep's blood is like the taste for liquor in men, and the dogs will travel as far to get their fun as the men will travel for theirs. They've got it in them, and you can't get it out."

We had come to a turn in the road where the ground sloped gently upward. We turned in at the gate, and drove between rows of trees up to a long, low, red house, with a veranda all around it. There was a wide lawn in front, and away on our right were the farm buildings. They too, were painted red, and there were some trees by them that Mr. Wood called his windbreak, because they kept the snow from drifting in the winter-time.

I thought it was a beautiful place. Miss Laura had been here before, but not for some years, so she too was looking about quite eagerly.

"Welcome to Dingley Farm, Joe," said Mrs. Wood, with her jolly laugh, as she watched me jump from the carriage seat to the ground. "Come in, and I'll introduce you to Pussy."

"Aunt Hattie, why is the farm called Dingley Farm?" said Miss Laura, as we went into the house. "It ought to be Wood Farm."

"Dingley is made out of 'dingle,' Laura. You know that pretty hollow back of the pasture? It is what they call a 'dingle.' So this farm was called Dingle Farm till the people round about got saying 'Dingley' instead. I suppose they found it easier. Why here is Lolo coming to see Joe."

Walking along the wide hall that ran through the house was a large tortoise-shell cat. She had a prettily marked face, and she was waving her large tail like a flag, and mewing kindly to greet her mistress. But when she saw me, what a face she made. She flew on the hall-table, and putting up her back till it almost lifted her feet from the ground, began to spit at me and bristle with rage.

"Poor Lolo," said Mrs. Wood, going up to her.
"Joe is a good dog, and not like Bruno. He
won't hurt you."

I wagged myself about a little, and looked
kindly at her, but she kept on saying bad words
to me. It was weeks before I made friends with
that cat. She was a young thing, and had known
only one dog, and he was a bad one, so she supposed all dogs were like him.

There were several rooms opening off the hall,
and one of them was the dining-room, where they
had tea. I lay on a rug outside the door and
watched them. There was a small table spread
with a white cloth, and it had pretty dishes and
glassware on it, and a good many different kinds
of things to eat. A little French girl, called
Adèle, kept coming and going from the kitchen
to give them hot cakes, and fried eggs, and hot
coffee. As soon as they finished their tea, Mrs.
Wood gave me one of the best meals that I ever
had in my life.

CHAPTER XVII

MR. WOOD AND HIS HORSES

HE morning after we arrived in Riverdale
I was up very early and walking around
the house. I slept in the woodshed, and
could run outdoors whenever I liked.

The woodshed was at the back of the house,
and near it was the tool-shed. Then there was a
carriage-house, and a plank walk leading to the
barnyard.

I ran up this walk, and looked into the first
building I came to. It was the horse-stable. A
door stood open, and the morning sun was glancing in. There were several horses there, some
with their heads toward me, and some with their
tails. I saw that instead of being tied up, they
were in box-stalls, and could stand any way they
liked.

There was a man moving about at the other
end of the stable, and long before he saw me, I
knew that it was Mr. Wood. What a nice, clean
stable he had! There was always a foul smell
coming out of Jenkins' stable, but here the air
seemed as pure inside as outside. There were
many little gratings in the wall to let in the
fresh air, and they were so placed that draughts

149

would not blow on the horses. Mr. Wood was going from one horse to another, giving them hay, and talking to them in a cheerful voice. At last he spied me, and cried out: "The top of the morning to you, Joe! You are up early. Don't come too near the horses, good dog," as I walked in beside him; "they might think you are another Bruno, and give you a sly bite or kick. I should have shot him long ago. It's hard to make a good dog suffer for a bad one, but that's the way of the world. Well, old fellow, what do you think of my horse-stable? Pretty fair, isn't it?"

Mr. Wood went on talking to me, as he fed and groomed his horses, till I soon found out that his chief pride was in them.

I like to have human beings talk to me. Mr. Morris often reads his sermons to me, and Miss Laura tells me secrets that I don't think she would tell to any one else.

I watched Mr. Wood carefully, while he groomed a huge, gray cart-horse, that he called Dutchman. He took a brush in his right hand, and a curry-comb in his left, and he curried and brushed every part of the horse's skin, and afterward wiped him with a cloth. "A good grooming is equal to two quarts of oats, Joe," he said.

Then he stooped down and examined the horse's hoofs. "Your shoes are too heavy, Dutchman," he said; "but that pig-headed blacksmith thinks he knows more about horses than I do. 'Don't cut the sole or the frog,' I say to him. 'Don't pare the hoof so much, and don't rasp it; and fit your shoe to the foot, and not the foot to the shoe,' and he looks as if he wanted to say, 'Mind your own business.' We'll not go to him again. ''Tis hard to teach an old dog new tricks.' I got you to work for me, not to wear out your strength in lifting about his weighty shoes."

Mr. Wood stopped talking for a few minutes, and whistled a tune. Then he began again. "I've made a study of horses, Joe. Over forty years I've studied them, and it's my opinion that the average horse knows more than the average man that drives him. When I think of the stupid fools that are goading patient horses about, beating them and misunderstanding them, and thinking they are only clods of earth with a little life in them, I'd like to take their horses out of the shafts and harness the men in, and I'd trot them off at a pace, and slash them, and jerk them, till I guess they'd come out with a little less patience than the animal does.

"Look at this Dutchman—see the size of him. You'd think he hadn't any more nerves than a bit of granite. Yet he's got a skin as sensitive as a girl's. See how he quivers if I run the curry-comb too harshly over him. The idiot I got him from didn't know what was the matter with him. He'd bought him for a reliable horse, and there he was, kicking and stamping whenever the boy went near him. 'Your boy's got too heavy a hand, Deacon Jones,' said I, when he described the horse's actions to me. 'You may depend upon it, a four-legged creature, unlike a two-legged one, has a reason for everything he does.' 'But he's only a draught-horse,' said Deacon Jones. 'Draught-horse or no draught-horse,' said I, 'you're describing a horse with a tender skin to me, and I don't care if he's as big as an elephant.' Well, the old man grumbled and said he didn't want any thoroughbred airs in his stable, so I bought you, didn't I, Dutchman?" and Mr. Wood stroked him kindly and went to the next stall.

In each stall was a small tank of water with a sliding cover, and I found out afterward that these covers were put on when a horse came in too heated to have a drink. At any other time he could drink all he liked. Mr. Wood believed in having plenty of pure water for all his animals.

Even I had a little bowl of water in the wood-shed, though I could easily have run up to the barnyard when I wanted a drink. As soon as I came, Mrs. Wood asked Adèle to keep it there for me, and when I looked up gratefully at her, she said: "Every animal should have its own feeding-place and its own sleeping-place, Joe; that is only fair."

The next horses Mr. Wood groomed were the black ones, Cleve and Pacer. Pacer had something wrong with his mouth, and Mr. Wood turned back his lips and examined it carefully. This he was able to do, for there were large windows in the stable and it was as light as the house.

"No dark corners here, eh Joe?" said Mr. Wood, as he came out of the stall and passed me to get a bottle from a shelf. "When this stable was built, I said no dirt holes for careless men here. I want the sun to shine in the corners, and I don't want my horses to smell bad smells, for they hate them, and I don't want them starting when they go into the light of day, just because they've been kept in a black hole of a stable, and I've never had a sick horse yet."

He poured something from the bottle into a saucer, and went back to Pacer with it. I followed him and stood outside. Mr. Wood seemed to be washing a sore in the horse's mouth. Pacer winced a little, and Mr. Wood said, "Steady, steady, my beauty, 'twill soon be over."

The horse fixed his intelligent eyes on his master and looked as if he knew that he was trying to do him good.

"Just look at these lips, Joe," said Mr. Wood, "delicate and fine like our own, and yet there are brutes that will jerk them as if they were made of iron. I wish the Lord would give horses voices just for one week. I tell you they'd scare some of us. Now, Pacer, that's over. I'm not going to dose you much, for I don't believe in it. If a horse has a serious trouble, get a good horse doctor, say I. If it's a simple thing, try a simple remedy. There's been many a good horse drugged and dosed to death. Well, Scamp, my beauty, how are you this morning?"

In the stall next to Pacer was a small jet-black mare, with a lean head, slender legs, and a curious, restless manner. She was a regular greyhound of a horse, no spare flesh, yet wiry and able to do a great deal of work. She was a wicked-looking little thing, so I thought I had better keep at a safe distance from her heels.

Mr. Wood petted her a great deal, and I saw that she was his favorite. "Scamp," he exclaimed, when she pretended to bite him, "you know if you bite me, I'll bite back again. I think I've conquered you," he said proudly, as he stroked her glossy neck, "but what a dance you led me. Do you remember how I bought you for a mere song, because you had a bad habit of turning around like a flash in front of anything that frightened you, and bolting off the other way? And how did I cure you, my beauty? Beat you and make you stubborn? Not I. I let you go round and round; I turned you and twisted you, the oftener the better for me, till at last I got it into your pretty head that turning and twisting was addling your brains, and you'd better let me be master.

"You've minded me from that day, haven't you? Horse, or man, or dog aren't much good till they learn to obey, and I've thrown you down, and I'll do it again if you bite me, so take care."

Scamp tossed her pretty head, and took little

pieces of Mr. Wood's shirt-sleeve in her mouth, keeping her cunning brown eye on him as if to see how far she could go. But she did not bite him. I think she loved him, for when he left her she whinnied shrilly, and he had to go back and stroke and caress her.

After that I often used to watch her as she went about the farm. She always seemed to be tugging and striving at her load, and trying to step out fast and do a great deal of work. Mr. Wood was usually driving her. The men didn't like her, and couldn't manage her. She had not been properly broken in.

After Mr. Wood finished his work he went and stood in the doorway. There were six horses altogether: Dutchman, Cleve, Pacer, Scamp, a bay mare called Ruby, and a young horse belonging to Mr. Harry, whose name was Fleetfoot.

"What do you think of them all?" said Mr. Wood, looking down at me. "A pretty fine-looking lot of horses, aren't they? Not a thoroughbred there, but worth as much to me as if each had a pedigree as long as this plank walk. There's a lot of humbug about this pedigree business in horses. Mine have their manes and tails anyway, and the proper use of their eyes, which is more liberty than some thoroughbreds get.

"I'd like to see the man that would persuade me to put blinders or check-reins or any other instrument of torture on my horses. Don't the simpletons know that blinders are the cause of—

well, I wouldn't like to say how many of our accidents, Joe, for fear you'd think me extravagant, and the check-rein drags up a horse's head out of its fine natural curve and presses sinews, bones, and joints together, till the horse is well-nigh mad. Ah, Joe, this is a cruel world for man or beast. You're a standing token of that, with your missing ears and tail; and now I have to go and be cruel, and shoot that dog. He must be disposed of before any one else is astir. How I hate to take life."

I ran away, because I could not help feeling sorry for Bruno.

Miss Laura's room was on one side of the house, and in the second story. There was a little balcony outside it, and when I got near I saw that she was standing on it, wrapped in a shawl. Her hair was streaming over her shoulders, and she was looking down into the garden, where there were a great many white and yellow flowers in bloom.

I barked, and she looked at me. "Dear old Joe, I will get dressed and come down."

She hurried into her room, and I lay on the veranda till I heard her step. Then I jumped up. She unlocked the front door, and we went for a walk down the lane to the road until we heard the breakfast-bell. Then we ran back to the house, and Miss Laura had such an appetite for her breakfast that her aunt said the country had done her good already.

CHAPTER XVIII

MRS. WOOD'S POULTRY

FTER breakfast Mrs. Wood put on a large apron, and going into the kitchen, said: " Have you any scraps for the hens, Adèle? Be sure and not give me anything salty."

The French girl gave her a dish of food, then Mrs. Wood asked Miss Laura to go and see her chickens, and away we went to the poultry-house.

On the way we saw Mr. Wood. He was sitting on the step of the tool-shed cleaning his gun. " Is the dog dead?" asked Miss Laura.

" Yes," he replied.

She sighed and said: " Poor creature, I am sorry he had to be killed. Uncle, what is the most merciful way to kill a dog? Sometimes, when they get old, they should be put out of the world."

" You can shoot them," he said, " poison them, or put them in an electric cage. In shooting, there's a right place at which to aim. It's a little to one side of the top of the skull. If you'll remind me, I'll show you a circular I have that tells the proper way to kill animals. The American Humane Education Society in Boston puts it out.

" You don't know anything about the slaughtering of animals, Laura, and it's well you don't.

157

There's an awful amount of cruelty practised, and practised by some people that think themselves pretty good. I wouldn't have my lambs killed the way my father had his for a kingdom. I'll never forget the first one I saw butchered. I wouldn't feel worse at a hanging now. And that white ox, Hattie—you remember my telling you about him. He had to be killed, and father sent for the butcher. I was only a lad, and I was all of a shudder to have the life of the creature I had known taken from him. The butcher, stupid clown, gave him several blows before he struck the right place."

Miss Laura turned away, and Mrs. Wood followed her, saying: "If ever you want to kill a cat, Laura, give it cyanide of potassium. I killed a poor old sick cat for Mrs. Windham the other day. We put the potassium in a long-handled wooden spoon and dropped it on the cat's tongue, as near the throat as we could. Poor pussy—she died in a few seconds. Here we are at the hen-house, or rather one of the hen-houses."

"Don't you keep all your hens together?" asked Miss Laura.

"Only in the wintertime," said Mrs. Wood. "I divide my flock in the spring. Part of them stay here and part go to the orchard to live in little movable houses that we put about in different places. I feed each flock morning and evening at their own little house. They know they'll get no food even if they come to my house, so they stay at home. And they know they'll get no food between times, so all day long they pick and scratch in the orchard, and destroy so many bugs and insects that it more than pays for the trouble of keeping them there."

"Doesn't this flock want to mix up with the other?" asked Miss Laura, as she stepped into the little wooden house.

"No; they seem to understand. I keep my eye on them for a while at first, and they soon find out that they're not to fly either over the garden fence or the orchard fence. They roam over the farm and pick up what they can get. There's a good deal of sense in hens, if one manages them properly. I love them, because they are such good mothers."

We were in the little wooden house by this time, and I looked around it with surprise. It was better than some of the poor people's houses in Fairport. The walls were white and clean. So were the little ladders that led up to different kinds of roosts, where the fowls sat at night. Some roosts were thin and round, and some were broad and flat. Mrs. Wood said that the broad ones were for a heavy fowl called the Brahma. Every part of the little house was almost as light as it was outdoors, on account of the large windows.

Miss Laura spoke of it. "Why, auntie, I never saw such a light hen-house."

Mrs. Wood was diving into a partly shut-in

place, where it was not so light, and where the nests were. She straightened herself, her face redder than ever, and looked at the windows with a pleased smile.

"Yes, there's not a hen-house in New Hampshire with such big windows. Whenever I look at them I think of my mother's hens, and wish that they could have had a place like this. They would have thought themselves in a hen's paradise. When I was a girl, we didn't know that hens loved light and heat, and all winter they used to sit in a dark hencoop, and the cold was so bad that their combs would freeze stiff, and the tops of them would drop off. We never thought about it. If we'd had any sense, we might have watched them on a fine day go and sit on the compost heap and sun themselves, and then have concluded that if they liked light and heat outside, they'd like it inside. Poor biddies, they were so cold that they wouldn't lay us any eggs in winter."

"You take a great interest in your poultry, don't you, auntie?" said Miss Laura.

"Yes, indeed, and well I may. I'll show you my brown Leghorn, Jenny, that lays eggs enough in a year to pay for the newspapers I take to keep myself posted in poultry matters. I buy all my own clothes with my hen money, and lately I've opened a bank-account, for I want to save up enough to start a few stands of bees. Even if I didn't want to be kind to my hens, it would pay me to be so for the sake of the profit they yield. Of course they're quite a lot of trouble. Sometimes they get vermin on them, and I have to grease them and spray carbolic acid on them, and try some of my numerous cures. Then I must keep ashes and dust wallows for them, and be very particular about my eggs when hens are setting, and see that the hens come off regularly for food and exercise. Oh, there are a hundred things I have to think of, but I always say to any one that thinks of raising poultry, 'If you are going into the business for the purpose of making money it pays to take care of them.'"

"There is one thing I notice," said Miss Laura, "and that is, your drinking-fountains must be a great deal better than the shallow pans that I have seen some people use for their hens."

"Dirty things they are." said Mrs. Wood; "I wouldn't have one of them. I don't think there is anything worse for hens than drinking dirty water. My hens must have as clean water as I drink myself, and in winter I heat it for them. Now let us go and see my beautiful bronze turkeys. They don't need any houses, for they roost in the trees the year round."

We found the flock of turkeys, and Miss Laura admired their changeable colors. Some of them were very large, and I did not like them, for the gobblers ran at me, and made a dreadful noise in their throats.

Every place she took us to was as clean as pos-

L

sible. " No one can be successful in raising poultry in large numbers," she said, " unless they keep
their quarters clean and comfortable."

As yet we had seen no hens, except a few on
the nests, and Miss Laura said: " Where are they?
I should like to see them."

" They are coming," said Mrs. Wood. " It is
just their breakfast time, and they are as punctual
as clockwork. They go off early in the morning,
to scratch about a little for themselves first."

As she spoke she stepped off the plank walk
and looked off toward the fields.

Miss Laura burst out laughing. Away beyond
the barns the hens were coming. Seeing Mrs.
Wood standing there, they thought they were
late, and began to run and fly, jumping over each
other's backs, and stretching out their necks, in a
state of great excitement. Some of their legs
seemed sticking straight out behind. It was very
funny to see them.

They were a fine-looking lot of poultry, mostly
white, with glossy feathers and bright eyes. They
greedily ate the food scattered to them, and Mrs.
Wood said: " They think I've changed their break-
fasttime, and tomorrow they'll come earlier. And
yet people say hens have no sense."

CHAPTER XIX

A BAND OF MERCY

FEW evenings after we came to Dingley Farm, Mrs. Wood and Miss Laura were sitting out on the veranda, and I was lying at their feet.

"Auntie," said Miss Laura, "what do those letters mean on that silver pin that you wear with that piece of ribbon?"

"You know what the white ribbon means, don't you?" asked Mrs. Wood.

"Yes; that you are a temperance woman, doesn't it?"

"It does; and the star pin means that I am a member of a Band of Mercy. Do you know what a Band of Mercy is?"

"No," said Miss Laura.

"How strange! I should think that you would have several in Fairport. A cripple boy, the son of a Boston artist, started this one here. It has done a great deal of good. There is a meeting tomorrow, and I will take you to it if you like."

It was on Monday that Mrs. Wood had this talk with Miss Laura, and the next afternoon, after all the work was done, they got ready to walk to the village.

"May Joe go?" asked Miss Laura.

"Certainly," said Mrs. Wood; "he is such a good dog that he won't be any trouble."

I was very glad to hear this, and trotted along by them down the lane to the road. The lane was a very cool and pleasant place. There were tall trees growing on each side, and under them, among the grass, pretty wild flowers were peeping out to look at us as we went by.

Mrs. Wood and Miss Laura talked about the Band of Mercy all the way to the village. Miss Laura was much interested, and said that she would like to start one in Fairport.

"It is a very simple thing," said Mrs. Wood. "All you have to do is to write the pledge at the top of a piece of paper, 'I will try to be kind to all harmless living creatures, and try to protect them from cruel usage,' and get thirty people to sign it. That makes a Band.

"I have formed two or three Bands by keeping slips of paper ready, and getting people that come to visit me to sign them. I call them 'Corresponding Bands,' for they are too far apart to meet. I send the members 'Band of Mercy' papers, and I get such nice letters from them, telling me of kind things they do for animals.

"A Band of Mercy in a place is a splendid thing. There's the greatest difference in Riverdale since this one was started. A few years ago, when a man beat or ill-used his horse, and any one interfered, he said, 'This horse is mine, I'll do

what I like with him.' Most people thought he
was right, but now they're all for the poor horse,
and there isn't a man anywhere around who would
dare to abuse any animal.

"It's all the children. They're doing a grand
work, and I say it's a good thing for them. Since
we've studied this subject, it's enough to frighten
one to read what is sent us about our American
boys and girls. Do you know, Laura, that with
all our boasting about our schools and colleges,
that really are wonderful, we're turning out an
alarming number of criminals. The cause of it is
said to be lack of proper training for the youth
of our land. Immigration has something to do
with it too. We're thinking too much about edu-
cating the mind, and forgetting about the heart
and soul. So I say now, while we've got all our
future population in our schools, let us try to
slip in something between the ; ography, and history, and grammar that will go a little deeper, and
touch them so much that when they are grown up
and go out in the world, they will carry with them
lessons of love and good-will to men.

"A little child is such a tender thing. You can
bend it any way you like. Speaking of this heart
education of children as combined with mind education, I notice many school-teachers say that there
is nothing better than to give them lessons on
kindness to animals. Children who are taught to
love and protect dumb creatures will be kind to
their fellow men when they grow up."

I was very much pleased with this talk between
Mrs. Wood and Miss Laura, and kept close to
them, so that I should not miss a word.

As we went along, houses began to appear here
and there, set back from the road among the
trees. Soon they got quite close together, and
I saw some shops.

This was the village of Riverdale, and nearly
all the buildings were along this winding street.
The river was away back of the village. We had
already driven there several times.

We passed the school on our way. It was a
square, white building, standing in the middle of
a large yard. Boys and girls with their arms full
of books were hurrying down the steps, and coming into the street. Two quite big boys came behind us, and Mrs. Wood turned around and spoke
to them, and asked if they were going to the Band
of Mercy.

" Oh, yes, ma'am," said the younger one. " I've
got a recitation, don't you remember? "

" Yes, yes, excuse me for forgetting," said Mrs.
Wood, with her jolly laugh. " And here are Dolly,
and Jennie, and Martha," she went on, as some
little girls came running out of a house that we
were passing.

The little girls joined us, and looked so hard
at my head, and stump of a tail, and my fine collar, that I felt quite shy, and walked with my
head against Miss Laura's dress.

She stooped down and patted me, and then I

felt as if I didn't care how much they stared. Miss Laura never forgot me. No matter how earnestly she was talking, or playing a game, or doing anything, she always stopped occasionally to give me a word or look, to show that she knew I was near.

Mrs. Wood paused in front of a building on the main street. A great many boys and girls were going in, and we went with them. We found ourselves in a large room, with a platform at one end of it. There were some chairs on this platform, and a small table.

A boy stood by this table with his hand on a bell. Presently he rang it, and then every one kept still. Mrs. Wood whispered to Miss Laura that this boy was the president of the band, and the young man with the pale face and curly hair who sat in front of him was Mr. Maxwell, the artist's son, who had formed this Band of Mercy.

The lad who presided had a ringing, pleasant voice. He said they would begin their meeting by singing a song. There was an organ near the platform, and a young girl played on it, while all the other boys and girls stood up, and sang very sweetly and clearly.

Then the president asked for the report of their last meeting.

A little girl, blushing and hanging her head, came forward, and read what was written on a paper that she held in her hand.

The president made some remarks after she

had finished, and then every one had to vote. It was just like a meeting of grown people, and I was surprised to see how good those children were. They did not frolic or laugh, but all seemed sober and listened attentively.

After the voting was over, the president called upon John Turner to give a recitation. This was the boy whom we met on the way there. He walked up to the platform, made a bow, and said that he had learned two stories for his recitation, out of the paper, "Our Dumb Animals." One story was about a horse, and the other was about a dog, and he thought that they were two of the best animal stories on record. He would tell the horse story first.

"A man in Missouri had to go to Nebraska to see about some land. He went on horseback, on a horse that he had trained himself, and that came at his whistle like a dog. On getting into Nebraska, he came to a place where there were two roads. One went by a river, and the other went over the hill. The man saw that the traffic went over the hill, but thought he'd take the river road. He didn't know that there was a quicksand across it, and that people couldn't use it in spring and summer. There used to be a signboard to tell strangers about it, but it had been taken away.

"The man got off his horse to let him graze, and walked along till he got so far ahead of the horse, that he had to sit down and wait for him.

Suddenly he found that he was on a quicksand. His feet had sunk in the sand, and he could not get them out. He whistled for his horse, and shouted for help, but no one came. He could hear some young people singing out on the river, but they could not hear him. The terrible sand drew him in almost to his waist, and he thought he was lost. At that moment the horse came running up, and stood by his master. The man was too low down to get hold of the saddle or bridle, so he took hold of the horse's tail, and told him to go. The horse gave an awful pull, and landed his master on safe ground."

Everybody clapped and stamped when this story was finished, and called out, "The dog story—the dog story."

The boy bowed and smiled, and began again. "You all know what a 'round up' of cattle is, so I need not explain. Once a man down South was going to have one, and he and his boys and friends were talking it over. There was an ugly black steer in the herd, and they were wondering whether their old yellow dog would be able to manage him. The dog's name was Tige, and he lay and listened wisely to their talk. The next day there was a scene of great confusion. The steer raged and tore about, and would allow no one to come within whip touch of him.

"Tige, who had always been brave, skulked about for a while, and then, as if he had got up a little spirit, he made a run at the steer. The steer sighted him, gave a bellow, and lowering his horns, ran at him. Tige turned tail, and the young men that owned him were nearly frantic. They'd been praising him, and thought they were going to have it proved false. Their father called out, 'Don't shoot Tige till you see where he's running to.' The dog ran right to the cattle-pen. The steer was so enraged that he never noticed where he was going, and dashed in after him. Tige leaped the wall, and came back to the gate, barking for the men to come and shut the steer in. They closed the gate and petted Tige, and bought him a collar with a silver plate."

The boy was loudly cheered, and went to his seat. The president said he would like to have remarks made about these two stories.

Several children put up their hands, and he asked each one to speak in turn. One said that if that man's horse had had a docked tail, his master wouldn't have been able to reach it, and would have perished. Another said that if the man hadn't treated his horse kindly, he never would have come at his whistle, and stood over him to see what he could do to help him. A third child said that the people on the river weren't as quick at hearing the voice of the man in trouble as the horse was.

When this talk was over, the president called for some stories of foreign animals.

Another boy came forward, made his bow, and said, in a short, abrupt voice: "My uncle's name is Henry Worthington. He is an Englishman, and once he was a soldier in India. One day when he was hunting in the Punjab, he saw a mother monkey carrying a little dead baby monkey. Six months after, he was in the same jungle. Saw same monkey still carrying dead baby monkey, all shriveled up. Mother monkey loved her baby monkey, and wouldn't give it up."

The boy went to his seat, and the president, with a queer look on his face, said, "That's a very good story, Ronald—if it is true."

None of the children laughed, but Mrs. Wood looked amused, Miss Laura bit her lip, and there was a smile on Mr. Maxwell's face.

The boy who told the story looked very angry. He jumped up again: "My uncle's a true man, Phil Dodge, and never told a lie in his life."

The president remained standing, his face a deep scarlet, and a tall boy at the back of the room got up and said: "Mr. President, what would be impossible in this climate might be possible in a hot country like India. Doesn't heat sometimes shrivel and preserve things?"

The president's face cleared. "Thank you for the suggestion," he said. "I don't want to hurt anybody's feelings; but you know there is a rule in the Band that only true stories are to be told here."

CHAPTER XX

MRS. WOOD asked permission to say a few words just here, and the president said, "Certainly, we are always glad to hear from you."

She went up on the platform, and faced the roomful of children. "Dear boys and girls," she began. "You all know that nearly every tree and plant that grows swarms with insect life, and that they couldn't grow if the birds didn't eat the insects that would devour their foliage. All day long, the little beaks of the birds are busy. The dear little rose-breasted grosbeak carefully examines the potato plants, and picks off the beetles, the martins destroy weevil, the quail and grouse family eats the chinchbug, the woodpeckers dig the worms from the trees, and many other birds devour the flies and gnats and mosquitoes that torment us so. No flying or crawling creature escapes their sharp little eyes. A great Frenchman says that if it weren't for the birds, human beings would quickly perish from the face of the earth. They are doing all this for us, and how are we rewarding them? All over America they are hunted and killed.

172

"Every bird of the rarer kinds that is killed, such as humming-birds, orioles, and kingfishers, means the death of several others—that is, the young that starve to death, the wounded that fly away to die, and those whose plumage is so torn that it is not fit to put in a fine lady's hat. In some cases where birds have gay wings, and the hunters do not need the rest of the body, they tear off the wings from the living bird, and throw it away to die.

"I am sorry to tell you such painful things, but I think you ought to know them. You will soon be men and women. Do what you can to stop this dreadful trade. Our beautiful birds are being taken from us, and the insect pests are increasing. The State of Massachusetts has lost thousands of dollars because it did not protect its birds. The gipsy-moth stripped the trees near Boston, and the State had to pay out enormous sums of money, and even then could not get rid of the moths. The birds could have done it better than the State, but they were mostly gone. My last words to you are, 'Protect the birds.'"

Mrs. Wood went to her seat, and though the boys and girls had listened very attentively, none of them cheered her. Their faces looked sad, and they kept very quiet for a few minutes. I saw one or two little girls wiping their eyes. I think they felt sorry for the birds.

"Has any boy done anything about blinders and check-reins?" asked the president, after a time.

A brown-faced boy stood up. "I had a picnic last Monday," he said; "father let me cut all the blinders off our head-stalls with my penknife."

"How did you get him to consent to that?" asked the president.

"I told him," said the boy, "that I couldn't get to sleep for thinking of him. You know he drives a good deal late at night. I told him that every dark night he came from Sudbury I thought of the deep ditch alongside the road, and wished his horses hadn't blinders on. Then every night he comes from the Junction, and has to drive along the river bank where the water has washed away the earth till the wheels of the wagon are within a foot or two of the edge, I have wished again that his horses could see each side of them, for I knew they'd have sense enough to keep out of danger if they could see it.

"Father said that might be very true, and yet his horses had been broken in with blinders, and didn't I think they would be inclined to shy if he took them off; and wouldn't they be frightened to look around and see the wagon wheels so near? I told him that for every accident that happened to a horse without blinders, several happened to a horse with them; and then I gave him Mr. Wood's opinion—Mr. Wood out at Dingley Farm. He says that the worst thing against blinders is that a frightened horse never knows when he has passed the thing that scared him. He always thinks it is behind him. The blinders are there, and he can't see that he has passed it, and he can't turn his head to have a good look at it. So often he goes tearing madly on; and sometimes lives are lost all on account of a little bit of leather fastened over a beautiful eye that ought to look out full and free at the world. That finished father. He said he'd take off the blinders, and if he had an accident, he'd send the bill for damages to Mr. Wood. But we've had no accident. The horses did act rather queerly at first, and started a little; but they soon got over it, and now they go as steady without blinders as they ever did with them."

The boy sat down, and the president said: " I think it is time we threw off this foolishness of half covering our horses' eyes. Just put your hands up to your eyes, members of the band. Half cover them, and see how shut in you will feel; and how curious you will be to know what is going on beside you. Suppose a girl saw a mouse with her eyes half covered, wouldn't she run?"

Everybody laughed, and the president asked some one to tell him who invented blinders.

" A very rich man," shouted a boy, " who had a wall-eyed horse! He wanted to cover up the defect, and I think it is a great shame that so many horses have to suffer because that one had an ugly eye."

" So do I," said the president. " Three groans for blinders, boys."

All the children in the room made three dreadful noises away down in their throats. Then they had another good laugh, and the president became sober again. "Only seven more minutes," he said; "this meeting has got to be let out at five sharp."

A tall girl at the back of the room rose, and said, "My little cousin has two stories that she would like to tell the Band."

"Very well," said the president, "bring her right along."

The big girl came forward, leading a tiny child whom she placed in front of the boys and girls. The child stared up into her cousin's face, turning and twisting her white pinafore through her fingers. Every time the big girl took her pinafore away from her, she picked it up again. "Begin, Nannie," said the big girl kindly.

"Well, Cousin Eleanor," said the child, "you know Topsy, Graham's pony. Well, Topsy *would* run away, and a big, big man came out to papa and said he would train Topsy. So he drove her every day, and beat her, and beat her, till he was tired, but still Topsy would run away. Then papa said he would not have the poor pony whipped so much, and he took her out a piece of bread every day, and he petted her, and now Topsy is very gentle, and never runs away."

"Tell about Tiger," said the girl.

"Well, Cousin Eleanor," said the child, "you know Tiger, our big dog. He used to be a bad dog, and when Doctor Fairchild drove up to the house he jumped up and bit at him. Doctor Fairchild used to speak kindly to him, and throw out bits of meat, and now when he comes, Tiger follows behind and wags his tail. Now give me a kiss."

The girl had to give her a kiss, right up there before every one, and what a stamping the boys made. The larger girl blushed deeply and hurried back to her seat, with the child clinging to her hand.

There was one more story, about a brave Newfoundland dog, that saved eight lives by swimming out to a wrecked sailing vessel, and getting a rope by which the men came ashore, and then a lad got up whom they all greeted with cheers, and cries of, "The Poet! the Poet!" I didn't know what they meant, till Mrs. Wood whispered to Miss Laura that he was a boy who made rhymes, and the children would rather hear him speak than any one else in the room.

He had a snub nose and freckles, and I think he was the plainest boy there, but that didn't matter, if the other children loved him. He sauntered up to the front, with his hands behind his back, and a very grand manner.

"The beautiful poetry recited here today," he drawled, "put some verses in my mind that I never had till I came here today." Every one present cheered wildly, and he began, in a singsong voice:

M

" I am a Band of Mercy boy,
    I would not hurt a fly,
I always speak to dogs and cats,
    Whene'er I pass them by.

" I always let the birdies sing,
    I never throw a stone,
I always give a hungry dog
    A nice, fat, meaty bone.

" I wouldn't drive a bob-tailed horse,
    Nor hurry up a cow,
I——"

Then he forgot the rest. The boys and girls
were so sorry. They called out, " Pig," " Goat,"
" Calf," " Sheep," " Hens," " Ducks," and all the
other animals' names they could think of, but
not one of them was right, and as the boy had just
made up the poetry, no one knew what the next
could be. He stood for a long time staring at the
ceiling, then he said, " I guess I'll have to give
it up."

The children looked dreadfully disappointed.
" Perhaps you will remember it by our next meeting," said the president anxiously.

" Possibly," said the boy, " but probably not. I
think it is gone forever." And he went to his
seat.

The next thing was to call for new members.
Miss Laura got up and said she would like to
join their Band of Mercy. I followed her to the

platform, while they pinned a little badge on her, and every one laughed at me. Then they sang, "God bless our native land," and the president told us that we might all go home.

It seemed to me a lovely thing for those children to meet together to talk about kindness to animals. They all had bright and good faces, and many of them stopped to pat me as I came out. One little girl gave me a biscuit from her school bag.

Mrs. Wood waited at the door till Mr. Maxwell came limping out on his crutches. She introduced him to Miss Laura, and invited him to go and take tea with them. He said he would be very happy to do so, and then Mrs. Wood laughed, and asked him if he hadn't better empty his pockets first. She didn't want a little toad jumping over her tea-table, as one did the last time he was there.

CHAPTER XXI

MR. MAXWELL AND MR. HARRY

R. MAXWELL wore a coat with loose pockets, and while she was speaking, he rested on his crutches, and began to slap them with his hands. "No; there's nothing here today," he said, "I think I emptied my pockets before I went to the meeting."

Just as he said that there was a loud squeal. "Oh, my guinea-pig," he exclaimed, "I forgot him," and he pulled out a little spotted creature a few inches long. "Poor Derry, did I hurt you?" and he soothed it very tenderly.

I stood and looked at Mr. Maxwell, for I had never seen any one like him. He had thick curly hair and a white face, and he looked just like a girl. While I was staring at him, something rose up from one of his pockets and ran out its tongue at me so fast that I could scarcely see it, and then drew back again. I was thunderstruck. I had never seen such a creature before. It was long and thin, and of a bright green color like grass, and it had queer shiny eyes. Its tongue was the strangest part of it, and came and went like lightning. I became more and more uneasy and began to bark.

"What's the matter, Joe?" said Mrs. Wood, "the pig won't hurt you."

But it wasn't the pig I was afraid of, and I kept on barking. And all the time that strange live thing kept sticking up its head and putting out its tongue at me, and none of them noticed it.

"It's getting on toward six," said Mrs. Wood, "we must be going home. Come, Mr. Maxwell."

The young man put the guinea-pig in his pocket, picked up his crutches, and we started down the sunny village street. He left his guinea-pig at his boarding-house as he went by, but he said nothing about the other creature, so I knew he did not know it was there.

I was very much taken with Mr. Maxwell. He seemed so bright and happy, in spite of his lameness, which kept him from running about like other young men. He looked a little older than Miss Laura, and one day, a week or two later, when they were sitting on the veranda, I heard him tell her that he was just nineteen. He told her too, that his lameness made him love animals. They never laughed at him, or slighted him, or got impatient, because he could not walk quickly. They were always good to him, and he said he loved all animals while he liked very few people.

On this day, as he was limping along, he said to Mrs. Wood: "I am getting more absent-minded every day. Have you heard of my latest escapade?"

"No," she said.

"I am glad," he replied. "I was afraid that it
would be all over the village by this time. I went
to church last Sunday with my poor guinea-pig
in my pocket. He hasn't been well, and I was
attending to him before church, and put him in
there to get warm, and forgot about him. Unfortunately I was late, and the back seats were all
full, so I had to sit farther up than I usually do.
During the first hymn I happened to strike Piggy
against the side of the seat. Such an ear-splitting
squeal as he set up. It sounded as if I was mur-
dering him. The people stared and stared, and
I had to leave the church, overwhelmed with confusion."

Mrs. Wood and Miss Laura laughed, and then
they got to talking about other matters that were
not interesting to me, so I did not listen. But I
kept close to Miss Laura, for I was afraid that
green thing might hurt her. I wondered very
much what its name was. I don't think I should
have feared it so much if I had known what it
was.

"There's something the matter with Joe," said
Miss Laura, when we got into the lane. "What
is it, dear old fellow?" She put down her little
hand, and I licked it, and wished so much that I
could speak.

Sometimes I wish very much that I had the
gift of speech, and then at other times I see how
little it would profit me, and how many foolish
things I should often say. And I don't believe

human beings would love animals so well, if they could speak.

When we reached the house, we had a joyful surprise. There was a trunk standing on the veranda, and as soon as Mrs. Wood saw it, she gave a little shriek: "My dear boy!"

Mr. Harry was there, sure enough, and stepped out through the open door. He took his mother in his arms and kissed her, then he shook hands with Miss Laura and Mr. Maxwell, who seemed to be an old friend of his. They all sat down on the veranda and talked, and I lay at Miss Laura's feet and looked at Mr. Harry. He was a handsome young man, and had such a noble face. He was older and graver-looking than when I saw him last, and he had a light, brown mustache that he did not have when he was in Fairport.

He seemed very fond of his mother and of Miss Laura, and however grave his face might be when he was looking at Mr. Maxwell, it always lighted up when he turned to them. "What dog is that?" he asked at last, in a puzzled way, and pointing to me.

"Why, Harry," exclaimed Miss Laura, "don't you know Beautiful Joe, that you rescued from that wretched milkman?"

"Is it possible," he said, "that this well-conditioned creature is the bundle of dirty skin and bones that we nursed in Fairport? Come here, sir. Do you remember me?"

Indeed I did remember him, and licked his

hands and looked up gratefully into his face. "You're almost handsome now," he said, caressing me with a firm, kind hand, "and of a solid build too. You look like a fighter—but I suppose you wouldn't let him fight, even if he wanted to, Laura," and he smiled and glanced at her.

"No," she said, "I don't think I should; but he can fight when the occasion requires it;" and she told him about our night with Jenkins.

All the time she was speaking, Mr. Harry held me by the paws, and stroked my body over and over again. When she finished, he put his head down to me, and murmured, "Good dog," and I saw that his eyes were red and shining.

"That's a capital story, we must have it at the Band of Mercy," said Mr. Maxwell. Mrs. Wood had gone to help prepare the tea, so the two young men were alone with Miss Laura. When they had done talking about me, she asked Mr. Harry a number of questions about his college life, and his trip to New York, for he had not been studying all the time that he was away.

"What are you going to do with yourself, Gray, when your college course is ended?" asked Mr. Maxwell.

"I'm going to settle right down here," said Mr. Harry.

"What, be a farmer?" asked his friend.

"Yes, why not?"

"Nothing, only I imagined that you would take a profession."

"Suppose I did and went to a city. I shouldn't like it. The heat and dust, and crowds of people, and buildings overtopping one another, and the rush of living, take my breath away. You know I am not an intellectual giant. I should never distinguish myself in any profession. I should be a poor lawyer or doctor, living in a back street all the days of my life, and never watch a tree or flower grow, or tend an animal, or have a drive unless I paid for it. No, thank you. I agree with President Eliot, of Harvard. He says, scarcely one person in ten thousand betters himself permanently by leaving his rural home and settling in a city."

"But most farmers lead such a dog's life," said Mr. Maxwell.

"So they do; farming isn't made one-half as attractive as it should be," said Mr. Harry.

Mr. Maxwell smiled. "Attractive farming. Just sketch an outline of that, will you, Gray?"

"In the first place," said Mr. Harry, "I should like to tear out of the heart of the farmer the thing that is as firmly implanted in him as it is in the heart of his city brother—the thing that is doing more to harm our nation than anything else under the sun."

"What is that?" asked Mr. Maxwell, curiously.

"The thirst for gold. The farmer wants to get rich, and he works so hard to do it that he wears himself out soul and body, and the young people around him get so disgusted with that way of

getting rich, that they go off to the cities to find
out some other way, or at least to enjoy themselves, for I don't think many young people are
animated by a desire to heap up money."

Mr. Maxwell looked amused. "There is certainly a great exodus from country places city-
ward," he said. "What would be your plan for
checking it?"

"I would make the farm so pleasant, that you
couldn't hire the boys and girls to leave it. I
would have them work, and work hard too, but
when their work was over, let them have some
fun. That is what they go to the city for. They
want amusement and society, and to get into some
kind of a crowd when their work is done. The
young men and young women want to get together, as is only natural. Now that could be
done in the country. If farmers would be contented with smaller profits and smaller farms,
their houses could be nearer together. Their children would have opportunities of social intercourse,
there could be societies and clubs, and that would
tend to a distribution of literature. A farmer
ought to take five or six papers and two or three
magazines. It would be sure to pay him in the
long run."

Mr. Maxwell smiled. "And you ought to make
him mend his roads as well as mend his ways.
I tell you, Gray, the bad roads would put an end
to all these fine schemes of yours. Imagine farmers calling on each other on a dark evening after

a spring freshet. I can see them mired and bogged, and the house a mile ahead of them."

" That is true," said Mr. Harry, " the road question is a serious one. Do you know how father and I settled it? "

" No," said Mr. Maxwell.

" We got so tired of the whole business, and the farmers around here spent so much time discussing whether we needed this or that number of stump extractors, and how many shovels and crushers and ditchers would be necessary to keep our roads in order, and so on, that we simply withdrew. Once a year, father gets a gang of men and tackles every section of road that borders upon our land, and our roads are the best around here. I wish the government would take up this matter of making roads and settle it. If we had good, smooth, country roads, such as they have in some parts of Europe, we should be able to travel comfortably over them all through the year, and our draught animals would last longer, for they would not expend so much energy in drawing their loads."

CHAPTER XXII

WHAT HAPPENED AT THE TEA-TABLE

FROM my place under Miss Laura's chair, I could see that all the time Mr. Harry was speaking, Mr. Maxwell, although he spoke rather as if he was laughing at him, was yet glancing at him admiringly.

When Mr. Harry was silent, he exclaimed: "You are right, you are right, Gray. With your smooth highways, and plenty of schools, and churches, and libraries, and meetings for young people, and cheap telephones and free rural postal delivery, you would make country life a paradise, and I tell you what you would do too: you would empty the slums of the cities. It is the slowness and dulness of country life, and not their poverty alone, that keep the poor in dirty lanes and tenement houses. They want stir and amusement too, poor souls, when their day's work is over. I believe they would come to the country if it was made more pleasant for them."

"That is another question," said Mr. Harry, "a burning question in my mind—the one of labor and capital. When I was in New York, Maxwell, I was in a hospital, and saw a number of men who had been day-laborers. Some of them were young men broken down in the prime of life. Their limbs were shrunken and drawn. They had been digging in the earth, and working on high buildings, and confined in dingy basements, and had done all kinds of hard labor for other men. They had given their lives and strength for others, and this was the end of it all—that they should die poor and forsaken.

"I looked at them, and they reminded me of the martyrs of old. Ground down, living from hand to mouth, separated from their families in many cases—they had had a bitter lot. I tell you there is something wrong. We don't do enough for the people that slave and toil for us. We should take better care of them, we should not herd them together like cattle, and when we get rich, we should carry them along with us, and give them a part of our gains, for without them we would be as poor as they are."

"Good, Harry—I'm with you there," said a voice behind him, and looking around, we saw Mr. Wood standing in the doorway, gazing down proudly at his stepson.

Mr. Harry smiled, and getting up, said, "Won't you have my chair, sir?"

"No, thank you, your mother wishes us to come to tea. There are muffins, and you know they won't improve with keeping."

They all went into the dining-room, and I followed them. On the way, Mr. Wood said, "Right on top of that talk of yours, Harry, I've got to tell you of another person who is going to Boston to live."

"Who is it?" said Mr. Harry.

"Lazy Dan Wilson. I've been to see him this afternoon. You know his wife is sick, and they're half starved. He says he is going to the city, for he hates to chop wood and work, and he thinks maybe he'll get some light job there."

Mr. Harry looked grave, and Mr. Maxwell said, "He will starve, that's what he will do."

"Precisely," said Mr. Wood, spreading out his hard, brown hands, as he sat down at the table. "I don't know why it is, but the present generation has a marvelous way of skimming around any kind of work with their hands. They'll work their brains till they haven't got any more backbone than a caterpillar, but as for manual labor, it's old-timey and out of fashion. I wonder how these farms would ever have been carved out of the backwoods, if the old Puritans had sat down on the rocks with their noses in a lot of books, and tried to figure out just how little work they could do, and yet exist."

"Now, father," said Mrs. Wood, "you are trying to insinuate that the present generation is lazy, and I'm sure it isn't. Look at Harry. He works as hard as you do."

"Isn't that like a woman?" said Mr. Wood with a good-natured laugh. "The present generation consists of her son, and the past of her husband. I don't think all our young people are lazy, Hattie; but how in creation, unless the Lord rains down a few farmers, are we going to support all our young lawyers and doctors? They say the world is getting healthier and better, but we've got to fight a little more, and raise some more criminals, and we've got to take to eating pies and doughnuts for breakfast again, or some of our young sprouts from the colleges will go a begging."

"You don't mean to undervalue the advantages of a good education, do you, Mr. Wood?" said Mr. Maxwell.

"No, no, look at Harry there. Isn't he pegging away at his studies with my hearty approval? and he's going to be nothing but a plain, common farmer. But he'll be a better one than I've been, because he's got a trained mind. I found that out when he was a lad going to the village school. Education's a help to any man. What I am trying to get at is this, that in some way or other we're running more to brains and less to hard work than our forefathers did."

Mr. Wood was beating on the table with his forefinger while he talked, and every one was laughing at him. "When you've quite finished speechifying, John," said Mrs. Wood, "perhaps you'll serve the berries and pass the cream and sugar. Do you get yellow cream like this in the village, Mr. Maxwell?"

"No, Mrs. Wood," he said, "ours is a much paler yellow," and then there was a great tinkling of china, and passing of dishes, and talking and laughing, and no one noticed that I was not in my usual place in the hall. I could not get over my dread of the green creature, and I had crept under the table, so that if it came out and frightened Miss Laura, I could jump up and catch it.

When tea was half over, she gave a little cry. I sprang up on her lap, and there, gliding over the table toward her, was the wicked-looking, green thing. I stepped on the table, and had it by the middle before it could get to her. One of my hind legs was in a dish of jelly, and one of my front ones was in a plate of cake, and I was very uncomfortable. The tail of the green thing hung in a milk pitcher, and its tongue was still going at me, but I held it firmly and stood quite still.

"Drop it, drop it," cried Miss Laura, in tones of distress, and Mr. Maxwell struck me on the back, so I let the thing go, and stood sheepishly looking about me. Mr. Wood was leaning back in his chair, laughing with all his might, and Mrs. Wood was staring at her untidy table with rather a long face. Miss Laura told me to jump on the floor, and then she helped her aunt to take the spoiled things off the table.

I felt that I had done wrong, so I slunk out into the hall. Mr. Maxwell was sitting on the lounge, tearing his handkerchief in strips and tying them around the creature where my teeth had stuck in. I had been careful not to hurt it much, for I knew it was a pet of his; but he did not know that, and scowled at me, saying, "You rascal, you've hurt my poor snake terribly."

I felt so badly to hear this that I went and stood with my head in a corner. I had rather be whipped than scolded. After a while Mr. Maxwell went back into the room, and they all went on with their tea. I could hear Mr. Wood's loud, cheery voice: "The dog did quite right. Some snakes are poisonous creatures, and his instinct told him to protect his mistress. Where is he? Joe, Joe."

I would not move till Miss Laura came and spoke to me. "Dear old dog," she whispered, "you knew the snake was there all the time, didn't you?" Her words made me feel better, and I followed her to the dining-room, where Mr. Wood made me sit beside him and eat scraps from his hand all through the rest of the meal.

Mr. Maxwell had got over his ill humor, and was chatting in a lively way. "Good Joe," he said; "I was cross to you, and I beg your pardon. It always riles me to have any of my pets injured. You didn't know my poor snake was only after something to eat. Mrs. Wood has pinned him in my pocket so he won't come out again. Do you know where I got that snake, Mrs. Wood?"

"No," she said; "you never told me."

"It was across the river by Blue Ridge," he said. "One day last summer I was out rowing, and, getting very hot, tied my boat in the shade

N

of a big tree. Some village boys were in the woods, and hearing a great noise, I went to see what it was all about. They were Band of Mercy boys, and finding a country boy beating a snake to death, they were remonstrating with him for his cruelty, telling him that some kinds of snakes are a help to the farmer, and destroy large numbers of field-mice and other vermin. The boy was obstinate. He had found the snake, and he insisted upon his right to kill it, and they were having rather a lively time when I appeared. I persuaded them to make the snake over to me. Apparently it was already dead. Thinking it might revive, I put it on some grass in the bow of the boat. It lay there motionless for a long time, and I picked up my oars and started for home. I had got half-way across the river, when I turned around and saw that the snake was gone. It had just dropped into the water, and was swimming toward the bank we had left. I turned and followed it.

"It swam slowly and with evident pain, lifting its head every few seconds high above the water, to see which way it was going. On reaching the bank it coiled itself in the grass, throwing up blood and water. I took it up carefully, carried it home, and nursed it. It soon got better, and has been a pet of mine ever since."

After tea was over, and Mrs. Wood and Miss Laura had helped Adèle finish the work, they all gathered in the parlor. The day had been quite warm, but now a cool wind had sprung up, and Mr. Wood said that it was blowing up rain.

Mrs. Wood said a fire would be pleasant; so they lighted the wood in the open grate, and all sat round the blazing logs.

Mr. Maxwell tried to get me to make friends with the little snake that he held in his hands toward the blaze, and now that I knew it was harmless I was not afraid of it; but it did not like me, and put out its funny little tongue whenever I looked at it.

By and by the rain began to strike against the windows, and Mr. Maxwell said: "This is just the night for a story. Tell us something out of your experience, won't you, Mr. Wood?"

"What shall I tell you?" he asked good-humoredly. He was sitting between his wife and Mr. Harry, and had his hand on Mr. Harry's knee.

"Something about animals," said Mr. Maxwell. "We seem to be on that subject today."

"Well," said Mr. Wood, "I'll talk about something that has been running in my head for many a day. There is a good deal of talk nowadays about kindness to domestic animals, but I do not hear much about kindness to wild ones. The same Creator formed them both. I do not see why you should not protect one as well as the other. I have no more right to torture a bear than a cow. Our wild animals around here are getting pretty well killed off, but there are lots in other places. I used to be fond of hunting when I was a boy, but I have got rather disgusted with killing these late years; and unless the wild creatures ran in our streets, I would lift no hand against them. Shall I tell you some of the sport we had when I was a youngster?"

"Yes, yes," they all exclaimed.

CHAPTER XXIII

TRAPPING WILD ANIMALS

ELL," Mr. Wood began, "I was brought up, as you all know, in the eastern part of Maine, and we often used to go over into New Brunswick for our sport. Moose were our best game. Did you ever see one, Laura?"

"No, uncle," she said.

"When I was a boy there was no more beautiful sight to me in the world than a moose with his dusky hide, and long legs, and branching antlers, and shoulders standing higher than a horse's. Their legs are so long that they can't eat close to the ground. They browse on the tops of plants, and the tender shoots and leaves of trees. They walk among the thick underbrush, carrying their horns adroitly to prevent their catching in the branches, and they step so well, and aim so true, that you'll scarcely hear a twig fall as they go.

"They're a timid creature except at times. Then they'll attack with hoofs and antlers whatever comes in their way. They hate mosquitoes, and when they're tormented by them it's just as well to be careful about approaching them. Like all other animals, the Lord has put into them a won-

197

derful amount of sense, and when a female moose
has her one or two fawns she goes into the deepest
part of the forest, or swims to islands in large
lakes, where she stays till they are able to look
out for themselves.

"Well, we used to like to catch a moose, and
we had different ways of doing it. One way was
to snare them. We'd make a loop in a rope and
hide it on the ground under the dead leaves in one
of their paths. This was connected with a young
sapling whose top was bent down. When the
moose stepped on the loop it would release the
sapling, and up it would bound, catching him by
the leg. These snares were always set deep in
the woods, and we couldn't visit them very often.
Sometimes the moose would be there for days,
raging around, and scratching the skin off his legs.
That was cruel. I wouldn't catch a moose in that
way now for a hundred dollars.

"Another way was to hunt them on snowshoes
with dogs. Some winter day when there was a
crust over the deep snow, we used to get our dogs
together and set out. Moose don't travel in herds.
In summer they wander about over the forest, and
in the autumn they come together in small groups,
and select one or two hundred acres where there
is plenty of heavy undergrowth, and to which they
usually confine themselves. They do this so that
their tracks won't tell their enemies where they are.

"Any of these places where there were several
moose we called a moose-yard. We went through

the woods till we got on the tracks of some of the animals belonging to it, then the dogs smelled them and went ahead to start them. If I shut my eyes now I can see one of our moose hunts. The moose running and plunging through the snow crust, and occasionally rising up and striking at the dogs that hang on his bleeding muzzle and legs. The hunters' rifles going crack, crack, crack, sometimes killing or wounding dogs, as well as moose. That too was cruel.

"Two other ways we had of hunting moose: Calling and stalking. The calling was done in this way: We took a bit of birch-bark and rolled it up in the shape of a horn. We took this horn and started out, either on a bright moonlight night or just at evening, or early in the morning. The man who carried the horn hid himself, and then began to make a lowing sound like a female moose. He had to do it pretty well to deceive them. Away in the distance some moose would hear it, and with answering grunts would start off to come to it. If a young male moose was coming, he'd mind his steps, I can assure you, on account of fear of the old ones; but if it was an old fellow, you'd hear him stepping out bravely and rapping his horns against the trees, and plunging into any water that came in his way. When he got pretty near, he'd stop to listen, and then the caller had to be very careful and put his trumpet down close to the ground, so as to make a lower sound. If the moose felt doubtful he'd turn; if not, he'd come on, and unlucky for him if he did, for he got a warm reception, either from the rifles in our hands as we lay hidden near the caller, or from some of the party stationed at a distance.

"In stalking, we crept on them the way a cat creeps on a mouse. In the daytime moose are usually lying down. We'd find their tracks and places where they'd been nipping off the ends of branches and twigs, and follow them up. They easily take the scent of men, and we'd have to keep well to the leeward. Sometimes we'd come upon them lying down, but if, in walking along, we broke a twig, or made the slightest noise, they'd think it was one of their mortal enemies— a bear—creeping on them, and they'd be up and away. Their sense of hearing is very keen, but they're not so quick to see. A fox is like that too. His eyes aren't equal to his nose.

"Stalking is the most merciful way to kill moose. Then they haven't the fright and suffering of the chase."

"I don't see why they should be killed at all," said Mrs. Wood. "If I knew that forest back of the mountains was full of wild animals, I think I'd be glad of it, and not want to hunt them, that is, if they were harmless and beautiful creatures like the deer."

"You're a woman," said Mr. Wood, "and women are more merciful than men."

"Please tell us some more about the dogs that

helped you catch the moose, uncle," said Miss Laura. I was sitting up very straight beside her, listening to every word Mr. Wood said, and she was fondling my head.

"Well, Laura, when we camped out on the snow and slept on spruce boughs while we were after moose, the dogs used to be a great comfort to us. They slept at our feet and kept us warm. Poor brutes, they mostly had a rough time of it. They enjoyed the running and chasing as much as we did, but when it came to broken ribs and sore heads, it was another matter. Then the porcupines bothered them. Our dogs would never learn to let them alone. If they were going through the woods where there were no signs of moose and found a porcupine, they'd kill it. The quills would get in their mouths and necks and chests, and we'd have to gag them and take bullet-molds or nippers, or whatever we had, sometimes our jack-knives, and pull out the nasty things. If we got hold of the dogs at once, we could pull out the quills with our fingers. Sometimes the quills had worked in, and the dogs would go home and lie by the fire with running sores till they worked out. I've seen quills work right through dogs— go in one side, and come out the other."

"Poor brutes," said Mrs. Wood. "I wonder you took them."

"We once almost lost a valuable hound while moose-hunting," said Mr. Wood. "The moose struck him with his hoof and the dog was terribly injured, and lay in the woods for days, till a neighbor of ours, who was looking for timber, found him and brought him home on his shoulders. Wasn't there rejoicing among us boys to see old Lion coming back? We took care of him and he got well again.

"It was good sport to see the dogs when we were hunting a bear. Bears are fine runners, and when dogs get after them, there is great skirmishing. They nip the bear behind, and when he turns, the dogs run like mad, for a hug from a bear means sure death to a dog. If they got a slap from his paws, over they'd go. Dogs new to the business were often killed by the bears."

"Were there many bears near your home, Mr. Wood," asked Mr. Maxwell.

"Lots of them, more than we wanted. They used to bother us dreadfully about our sheep and cattle. I've often had to get up in the night, and run out to the cattle. The bears would come out of the woods, and jump on the young heifers and cows, and strike them and beat them down, and they would roar as if the evil one were mauling them. If the cattle were too far away from the house for us to hear them, the bears would worry them till they were dead.

"As for the sheep, they never made any resistance. They'd meekly run in a corner when they saw a bear coming, and huddle together, and he'd strike at them, and scratch them with his claws, and perhaps wound a dozen before he got one firmly. Then he'd seize it in his paws, and walk off on his hind legs over fences and anything else that came in his way, till he reached a nice retired spot, and there he'd sit down and skin that sheep just like a butcher. He'd gorge himself with the meat, and in the morning we'd find the other sheep that he'd torn, and we'd vow vengeance against that bear. He'd be almost sure to come back for more, so for a while after that we always put the sheep in the barn at nights, and set a trap by the remains of the one he had eaten.

"Everybody hated bears, and hadn't much pity for them; still they were only getting their meat at other wild animals do, and we'd no right to set such cruel traps for them as the steel ones. They had a clog attached to them, and had long sharp teeth. We put them on the ground, and strewed leaves over them, and hung up some of the carcass left by the bear near-by. When he attempted to get this meat, he would tread on the trap, and the teeth would spring together, and catch him by the leg. They always fought to get free. I once saw a bear that had been making a desperate effort to escape. His leg was broken, the skin and flesh were all torn away, and he was held by the tendons. It was a foreleg that was caught, and he would put his hind feet against the jaws of the trap, and then draw by pressing with his feet, till he would stretch those tendons to the utmost.

"I have known them to work away till they

really pulled these tendons out of the foot, and got off. It was a great event in our neighborhood when a bear was caught. Whoever found him blew a horn, and the men and boys came trooping together to see the sight. I've known them to blow that horn on a Sunday morning, and I've seen the men turn their backs on the meeting-house to go and see the bear."

"Was there no more merciful way of catching them than by this trap?" asked Miss Laura.

"Oh, yes, by the deadfall—that is by driving heavy sticks into the ground, and making a box-like place, open on one side, where two logs were so arranged with other heavy logs upon them, that when the bear seized the bait, the upper log fell down and crushed him to death. Another way was to fix bait in a certain place, with cords tied to it, which cords were fastened to triggers of guns placed at a little distance. When the bear took the bait, the guns went off, and he shot himself.

"Sometimes it took a good many bullets to kill them. I remember one old fellow that we put eleven into, before he keeled over. It was one fall, over on Pike's Hill. The snow had come earlier than usual, and this old bear hadn't got into his den for his winter's sleep. A lot of us started out after him. The hill was covered with beech trees, and he'd been living all the fall on the nuts, till he'd got as fat as butter. We took dogs and worried him, and ran him from one place to another, and shot at him, till at last he dropped. We took his meat home, and had his skin tanned for a sleigh-robe.

"One day I was in the woods, and looking through the trees espied a bear. He was standing up on his hind legs sniffing in every direction, and just about the time I espied him, he espied me. I had no dog and no gun, so I thought I had better be getting home to my dinner. I was a small boy then, and the bear probably thinking I'd be a mouthful for him anyway, began to come after me in a leisurely way. I can see myself now going through those woods—hat gone, jacket flying, arms out, eyes rolling over my shoulder every little while to see if the bear was gaining on me. He was a benevolent-looking old fellow, and his face seemed to say, 'Don't hurry, little boy.' He wasn't doing his prettiest, and I soon got away from him, but I made up my mind then, that it was more fun to be the chaser than the chased.

"Another time I was out in our cornfield, and hearing a rustling, looked through the stalks, and saw a brown bear with two cubs. She was slashing down the corn with her paws to get at the ears. She smelled me, and getting frightened, began to run. I had a dog with me this time, and shouted and rapped on the fence, and set him on her. He jumped up and snapped at her flanks, and every minute or so she'd turn and give him a cuff, that would send him yards away. I followed her up, and just back of the farm she and her cubs took into a tree. I sent my dog home, and my father and some of the neighbors came. It had grown dark by this time, so we built a fire under the tree, and watched all night, and told stories to keep each other awake. Toward morning we got sleepy, and the fire burnt low, and didn't that old bear and one cub drop right down among us and start off to the woods. That waked us up. We built up the fire and kept watch, so that the one cub still in the tree couldn't get away. Until daylight the mother bear hung around, calling to the cub to come down."

"Did you let it go, uncle?" asked Miss Laura.

"No, my dear, we shot it."

"How cruel!" cried Mrs. Wood.

"Yes, weren't we brutes?" said her husband; "but there was some excuse for us, Hattie. The bears ruined our farms. The kind of hunting that hunts and kills for the mere sake of slaughter is very different from that. I'll tell you what I've no patience with, and that's with those rich folks that dress themselves up, and take fine horses and packs of dogs, and tear over the country after one little fox or rabbit. Bah, it's contemptible. Now if they were hunting man-eating tigers, or animals that destroy property, it would be a different thing."

CHAPTER XXIV

THE RABBIT AND THE HEN

"YOU had foxes up in Maine, I suppose, Mr. Wood, hadn't you?" asked Mr. Maxwell.

"Heaps of them. I always want to laugh when I think of our foxes, for they were so cute. Never a fox did I catch in a trap, though I set many a one. I'd take the carcass of some creature that had died, a sheep, for instance, and put it in a field near the woods, and the foxes would come and eat it. When no harm befell them, they would be unsuspecting. So just before a snowstorm I'd take a trap and put it in this spot. I'd handle it with gloves, and smoke it, and rub fir boughs on it to take away the human smell, and then the snow would come and cover it up, and yet those foxes would know it was a trap and walk all around it."

"What kind of traps were they, father?" asked Mr. Harry.

"Steel ones. They'd catch an animal by the leg and sometimes break the bone. The leg would bleed, and below the jaws of the trap it would freeze, there being no circulation. The people around here use one made on the same principle for catching rats. I wouldn't have them on my place for any money. I believe we shall have to give an account for all the unnecessary suffering we put on animals."

"You'll have some to answer for, John, according to your own story," said Mrs. Wood.

"I have suffered already," he said. "Many a night I've lain on my bed and groaned, when I thought of needless cruelties I'd put upon animals when I was a young, unthinking boy."

"Tell us some more about the foxes, Mr. Wood," said Mr. Maxwell.

"Well, in addition to trapping, we used to hunt them with fox-hounds. Sometimes in the early morning they'd find a track in the snow. The leader for scent would go back and forth, to find out which way the fox was going. All the time he ran he was silent, but kept his tail aloft, wagging it as a signal to the hounds behind. By and by he would decide which way the fox had gone. Then his tail, still high in the air, would wag more violently. The rest followed him in single file, going pretty slow, so that we could keep up to them. Presently they would come to a place where the fox was sleeping for the day. As soon as he was disturbed, he would leave his bed under some thick fir or spruce branches near the ground. This flung his fresh scent into the air. When the hounds sniffed it, they gave tongue in good earnest. While in the excitement of his first flight, the fox would run fast for a mile or two, till he found it an easy matter to keep out of the way of the hounds. Then he, cunning creature, would begin to bother them. He would mount to the top pole of the worm fence dividing the fields from the woods. He could trot along here quite a distance and then make a long jump into the woods. The hounds would come up, but could not walk the fence, and they would have difficulty in finding where the fox had left it. Scattering in all directions, they made long detours into the woods and fields. As soon as the track was lost, they ceased to bay, but the instant a hound found it again, he bayed to give the signal to the others. All would hurry to the spot, and off they would go, baying as they went.

"Then Mr. Fox would try a new trick. He would climb a leaning tree, and jump to the ground. This trick would soon be found out. Then he'd try another. He would make a circle of a quarter of a mile in circumference. By making a loop in his course, he would come in behind the hounds, and puzzle them between the scent of his first and following tracks. If the snow was deep, the hounds had made a good track for him. Over this he could run easily, and they would have to feel their way along, for after he had gone around the circle a few times, he would jump from the beaten path as far as he could, and make off to other cover in a straight line. Before this was done it was my plan to get near the circle, taking care to approach it on the leeward side. If the fox got a sniff of human scent, he would leave his circle very quickly, and make tracks fast to

o

be out of danger. By the baying of the hounds, the circle in which the race was kept up could be easily located. The last runs to get near enough to shoot, had to be done when the hounds' baying came from the side of the circle nearest to me. For then the fox would be on the opposite side farthest away. As soon as I got near enough to see the hounds when they passed, I stopped. When they got on the opposite side. I then kept a bright lookout for the fox. Sometimes when the brush was thick, the sight of him would be indistinct. The shooting had to be quick. As soon as the report of the gun was heard, the hounds ceased to bay, and made for the spot. If the fox was dead, they enjoyed the scent of his blood. If only wounded, they went after him with all speed. Sometimes he was overtaken and killed, and sometimes he got into his burrow in the earth, or in a hollow log, or among the rocks.

"One day, I remember, when I was standing on the outside of the circle, the fox came in sight. I fired. He stopped in the snow and fell dead in his tracks."

"Poor little fox," said Miss Laura. "I wish you had let him get away."

"Here's one that nearly got away," said Mr. Wood. "One winter's day, I was chasing him with the hounds. There was a crust on the snow, and the fox was light, while the dogs were heavy. They ran along, the fox trotting nimbly on the top of the crust and the dogs breaking through,

and every few minutes that fox would stop and
sit down to look at the dogs. They were in a
fury, and the wickedness of the fox in teasing
them made me laugh so much that I was very
unwilling to shoot him."

"You said your steel traps were cruel things,
uncle," remarked Miss Laura. "Why didn't you
have a deadfall for the foxes as you had for the
bears?"

"They were too cunning to go into deadfalls.
There was a better way to catch them. Foxes
hate water, and never go into it unless they are
obliged to, so we used to find a place where a
tree had fallen across a river, and made a bridge
for them to go back and forth. Here we set
snares, with spring poles that would throw them
into the river when they made struggles to get
free, and drown them. Did you ever hear of the
fox, Laura, that wanted to cross a river, and lay
down on the bank pretending that he was dead,
and a countryman came along, and thinking he
had a prize, threw him in his boat and rowed
across, when the fox got up and ran away?"

"Now, uncle," said Miss Laura, "you're laughing at me. That couldn't be true."

"Well!" said Mr. Wood chuckling, "they're
mighty cute at pretending they're dead. I once
shot one in the morning, carried him a long way
on my shoulders, and started to skin him in the
afternoon, when he turned around and bit me
enough to draw blood."

"What other animals did you catch when you were a boy?" asked Mr. Maxwell.

"Oh, a number. Otters and beavers—we caught them in steel traps. A mink we usually took in a deadfall, smaller, of course, than the ones we used for the bears. The musk-rat we caught in box traps like a mouse trap. The wild-cat we ran down like the lucivee——"

"What kind of an animal is that?" asked Mr. Maxwell.

"The lucivee is a lynx, an animal of the cat tribe. They used to prowl about the country killing hens, geese, and sometimes sheep. They'd fix their tushes in the sheep's neck and suck the blood. They did not think much of the sheep's flesh. We ran them down with dogs. They'd often run up trees, and we'd shoot them. Then there were rabbits that we caught, mostly in snares. For musk-rats, we'd put a parsnip or an apple on the spindle of a box-trap. When we snared a rabbit, I always wanted to find it caught around the neck and strangled to death. If they got half through the snare and were caught around the body, or by the hind legs, they'd live for some time, and they'd cry just like a child. I liked shooting them better, just because I hated to hear their pitiful cries. It's a bad business this of killing dumb creatures, and the older I get, the more chicken-hearted I am about it."

"'Chicken-hearted'—I should think you are," said Mrs. Wood. "Do you know, Laura, he won't even kill a fowl for dinner. He gives it to one of the men to do."

" ' Blessed are the merciful,' " said Miss Laura, throwing her arm over her uncle's shoulder. " I love you, dear Uncle John, because you are so kind to every living thing."

"I'm going to be kind to you now," said her uncle, " and send you to bed. You look tired."

"Very well," she said with a smile. Then bidding them all good night, she went up-stairs. Mr. Wood turned to Mr. Maxwell. "You're going to stay all night with us, aren't you? "

" So Mrs. Wood says," replied the young man.

"Of course," she said. " I couldn't think of letting you go back to the village such a night as this. It's raining cats and dogs—but I mustn't say that, or there'll be no getting you to stay. I'll go and prepare your old room next to Harry's." And she bustled away.

The two young men went to the pantry for doughnuts and milk, and Mr. Wood stood gazing down at me. " Good dog," he said, " you looked as if you sensed that talk to-night. Come, get a bone, and then away to bed."

He gave me a very large mutton bone, and I held it in my mouth, and watched him opening the wood-shed door. I love human beings; and the saddest times of day for me is when I have to be separated from them while they sleep.

"Now go to bed and rest well, Beautiful Joe," said Mr. Wood, " and if you hear any stranger round the house, run out and bark. Don't be chasing wild animals in your sleep, though. They say a dog is the only animal that dreams. I wonder whether it's true?" Then he went into the house and shut the door.

I had a sheepskin to lie on, and a very good bed it made. I slept soundly for a long time; then I waked up and found that, instead of rain pattering against the roof, and darkness everywhere, it was quite light. The rain was over, the morning had come, and the sun was shining beautifully. I ran to the door and looked out. It was a very fine day, but it was early yet, and as I gazed all about the house and farm buildings I could see that there was no one stirring. I took a turn about the yard, and walked to the side of the house to glance up at Miss Laura's window. I always did this several times through the night, and very early in the morning, just to see if she was quite safe. I was on my way back to my bed for another nap, when I discovered two small white things moving away down the lane. I stood on the veranda and watched them. When they got nearer, I saw that there was a white rabbit hopping up the road followed by a white hen.

It seemed to me a very strange thing for these two creatures to be together, and why were they coming to Dingley Farm so early in the morning? This wasn't their home. I ran down on the road and stood in front of them.

Just as soon as the hen saw me she fluttered before the rabbit, and spreading out her wings, clucked angrily, and acted as if she would peck my eyes out if I went nearer.

I saw that they were harmless creatures, and remembering my adventure with the snake, I stepped aside. Besides that, I knew by their smell that they had been near Mr. Maxwell, so perhaps they were after him.

They understood quite well that I would not hurt them and passed by me. The rabbit went ahead again, and the hen fell behind. It seemed to me that the hen was worried at being in a strange place, and was following the rabbit only because she thought it was her duty and wanted to keep in his company.

He was going along in a very queer fashion, putting his head to the ground, and rising up on his hind legs, and sniffing the air, first on this side, and then on the other, and his nose was going, going, all the time.

He smelled all around the house till he came to Mr. Maxwell's room at the back. It opened on the veranda by a glass door, and the door stood ajar. The rabbit squeezed himself in and the hen stayed out. She watched for a while, and when he did not return, she flew up on the back of a chair that stood near the door, and stuck her feathers all out as if she felt cold or uncomfortable.

I went back to my bed, for I knew they would do no harm. Later in the morning, when I was walking around the house, I heard a great shouting and

laughing from Mr. Maxwell's room. He and Mr.
Harry had just discovered the hen and the rabbit,
and Mr. Harry was calling his mother to come and
look at them. The rabbit had hopped to the foot
of the bed, and the hen had flown on a table.

Mr. Harry was chaffing Mr. Maxwell very
much, and was telling him that any one who en-
tertained him was in for a traveling menagerie.
They had a great deal of fun over it, and Mr.
Maxwell said that he had had that pretty, white
hen as a pet for a long time in Boston. Once
when she had some little chickens, a frightened
rabbit, that was being chased by a dog, ran into
the yard. In his terror he got right under the
hen's wings, and she sheltered him, and pecked
at the dog's eyes, and kept him off till help came.
The rabbit belonged to a neighbor's boy, and Mr.
Maxwell bought it from him. From the day the
hen protected him, she became his friend, and
followed him everywhere.

I did not wonder that the rabbit wanted to see
his master. There was something about that young
man that made dumb animals just delight in him.
When Mrs. Wood mentioned this to him he said,
" I don't know why they should—I don't do anything to fascinate them."

" You love them," she said, " and they know it.
That is the reason."

CHAPTER XXV

A HAPPY HORSE

OR a good while after I went to Dingley Farm I was very shy of the horses, because I was afraid they might kick me, thinking that I was a bad dog like Bruno. However, they all had such good faces, and looked at me so kindly, that I was beginning to get over my fear of them.

Fleetfoot, Mr. Harry's colt, was my favorite, and one afternoon, when Mr. Harry and Miss Laura were going out to see him, I followed them. Fleetfoot was amusing himself by rolling over and over on the grass under a tree, but when he saw Mr. Harry he gave a shrill whinny, and running to him, began nosing about his pockets.

"Wait a bit," said Mr. Harry, holding him by the forelock. "Let me introduce you to this young lady, Miss Laura Morris. I want you to make her a bow." He gave the colt some sign, and immediately he began to paw the ground and shake his head.

Mr. Harry laughed and went on: "Here is her dog Joe. I want you to like him too. Come here, Joe."

I was not at all afraid, for I knew Mr.

217

Harry would not let him hurt me, so I stood in front of him, and for the first time had a good look at him. They called him the colt, but he was really a full-grown horse, and had already been put to work. He was of a dark chestnut color, and had a well-shaped body and a long, handsome head, and I never saw in the head of a man or beast a more beautiful pair of eyes than that colt had—large, full, brown eyes that he turned on me almost as a person would. He looked me all over as if to say, "Are you a good dog, and will you treat me kindly, or are you a bad one like Bruno, and will you chase me and snap at my heels and worry me, so that I shall want to kick you?"

I looked at him very earnestly and wagged my body, and lifted myself on my hind legs toward him. He seemed pleased and put down his nose to sniff at me, and then we were friends, and such good friends, for next to Jim and Billy, I have loved Fleetfoot.

Mr. Harry pulled some lumps of sugar out of his pocket, and giving them to Miss Laura, told her to put them on the palm of her hand and hold it out flat toward Fleetfoot. The colt ate the sugar, and all the time eyed her with his quiet, observing glance, that made her exclaim, "What a wise-looking colt!"

"He is like an old horse," said Mr. Harry. "When he hears a sudden noise, he stops and looks all about him to find an explanation."

"He has been well trained," said Miss Laura.

"I have brought him up carefully," said Mr. Harry. "Really, he has been treated more like a dog than a colt. He follows me about the farm and smells everything I handle, and seems to want to know the reason of things."

"Your mother says," replied Miss Laura, "that she found you both asleep on the lawn one day last summer, and the colt's head was on your arm."

Mr. Harry smiled and threw his arm over the colt's neck. "We've been comrades, haven't we, Fleetfoot? I've been almost ashamed of his devotion. He has followed me to the village, and he always wants to go fishing with me. He's four years old now, so he ought to get over those coltish ways. I've driven him a good deal. We're going out in the buggy this afternoon, will you come?"

"Where are you going?" asked Miss Laura.

"Just for a short drive back of the river to collect some money for father. I'll be home long before teatime."

"Yes, I should like to go," said Miss Laura. "I will run to the house and get my other hat."

"Come on, Fleetfoot," said Mr. Harry. And he led the way from the pasture, the colt following behind with me. I waited about the veranda, and in a short time Mr. Harry drove up to the front door. The buggy was black and shining, and Fleetfoot had on a silver-mounted harness that made him look very fine. He stood gently switching his long tail to keep the flies away, and with his head turned to see who was getting into the buggy. I stood by him, and as soon as he saw that Miss Laura and Mr. Harry had seated themselves, he acted as if he wanted to be off. Mr. Harry spoke to him and away he went, I racing down the lane by his side, so happy to think he was my friend. He liked having me beside him, and every few seconds put down his head toward me. Animals can tell each other things without saying a word. When Fleetfoot gave his head a little toss in a certain way, I knew that he wanted to have a race. He had a beautiful even gait, and went very swiftly. Mr. Harry kept speaking to him to check him.

"You don't like him to go too fast, do you?" said Miss Laura.

"No," he returned. "I think we could make a racer of him if we liked, but father and I don't go in for fast horses. There is too much said about fast trotters and race-horses. On some of the farms around here the people have gone mad on breeding fast horses. An old farmer out in the country had a common cart-horse that he suddenly discovered had great powers of speed and endurance. He sold him to a speculator for a big price, and it has set everybody wild. If the people who give all their time to it can't raise fast horses, I don't see how the farmers can. A fast horse on a farm is ruination to the boys, for it

starts them racing and betting. Father says he
is going to offer a prize for the fastest walker that
can be bred in New Hampshire. That Dutchman
of ours, heavy as he is, is a fair walker, and Cleve
and Pacer can each walk four and a half miles an
hour."

"Why do you lay such stress on their walking
fast?" asked Miss Laura.

"Because so much of the farm work must be
done at a walk. Plowing, teaming, and drawing produce to market, and going up and down
hills. Even for the cities it is good to have fast
walkers. Trotting on city pavements is very hard
on the dray-horses. If they are allowed to go at a
quick walk, their legs will keep strong much
longer. It is shameful the way horses are used
up in big cities. Our pavements are so bad that
cab-horses are ruined in three years. In many
ways we are a great deal better off in this new
country than the people in Europe; but we are
not in respect of cab-horses, for in London and
Paris they last for five years. I have seen horses
drop down dead in New York, just from hard
usage. Poor brutes, there is a better time coming
for them, though. Well, Fleetfoot, do you want
another spin? All right, my boy, go ahead."

Away we went again along a bit of level road.
Fleetfoot had no check-rein on his beautiful neck,
and when he trotted, he could hold his head in an
easy, natural position. With his wonderful eyes
and flowing mane and tail, and his glossy, reddish-

brown body, I thought that he was the hand-
somest horse I had ever seen. He loved to go
fast, and when Mr. Harry spoke to him to slow
up again, he tossed his head with impatience.
But he was too sweet-tempered to disobey. In
all the years that I have known Fleetfoot, I have
never once seen him refuse to do as his master
told him.

"You have forgotten your whip, haven't you,
Harry?" I heard Miss Laura say, as we jogged
slowly along, and I ran by the buggy panting and
with my tongue hanging out.

"I never use one," said Mr. Harry; "if I saw
any man lay one on Fleetfoot, I'd knock him
down." His voice was so severe that I glanced
up into the buggy. He looked just as he did the
day that he stretched Jenkins on the ground and
gave him a beating.

"I am so glad you don't," said Miss Laura.
"You are like the Russians. Many of them control their horses by their voices, and call them
such pretty names. But you have to use a whip
for some horses, don't you, Cousin Harry?"

"Yes, Laura. There are many vicious horses
that can't be controlled otherwise, and then with
many horses one requires a whip in case of neces-
sity for urging them forward."

"I suppose Fleetfoot never balks," said Miss
Laura.

"No," replied Mr. Harry; "Dutchman sometimes does, and we have two cures for him, both

equally good. We take up a forefoot and strike
his shoe two or three times with a stone. The
operation always interests him greatly, and he
usually starts. If he doesn't go for that, we pass
a line around his forelegs, at the knee joint, then
step in front of him and draw on the line. Father
won't let the men use a whip, unless they are
driven to it."

"Fleetfoot has had a happy life, hasn't he?"
said Miss Laura, looking admiringly at him.
"How did he get to like you so much, Harry?"

"I broke him in after a fashion of my own.
Father gave him to me, and the first time I saw
him on his feet, I went up carefully and put my
hand on him. His mother was rather shy of me,
for we hadn't had her long, and it made him shy
too, so I soon left him. The next time I stroked
him; the next time I put my arm around him.
Soon he acted like a big dog. I could lead him
about by a strap, and I made a small halter and a
bridle for him. I didn't see why I shouldn't train
him a little while he was young and manageable.

"I think it is cruel to let colts run till one has to
employ severity in mastering them. Of course, I
did not let him do much work. Colts are like
boys—a boy shouldn't do a man's work, but he
had exercise every day, and I trained him to draw
a light cart behind him. I used to do all kinds of
things to accustom him to unusual sounds. Father
talked a good deal to me about Rarey, the great
horse-tamer, and it put ideas into my head. He

said he once saw Rarey come on a stage in Boston with a timid horse that he was going to accustom to a loud noise. First a bugle was blown, then some louder instrument, and so on, till there was a whole brass band going. Rarey reassured the animal, and it was not afraid."

"You like horses better than any other animals, don't you, Harry?" asked Miss Laura.

"I believe I do, though I am very fond of that dog of yours. I think I know more about horses than dogs. Have you noticed Scamp?"

"Oh, yes; I often watch her. She is such an amusing little creature."

"She's the most interesting one we've got; that is, after Fleetfoot. Father bought her from a man who couldn't manage her, and she came to us with a legion of bad tricks. Father has taken solid comfort, though, in breaking her of them. She is his pet among our stock. I suppose you know that horses, more than any other animals, are creatures of habit. If they do a thing once, they will do it again. When she came to us, she had a trick of biting at a person who gave her oats. She would do it without fail, so father put a little stick under his arm, and every time she would bite he would give her a rap over the nose. She soon got tired of biting, and gave it up. Sometimes now, you'll see her make a snap at father as if she was going to bite, and then look under his arm to see if the stick is there.

"He cured some of her tricks in one way, and

some in another. One bad one she had was to start for the stable the minute one of the traces was unfastened when we were unharnessing. She pulled father over once, and another time she ran the shaft of the sulky clean through the barn door. The next time father brought her in he got ready for her. He twisted the lines around his hands, and the minute she began to bolt he gave a tremendous jerk, that pulled her back upon her haunches, and shouted, 'Whoa.' It cured her, and she never started again, till he gave her the word. Often now, you'll see her throw her head back when she is being unhitched. He did it only once, yet she remembers. If we'd had the training of Scamp, she'd be a very different animal. It's nearly all in the bringing up of a colt, whether it will turn out vicious or gentle. If any one were to strike Fleetfoot he would not know what it meant. He has been brought up differently from Scamp.

" She was probably trained by some brutal man who inspired her with distrust of the human species. She never bites an animal, and seems attached to all the other horses. She loves Fleetfoot and Cleve and Pacer. Those three are her favorites."

" I love to go for drives with Cleve and Pacer," said Miss Laura, " they are so steady and good. Uncle says they are the most trusty horses he has. He has told me about the man you had, who said that they knew more than most 'humans.'"

P

"That was old Davids," said Mr. Harry; "when we had him, he was courting a widow who lived over in Hoytville. About once a fortnight he'd ask father for one of the horses to go over to see her. He always stayed pretty late, and on the way home he'd tie the reins to the whip-stock and go to sleep, and never wake up till Cleve or Pacer, whichever one he happened to have, would draw up in the barnyard. They would pass any rigs they happened to meet, and turn out a little for a man. If Davids wasn't asleep, he could always tell by the difference in their gait, which they were passing. They'd go quickly past a man, and much slower, with more of a turn-out, if it was a team. But I dare say father told you this. He has a great stock of horse stories, and I am almost as bad. You will have to cry 'halt' when we bore you."

"You never do," replied Miss Laura. "I love to talk about animals. I think the best story about Cleve and Pacer is the one that uncle told me last evening. I don't think you were there. It was about stealing the oats."

"Cleve and Pacer never steal," said Mr. Harry. "Don't you mean Scamp? She's the thief."

"No, it was Pacer that stole. He got out of his box, uncle says, and found two bags of oats, and he took one in his teeth and dropped it before Cleve, and ate the other himself, and uncle was so amused that he let them eat a long time, and stood and watched them."

"That was a clever trick," said Mr. Harry. "Father must have forgotten to tell me. Those two horses have been mates ever since I can remember, and I believe if they were separated they'd pine away and die. You have noticed how low the partitions are between the boxes in the horse-stable. Father says you wouldn't put a lot of people in separate boxes in a room, where they couldn't see each other, and horses are just as fond of company as we are. Cleve and Pacer are always nosing each other.

"A horse has a long memory. Father has had horses recognize him that he has been parted from for twenty years. Speaking of their memories, reminds me of another good story about Pacer, that I never heard till yesterday, and that I would not talk about to any one but you and mother. Father wouldn't write me about it, for he never will put a line on paper where any one's reputation is concerned."

CHAPTER XXVI

"THIS story," said Mr. Harry, "is about one of the hired men we had last winter, whose name was Jacobs. He was a cunning fellow, with a hang-dog look, and a great cleverness at stealing farm produce from father on the sly, and selling it. Father knew perfectly well what he was doing, and was wondering what would be the best way to deal with him, when one day something happened that brought matters to a climax.

"Father had to go to Sudbury for farming tools, and took Pacer and the cutter. There are two ways of going there—one the Sudbury Road, and the other the old Post Road, which is longer and seldom used. On this occasion father took the Post Road. The snow wasn't deep, and he wanted to inquire after an old man who had been robbed and half frightened to death a few days before. He was a miserable old creature, known as Miser Jerrold, and he lived alone with his daughter. He had saved a little money that he kept in a box under his bed. When father got near the place, he was astonished to see by Pacer's actions that he had been on this road before, and

228

recently too. Father is so sharp about horses that they never do a thing that he doesn't understand. So he let the reins hang a little loose, and kept his eye on Pacer. The horse went along the road, and seeing father didn't direct him, turned into the lane leading to the house. There was an old red gate at the end of it, where he stopped and waited for father to get out. Then he passed through, and instead of going up to the house, turned around, and stood with his head toward the road.

"Father never said a word, but he was doing a lot of thinking. He went into the house, and found the old man sitting over the fire, rubbing his hands, and half crying about 'the few poor dollars' that he said he had had stolen from him. Father had never seen him before, but he knew he had the name of being half silly, and question him as much as he liked, he could make nothing of him. The daughter said that they had gone to bed at dark the night her father was robbed. She slept up-stairs, and he down below. About ten o'clock she heard him scream, and running downstairs she found him sitting up in bed, and the window wide open. He said a man had sprung in upon him, and dragging his box from under the bed, had made off with it. She ran to the door and looked out, but there was no one to be seen. It was dark, and snowing a little, so no traces of footsteps were to be perceived in the morning.

"Father found that the neighbors were drop-

ping in to bear the old man company, so he drove
on to Sudbury, and then returned home. When
he arrived, he said Jacobs was fussing about the
stable in a nervous way, and said he wanted to
speak to him. Father said, very good, but to put
the horse in first. Jacobs unhitched, and father
sat on one side of the stable benches and watched
him till he came lounging along with a straw in
his mouth, and said he'd made up his mind to go
West, and he'd like to set off at once.

"Father said again, very good, but first he had
a little account to settle with him, and he took
out of his pocket a paper, where he had jotted
down as far as he could, every quart of oats, and
every bag of grain, and every quarter of a dollar
of market money of which Jacobs had defrauded
him. Father said the fellow turned all the colors
of the rainbow, for he thought he had covered up
his tracks so cleverly that he would never be found
out. Then father said, 'Sit down, Jacobs, for I
have got to have a long talk with you.'

"He had him there about an hour, and when he
finished, the fellow was completely broken down.
Father told him that there were just two courses
in life for a young man to take, and he had
started on the wrong one. If he turned right
around now, there was a chance for him. If he
didn't, there was nothing but the State's prison
ahead of him, for he needn't think he was going
to gull and cheat all the world and never be found
out. Father said he'd give him all the help in

his power, if he had his word that he'd try to be an honest man. Then he tore up the paper, and said there was an end of his indebtedness to him.

"Jacobs was only a young fellow, twenty-three or thereabout, and father says he sobbed like a baby. Then, without looking at him, father gave an account of his afternoon's drive, just as if he was talking to himself. He said that Pacer never to his knowledge had been on that road before, and yet he seemed perfectly familiar with it, and that he stopped and turned all ready to leave again quickly, instead of going up to the door, and how he looked over his shoulder and started on a run down the lane, the minute father's foot was in the cutter again. In the course of his remarks, father mentioned the fact that on Monday, the evening that the robbery was committed, Jacobs had borrowed Pacer to go to the Junction, but had come in with the horse steaming, and looking as if he had been driven a much longer distance. Father said that when he got done Jacobs had sunk down all in a heap on the stable floor, with his hands over his face. Father left him to have it out with himself, and went to the house.

"The next morning Jacobs looked just the same as usual, and went about with the other men doing his work, but saying nothing about going West. Late in the afternoon, a farmer going by hailed father, and asked if he'd heard the news. Old Miser Jerrold's box had been left on his doorstep some time through the night, and he'd found

it in the morning. The money was all there, but
the old fellow was so cute that he wouldn't tell
any one how much it was. The neighbors had
persuaded him to bank it, and he was coming to
town the next morning with it, and that night
some of them were going to help him mount
guard over it. Father told the men at milking
time, and he said Jacobs looked as unconscious
as possible. However, from that day there was a
change in him. He never told father in so many
words that he'd resolved to be an honest man, but
his actions spoke for him. He had been a kind of
sullen, unwilling fellow, but now he turned handy
and obliging, and it was a real trial to father to
part with him."

Miss Laura was intensely interested in this story.
"Where is he now, Cousin Harry?" she asked
eagerly. "What became of him?"

Mr. Harry laughed in such amusement that I
stared up at him, and even Fleetfoot turned his
head around to see what the joke was. We were
going very slowly up a long, steep hill, and in the
clear, still air we could hear every word spoken
in the buggy.

"The last part of the story is the best, to my
mind," said Mr. Harry, "and as romantic as even
a girl could desire. The affair of the stolen box
was much talked about along Sudbury way, and
Miss Jerrold got to be considered quite a desir-
able young person among some of the youth near
there, though she is a frowsy-headed creature,

and not as neat in her personal attire as a young
girl should be. Among her suitors was Jacobs.
He cut out a blacksmith, and a painter, and several young farmers, and father said he never in
his life had such a time to keep a straight face as
when Jacobs came to him this spring and said he
was going to marry old Miser Jerrold's daughter. He wanted to quit father's employ, and he
thanked him in a real manly way for the manner
in which he had always treated him. Well,
Jacobs left, and mother says that father would sit
and speculate about him, as to whether he had
fallen in love with Eliza Jerrold, or whether he
was determined to regain possession of the box,
and was going to do it honestly, or whether he
was sorry for having frightened the old man into
a greater degree of imbecility, and was marrying
the girl so that she could take care of him, or
whether it was something else, and so on, and so
on. He had a dozen theories, and then mother
says he would burst out laughing, and say it was
one of the cutest tricks that he had ever heard of.

"In the end, Jacobs got married, and father and
mother went to the wedding. Father gave the
bridegroom a yoke of oxen, and mother gave the
bride a lot of household linen, and I believe
they're as happy as the day is long. Jacobs makes
his wife comb her hair, and he waits on the old
man as if he were his son, and he is improving the
farm that was going to rack and ruin, and I hear
he is going to build a new house."

"Harry," exclaimed Miss Laura, "can't you take me to see them?"

"Yes, indeed; mother often drives over to take them little things, and we'll go too, some time. I'd like to see Jacobs myself, now that he is a decent fellow. Strange to say, though he hadn't the best of characters, no one has ever suspected him of the robbery, and he's been cunning enough never to say a word about it. Father says Jacobs is like all the rest of us. There's a mixture of good and evil in him, and sometimes one predominates and sometimes the other. But we must go on and not talk here all day. Get up, Fleetfoot."

"Where did you say we were going?" asked Miss Laura, as we crossed the bridge over the river.

"A little way back here in the woods," he replied, "there's a man named Barron on a small clearing that he calls Penhollow. Father loaned him some money three years ago, and he won't pay either interest or principal."

"I think I've heard of him," said Miss Laura. "Isn't he the man whom the boys call Lord Chesterfield?"

"The same one. He's a queer specimen of a man. He lives alone, only coming occasionally to the village for supplies, and though he is poorer than poverty, he despises every soul within a ten-mile radius of him, and looks upon us as no better than an order of well-trained lower animals."

"Why is that?" asked Miss Laura in surprise.

"He is a gentleman, Laura, and we are only common people. My father can't hand a lady in and out of a carriage as Lord Chesterfield can, nor can he make so grand a bow, nor does he put on evening dress for a late dinner, and we never go to the opera nor to the theater, and know nothing of polite society, nor can we tell exactly from whom our great-great-grandfather sprang. I tell you, there is a gulf between us and that aristocrat, wider than the one young Curtius leaped into."

Miss Laura was laughing merrily. "How funny that sounds, Harry. So he despises you," and she glanced at her good-looking cousin, and his handsome buggy and well-kept horse, and then burst into another merry peal of laughter.

Mr. Harry laughed too. "It does seem absurd. Sometimes when I pass him jogging along to town in his rickety old cart, and look at his pale, cruel face, and know that he is a broken-down gambler and man of the world, and yet considers himself infinitely superior to me—a young man in the prime of life, with a good constitution and happy prospects, it makes me turn away to hide a smile."

By this time we had left the river and the meadows far behind us, and were passing through a thick wood. The road was narrow and very broken, and Fleetfoot was obliged to pick his way carefully. "Why does the man Barron live in

this out-of-the-way place, if he is so fond of city
life?" said Miss Laura.

"I don't know," said Mr. Harry. "Father is
afraid that he has committed some misdeed, and
is in hiding; but we say nothing about it. We
have not seen him for some weeks, and to tell the
truth, this trip is as much to see what has become
of him, as to make a demand upon him for the
money. As he lives alone, he might lie there ill,
and no one would know anything about it. The
last time that we knew of his coming to the village was to draw quite a sum of money from the
bank. It annoyed father, for he said he might
take some of it to pay his debts. I think his rich
relatives supply him with funds. Here we are at
the entrance to the mansion of Penhollow. I must
get out and open the gate that will admit us to
the winding avenue."

We had arrived in front of some bars that
were laid across an opening in the snake fence
that ran along one side of the road. I sat down
and looked about. It was a strange, lonely place.
The trees almost met overhead, and it was very
dim and quiet. The sun could send only little
straggling beams through the branches. There
was a pool of muddy water before the bars that
Mr. Harry was letting down, and he got his feet
wet in it. "Confound that man," he said, back-
ing out of the water, and wiping his boots on
the grass. "He hasn't even gumption enough to
throw down a load of stone there. Drive in,

Laura, and I'll put up the bars." Fleetfoot took her through, and then Mr. Harry jumped into the buggy and picked up the reins again.

We had to go very slowly up a narrow, rough road. The bushes scratched and scraped against the buggy, and Mr. Harry looked annoyed.

"No man liveth to himself," said Miss Laura softly. "This man's carelessness is giving you trouble. Why doesn't he cut these branches that overhang the road?"

"He can't do it because his abominable laziness won't let him," said Mr. Harry. "I'd like to be behind him for a week, and I'd make him step a little faster. We have arrived at last, thank goodness."

There was a small grass clearing in the midst of the woods. Chips and bits of wood were littered about, and across the clearing was a roughly built house of unpainted boards. The front door was propped open by a stick. Some of the panes of glass in the windows were broken, and the whole house had a melancholy, dilapidated look. I thought that I had never seen such a sad-looking place.

"It seems as if there was no one about," said Mr. Harry with a puzzled face. "Barron must be away. Will you hold Fleetfoot, Laura, while I go and see?"

He drew the buggy up near a small log building that had evidently been used for a stable, and I lay down beside it and watched Miss Laura.

CHAPTER XXVII

A NEGLECTED STABLE

HAD not been on the ground more than a few seconds, before I turned my eyes from Miss Laura to the log hut. It was deathly quiet, there was not a sound coming from it, but the air was full of queer smells, and I was so uneasy that I could not lie still. There was something the matter with Fleetfoot too. He was pawing the ground, and whinnying, and looking, not after Mr. Harry, but toward the log building.

"Joe," said Miss Laura, "what is the matter with you and Fleetfoot? Why don't you stand still? Is there any stranger about?" and she peered out of the buggy.

I knew there was something wrong somewhere, but I didn't know what it was; so I stretched myself up on the step of the buggy, and licked her hand, and barking, to ask her to excuse me, I ran off to the other side of the log hut. There was a door there, but it was closed, and propped firmly up by a plank that I could not move, scratch as hard as I liked. I was determined to get in, so I jumped against the door, and tore and bit at the plank, till Miss Laura came to help me.

238

"You won't find anything but rats in that ramshackle old place, Beautiful Joe," she said, as she pulled the plank away; "and as you don't hurt them, I don't see why you want to get in. However, you are a sensible dog, and usually have a reason for wanting your own way, so I am going to let you have it."

The plank fell down as she spoke, and she pulled open the rough door and looked in. There was no window inside, only the light that streamed through the door, so for an instant she could see nothing. "Is any one here?" she asked, in her clear, sweet voice. There was no answer, except a low moaning sound. "Why, some poor creature is in trouble, Joe," said Miss Laura cheerfully. "Let us see what it is," and she stepped inside.

I shall never forget seeing my dear Miss Laura going into that wet and filthy log house, holding up her white dress in her hands, her face a picture of pain and horror. There were two rough stalls in it, and in the first one was tied a cow, with a calf lying beside her. I could never have believed, if I had not seen it with my own eyes, that an animal could get as thin as that cow was. Her backbone rose up high and sharp, her hip-bones stuck away out, and all her body seemed shrunken in. There were sores on her sides, and the smell from her stall was terrible. Miss Laura gave one cry of pity, then with a very pale face she dropped her dress, and seizing a little penknife from her pocket, she hacked at the rope that tied the cow to the manger, and cut it so that the poor animal could lie down. The first thing the cow did was to lick her calf, but it was quite dead, I used to think Jenkins' cows were thin enough, but he never had one that looked like this. Her head was like the head of a skeleton, and her eyes had such a famished look, that I turned away, sick at heart, to think that she had suffered so.

When the cow lay down, the moaning noise stopped, for she had been making it. Miss Laura ran outdoors, snatched a handful of grass and took it in to her. The cow ate it gratefully, but slowly, for her strength seemed all gone.

Miss Laura then went into the other stall to see if there was any creature there. There had been a horse. There was now a lean, gaunt-looking animal lying on the ground, that seemed as if he were dead. There was a heavy rope knotted round his neck, and fastened to his empty rack. Miss Laura stepped carefully between his hoofs, cut the rope, and going outside the stall spoke kindly to him. He moved his ears slightly, raised his head, tried to get up, fell back again, tried again, and succeeded in staggering outdoors after Miss Laura, who kept encouraging him, and then he fell down on the grass.

Fleetfoot stared at the miserable-looking creature as if he did not know what it was. The horse had no sores on his body as the cow had, nor was he quite so lean; but he was the weakest, most distressed-looking animal that I ever saw. The flies settled on him, and Miss Laura had to keep driving them away. He was a white horse, with some kind of pale-colored eyes, and whenever he turned them on Miss Laura, she would look away. She did not cry, as she often did over sick and suffering animals. This seemed too bad for tears. She just hovered over that poor horse with her face as white as her dress, and an expression of fright in her eyes. Oh, how dirty he was! I would never have imagined that a horse could get in such a condition.

All this had taken only a few minutes, and just after she got the horse out, Mr. Harry appeared. He came out of the house with a slow step, that quickened to a run when he saw Miss Laura. "Laura!" he exclaimed, "what are you doing?" Then he stopped and looked at the horse, not in amazement, but very sorrowfully. "Barron is gone," he said, and crumpling up a piece of paper, he put it in his pocket. "What is to be done for these animals? There is a cow, isn't there? Have you found her?"

He stepped to the door of the log hut, glanced in, and said quickly, "Do you feel able to drive home?"

"Yes," said Miss Laura.

"Sure?" and he eyed her anxiously.

"Yes, yes," she returned, "what shall I get?"

"Just tell father that Barron has run away and left a starving pig, cow, and horse. There's not

Q

a thing to eat here. He'll know what to do. I'll
drive you to the road."

Miss Laura got into the buggy and Mr. Harry
jumped in after her. He drove her to the road
and put down the bars, then he said: "Go straight
on. You'll soon be on the open road, and there's
nothing to harm you. Joe will look after you.
Meanwhile I'll go back to the house and heat
some water."

Miss Laura let Fleetfoot go as fast as he liked
on the way home, and it seemed only a few minutes before we drove into the yard. Adèle came
out to meet us. "Where's uncle?" asked Miss
Laura.

"Gone to de big meadow," said Adèle.

"And auntie?"

"She had de colds and chills, and entered into
de bed to keep warm. She lose herself in sleep
now. You not go near her."

"Are there none of the men about?" asked
Miss Laura.

"No, mademoiselle. Dey all occupied way off."

"Then you help me, Adèle, like a good girl,"
said Miss Laura, hurrying into the house. "We've
found a sick horse and cow. What shall I take
them?"

"Nearly all animals like de bran mash," said
Adèle.

"Good," cried Miss Laura. "That is the very
thing. Put in the things to make it, will you
please, and I should like some vegetables for the

cow. Carrots, turnips, anything you have, take some of those you have prepared for dinner to-morrow, and please run up to the barn, Adèle, and get some hay, and corn, and oats, not much, for we'll be going back again; but hurry, for the poor things are starving, and have you any milk for the pig? Put it in one of those tin kettles with covers."

For a few minutes, Miss Laura and Adèle flew about the kitchen, then we set off again. Miss Laura took me in the buggy, for I was out of breath and wheezing greatly. I had to sit on the seat beside her, for the bottom of the buggy and the back were full of eatables for the poor sick animals. Just as we drove into the road, we met Mr. Wood. "Are you running away with the farm?" he said with a laugh, pointing to the carrot tops that were gaily waving over the dashboard.

Miss Laura said a few words to him, and with a very grave face he got in beside her. In a short time, we were back on the lonely road. Mr. Harry was waiting at the gate for us, and when he saw Miss Laura, he said: "Why did you come back again? You'll be tired out. This isn't a place for a sensitive girl like you."

"I thought I might be of some use," said she gently.

"So you can," said Mr. Wood. "You go into the house and sit down, and Harry and I will come to you when we want cheering up. What have you been doing, Harry?"

"I've watered them a little, and got a good fire going. I scarcely think the cow will pull through. I think we'll save the horse. I tried to get the cow outdoors, but she can't move."

"Let her alone," said Mr. Wood. "Give her some food and her strength will come to her. What have you got here?" and he began to take the things out of the buggy. "Bless the child, she's thought of everything, even the salt. Bring those things into the house, Harry, and we'll make a bran mash."

For more than an hour they were fussing over the animals. Then they came in and sat down. The inside of the house was as untidy as the outside. There was no up-stairs to it—only one large room with a dirty curtain stretched across it. On one side was a low bed with a heap of clothes on it, a chair and a washstand. On the other was a stove, a table, a shaky rocking-chair that Miss Laura was sitting in, a few hanging shelves with some dishes and books on them, and two or three small boxes that had evidently been used for seats.

On the walls were tacked some pictures of grand houses and ladies and gentlemen in fine clothes, and Miss Laura said that some of them were noble people. "Well, I'm glad this particular nobleman has left us," said Mr. Wood, seating himself on one of the boxes, "if nobleman he is. I should call him in plain English a scoundrel. Did Harry show you this note?"

"No, uncle," said Miss Laura.

"Read it aloud," said Mr. Wood. "I'd like to hear it again."

Miss Laura read:

"J. Wood, Esq. Dear Sir:—It is a matter of great regret to me that I am suddenly called away from my place at Penhollow, and shall, therefore, not be able to do myself the pleasure of calling on you and settling my little account. I sincerely hope that the possession of my live stock, which I make entirely over to you, will more than reimburse you for any trifling expense which you may have incurred on my account. If it is any gratification to you to know that you have rendered a slight assistance to the grandson of one of America's best known financiers, you have it. With expressions of the deepest respect, and hoping that my stock may be in good condition when you take possession,

I am, dear sir, ever devotedly yours,

HOWARD ALGERNON BARRON."

Miss Laura dropped the paper. "Uncle, did he leave those animals to starve?"

"Didn't you notice," said Mr. Wood grimly, "that there wasn't a wisp of hay inside that shanty, and that where the poor beasts were tied up the wood was gnawed and bitten by them in their torture for food? Wouldn't he have sent me that note, instead of leaving it here on the table, if he'd wanted me to know? The note isn't dated, but I judge he's been gone five or six days. He has had a spite against me ever since I lent him that hundred dollars. I don't know why, for

I've stood up for him when others would have run him out of the place. He intended me to come here and find every animal lying dead. He even had a rope around the pig's neck. Harry, my boy, let us go and look after them again. I love a dumb brute too well to let it suffer, but in this case I'd give two hundred dollars more if I could make them live, and have Barron know of it."

They left the room, and Miss Laura sat turning the sheet of paper over and over, with a kind of horror in her face. It was a very dirty piece of paper, but by and by she made a discovery. She took it in her hand and went outdoors. I am sure that the poor horse lying on the grass knew her. He lifted his head, and what a different expression he had now that his hunger had been partly satisfied. Miss Laura stroked and patted him, then she called to her cousin, "Harry, will you look at this?"

He took the paper from her, and said: "That is a crest shining through the different strata of dust and grime, probably that of his own family. We'll have it cleaned, and it will enable us to track the villain. You want him punished, don't you?" he said, with a sly laugh at Miss Laura.

She made a gesture in the direction of the suffering horse, and said frankly, "Yes, I do."

"Well, my dear girl," he said, "Father and I are with you. If we can hunt Barron down, we'll do it." Then he muttered to himself as she turned away: "She is a real Puritan, gentle, sweet, and good, and yet severe. Rewards for the virtuous, punishments for the vicious," and he repeated some poetry:

"She was so charitable and so piteous,
    She would weep if that she saw a mouse
Caught in a trap, if it were dead or bled."

Miss Laura saw that Mr. Wood and Mr. Harry were doing all that could be done for the cow and horse, so she wandered down to a hollow at the back of the house, where the runaway Barron had kept his pig. Just now, he looked more like a greyhound than a pig. His legs were so long, his nose so sharp, and hunger, instead of making him stupid like the horse and cow, had made him more lively. I think he had probably not suffered so much as they had, or perhaps he had had a greater store of fat to nourish him. Mr. Harry said that if he had been a girl, he would have laughed and cried at the same time when he discovered that pig. He must have been asleep or exhausted when we arrived, for there was not a sound out of him, but shortly afterward he had set up a yelling that attracted Mr. Harry's attention, and made him run down to him. Mr. Harry said he was raging around his pen, digging the ground with his snout, falling down and getting up again, and by a miracle, escaping death by choking from the rope that was tied around his neck.

Now that his hunger had been satisfied, he was gazing contentedly at his little trough that was half-full of good, sweet milk. Mr. Harry said that a starving animal, like a starving person, should be fed only a little at a time, but Mr. Barron's animals had always been fed poorly, and their stomachs had contracted so that they could not eat much at one time.

Miss Laura got a stick and scratched poor piggy's back a little, and then she returned to the house. In a short time we went home with Mr. Wood. Mr. Harry was going to stay all night with the sick animals, and his mother would send him things to make him comfortable. She was better by the time we got home, and was horrified to hear the tale of Mr. Barron's neglect. Later in the evening, she sent one of the men over with a whole boxful of things for her darling boy, and a nice, hot supper done up for him in a covered dish.

When the man came home, he said that Mr. Harry would not sleep in the dirty house, but had slung a hammock out under the trees. However, he would not be able to sleep much, for he had his lantern by his side, all ready to jump up and attend to the horse and cow. It was a very lonely place for him out there in the woods, and his mother said that she would be glad when the sick animals could be driven to their own farm.

CHAPTER XXVIII

THE END OF THE CRUEL MAN

N a few days, thanks to Mr. Harry's constant care, the horse and cow were able to walk. It was a mournful procession that came into the yard at Dingley Farm. The hollow-eyed horse, and lean cow, and funny little thin pig, staggering along in such a shaky fashion. Their hoofs were diseased, and had partly rotted away, so that they could not walk straight. Though it was only a mile or two from Penhollow to Dingley Farm, they were tired out, and dropped down exhausted on their comfortable beds.

Miss Laura was so delighted to think they had all lived, that she did not know what to do. Her eyes were bright and shining, and she went from one to another with such a happy face. The queer little pig that Mr. Harry had christened "Daddy Longlegs," had been washed, and he lay on his heap of straw in the corner of his neat little pen, and surveyed his clean trough and abundance of food with the air of a prince. Why, he would be clean and dry here, and all his life he had been used to dirty, damp Penhollow, with the trees hanging over him, and his little feet in a mass of filth and dead leaves. Happy little pig!

His ugly eyes seemed to blink and gleam with gratitude, and he knew Miss Laura and Mr. Harry as well as I did.

His tiny tail was curled so tight that it was almost in a knot. Mr. Wood said it was a sign that he was healthy and happy, and when poor Daddy was at Penhollow, he had noticed that his tail hung as limp and loose as the tail of a rat. He came and leaned over the pen with Miss Laura, and had a little talk with her about pigs. He said they were by no means the stupid animals that some people considered them. He had had pigs that were almost as clever as dogs. One little black pig he had once sold to a man away back in the country had found his way home, through the woods, across the river, up hill and down dale, and he'd been taken to the place with a bag over his head. Mr. Wood said he kept that pig, because he knew so much.

He said that the most knowing pigs he ever saw were Canadian pigs. One time he was having a trip on a sailing vessel, and it anchored in a long, narrow harbor in Canada, where the tide came in with a front four or five feet high called the "bore." There was a village opposite the place where the ship was anchored, and every day at low tide a number of pigs came down to look for shell-fish. Sometimes they went out for half a mile over the mud flats, but always a few minutes before the tide came rushing in they turned and hurried to the shore. Their instinct warned them that if they stayed any longer they would be drowned.

Mr. Wood had a number of pigs, and after a while Daddy was put in with them, and a fine time he had making friends with the other little grunters. They were often let out in the pasture or orchard, and when they were there, I could always single out Daddy from among them, because he was the smartest. Though he had been brought up in such a miserable way, he soon learned to take very good care of himself at Dingley Farm, and it was amusing to see him when a storm was coming on, running about in a state of great excitement, carrying little bundles of straw in his mouth to make himself a bed. He was a white pig, and was always kept very clean. Mr. Wood said that it is wrong to keep pigs dirty. They like to be clean as well as other animals, and if they were kept so, human beings would not get so many diseases from eating their flesh.

The cow, poor unhappy creature, never so long as she lived on Dingley Farm, lost a strange, melancholy look from her eyes. I have heard it said that animals forget past unhappiness, and perhaps some of them do. I know that I have never forgotten my one miserable year with Jenkins, and I have been a sober, thoughtful dog in consequence, and not playful like some dogs who have never known what it is to be really unhappy.

It always seemed to me that the Penhollow cow was thinking of her poor dead calf, starved to death by her cruel master. She got well herself, and came and went with the other cows, seemingly as happy as they, but often when I watched her standing chewing her cud, and looking away in the distance, I could see a difference between her face and the faces of the cows that had always been happy on Dingley Farm. Even the farm hands called her "Old Melancholy," and soon she got to be known by that name, or Mel, for short. Until she got well, she was put into the cow-stable, where Mr. Wood's cows all stood at night upon raised platforms of earth covered over with straw litter, and she was tied with a Dutch halter, so that she could lie down and go to sleep when she wanted to. When she got well, she was put out to pasture with the other cows.

The horse they named "Scrub," because he could never be, under any circumstances, anything but a broken-down, plain-looking animal. He was put into the horse-stable in a stall next Fleetfoot, and as the partition was low, they could look over at each other. In time, by dint of much doctoring, Scrub's hoofs became clean and sound, and he was able to do some work. Miss Laura petted him a great deal. She often took out apples to the stable, and Fleetfoot would throw up his beautiful head and look reproachfully over the partition at her, for she always stayed longer with Scrub than with him, and Scrub always got the larger share of whatever good thing was going.

Poor old Scrub! I think he loved Miss Laura.

He was a stupid sort of a horse, and always acted as if he were blind. He would run his nose up and down the front of her dress, nip at the buttons, and be very happy if he could get a bit of her watch-chain between his strong teeth. If he was in the field he never seemed to know her till she was right under his pale-colored eyes. Then he would be delighted to see her. He was not blind though, for Mr. Wood said he was not. He said he had probably not been an overbright horse to start with, and had been made more dull by cruel usage.

As for the former master of these animals, a very strange thing happened to him. He came to a terrible end, but for a long time no one knew anything about it. Mr. Wood and Mr. Harry were so very angry with him, that they said they would leave no stone unturned to have him punished, or at least to have it known what a villain he was. They sent the paper with the crest on it to New York. Some one there found out that it was the crest of a highly esteemed family who were all honorable people except this one man, who was the black sheep of them all. As a young man, he had led a wild and wicked life, and had ended by forging the name of one of his friends, so that he was obliged to leave his home and take refuge in entirely new surroundings. By the description of this man, Mr. Wood knew that he must be Mr. Barron, so he wrote to these people, and told them what a wicked thing their relative had done in leaving his animals to starve. In a short time, he got an answer from them which was very proud and very touching. It came from Mr. Barron's cousin, and he said quite frankly that he knew his relative was a man of evil habits, but it seemed as if nothing could be done to reform him. His family was accustomed to send a quarterly allowance to him, on condition that he lead a quiet life in some retired place, but their last remittance to him was lying unclaimed in Boston, and they thought he must be dead. Could Mr. Wood tell them anything about him?

Mr. Wood looked very thoughtful when he got this letter, then he said, "Harry, how long is it since Barron ran away?"

"About eight weeks," said Mr. Harry.

"That's strange," said Mr. Wood. "The money these relatives sent him would get to Boston just a few days after he left here. He is not the man to leave it long unclaimed. Something must have happened to him. Where do you suppose he would go from Penhollow?"

"I have no idea, sir," said Mr. Harry.

"And how would he go?" said Mr. Wood. "He did not leave Riverdale Station, because he would have been spotted by some of his creditors."

"Perhaps he would cut through the woods to the Junction," said Mr. Harry.

"Just what he would do," said Mr. Wood, slapping his knee. "I'll be driving over there tomorrow to see Thompson, and I'll make inquiries."

Mr. Harry spoke to his father the next night when he came home, and asked him if he had found out anything. "Only this," said Mr. Wood. "There's no one answering to Barron's description who has left Riverdale Junction within a twelvemonth. He must have struck some other station. We'll let him go. The Lord looks out for fellows like that."

"We will look out for him if ever he comes back to Riverdale," said Mr. Harry quietly. All through the village, and in the country, it was known what a dastardly trick the man had played, and he would have been arrested for cruelty to animals if he had dared return.

Months passed away, and nothing was heard of him. Late in the autumn, after Miss Laura and I had gone back to Fairport, Mrs. Wood wrote her about the end of the stranger at Penhollow. Some Riverdale lads were beating about the woods, looking for lost cattle, and in their wanderings came to an old stone quarry that had been disused for years. On one side there was a smooth wall of rock, many feet deep. On the other the ground and rock were broken away, and it was quite easy to get into it. They found that, by some means or other, one of their cows had fallen into this deep pit, over the steep side of the quarry. Of course, the poor creature was dead, but the boys, out of curiosity, resolved to go down and look at her. They clambered down, found the cow, and to their horror and amazement, discovered near-by the skeleton of a man. There was a heavy walking-stick by his side, which they recognized as one that Mr. Barron had carried.

He was a drinking man, and perhaps he had taken something that he thought would strengthen him for his morning's walk, but which had, on the contrary, bewildered him, and made him lose his way and fall into the quarry. Or he might have started before daybreak, and in the darkness have slipped and fallen down this steep wall of rock. One leg was doubled under him, and if he had not been instantly killed by the fall, he must have been so disabled that he could not move. In that lonely place, he would call for help in vain, so he may have perished by the terrible death of starvation—the death he had thought to mete out to his suffering animals.

Mrs. Wood said there was never a sermon preached in Riverdale that had the effect the death of this wicked man had, and it reminded her of a verse in the Bible: " He made a pit and he digged it, and is fallen into the ditch which he made." Mrs. Wood said that her husband had written about the finding of Mr. Barron's body to his relatives, and had received a letter from them in which they seemed relieved to hear that he was dead. They thanked Mr. Wood for his plain speaking in telling them of their relative's misdeeds, and said that from all they knew of Mr. Barron's past conduct, his influence would be for evil and not for good, in any place that he chose to live. They were having their money sent from Boston to Mr. Wood, and they wished him to expend it in the way he thought best fitted to counteract the evil effects of their namesake's doings in Riverdale.

When this money came, it amounted to some hundreds of dollars. Mr. Wood would have nothing to do with it. He handed it over to the Band of Mercy, and they formed what they call the "Barron Fund," which they drew upon when they wanted money for buying and circulating humane literature. Mrs. Wood said that the fund was being added to, and the children were sending all over the State leaflets and little books which preached the gospel of kindness to God's lower creation. A stranger picking up one of them, and seeing the name of the wicked man printed on the title-page, would think that he was a friend and benefactor to the Riverdale people—the very opposite of what he gloried in being.

R

CHAPTER XXIX

OUR RETURN HOME

IN October, the most beautiful of all the months, we were obliged to go back to Fairport. Miss Laura could not bear to leave the farm, and her face got very sorrowful when any one spoke of her going away. Still, she had grown well and strong, and was as brown as a berry, and she said that she knew she ought to go home, and get back to her lessons.

Mr. Wood called October the golden month. Everything was quiet and still, and at night and in the mornings the sun had a yellow, misty look. The trees in the orchard were loaded with fruit, and some of the leaves were floating down, making a soft covering on the ground.

In the garden there were a great many flowers in bloom, in flaming red and yellow colors. Miss Laura gathered bunches of them every day to put in the parlor. One day when she was arranging them, she said regretfully: "They will soon be gone. I wish it could always be summer."

"You would get tired of it," said Mr. Harry, who had come up softly behind her. "There's only one place where we could stand perpetual summer, and that's in heaven."

258

"Do you suppose that it will always be summer there?" said Miss Laura, turning around and looking at him.

"I don't know. I imagine it will be, but I don't think anybody knows much about it. We've got to wait."

Miss Laura's eyes fell on me. "Harry," she said, "do you think that dumb animals will go to heaven?"

"I shall have to say again, I don't know," he replied. "Some people hold that they do. In a Michigan paper, the other day, I came across one writer's opinion on the subject. He says that among the best people of all ages have been some who believed in the future life of animals. Homer and the later Greeks, some of the Romans and early Christians held this view—the last believing that God sent angels in the shape of birds to comfort sufferers for the faith. St. Francis called the birds and beasts his brothers. Doctor Johnson believed in a future life for animals, as also did Wordsworth, Shelley, Coleridge, Jeremy Taylor, Agassiz, Lamartine, and many Christian scholars. It seems as if they ought to have some compensation for their terrible sufferings in this world. Then to go to heaven, animals would only have to take up the thread of their lives here. Man is a god to the lower creation. Joe worships you, much as you worship your Maker. Dumb animals live in and for their masters. They hang on our words and looks, and are dependent on us in almost every way. For my own part, and looking at it from an earthly point of view, I wish with all my heart that we may find our dumb friends in paradise."

"And in the Bible," said Miss Laura, "animals are often spoken of. The dove and the raven, the wolf and the lamb, and the leopard, and the cattle that God says are his, and the little sparrow that can't fall to the ground without our Father's knowing it."

"Still, there's nothing definite about their immortality," said Mr. Harry. "However, we have nothing to do with that. If it's right for them to be in heaven, we'll find them there. All we have to do now is to deal with the present, and the Bible plainly tells us that 'a righteous man regardeth the life of his beast.'"

"I think I should be happier in heaven if dear old Joe were there," said Miss Laura, looking wistfully at me. "He has been such a good dog. Just think how he has loved and protected me. I think I should be lonely without him."

"That reminds me of some poetry, or rather doggerel," said Mr. Harry, "that I cut out of a newspaper for you yesterday," and he drew from his pocket a little slip of paper, and read this:

"Do doggies gang to heaven, Dad?
  Will oor auld Donald gang?
For noo to tak' him, faither, wi' us,
  Wad be maist awfu' wrang"

There were other verses, telling how many kind things old Donald the dog had done for his master's family, and then it closed with these lines:

"Withoot are dogs. Eh, faither, man,
    'Twould be an awfu' sin
To leave oor faithfu' doggie there,
    He's certain to win in.

"Oor Donald's no like ither dogs,
    He'll no be lockit oot,
If Donald's no let into heaven,
    I'll no gang there one foot."

"My sentiments exactly," said a merry voice behind Miss Laura and Mr. Harry, and looking up they saw Mr. Maxwell. He was holding out one hand to them, and in the other kept back a basket of large pears that Mr. Harry promptly took from him, and offered to Miss Laura. "I've been dependent upon animals for the most part of my comfort in this life," said Mr. Maxwell, "and I sha'n't be happy without them in heaven. I don't see how you would get on without Joe, Miss Morris, and I want my birds, and my snake, and my horse—how can I live without them? They're almost all my life here."

"If some animals go to heaven and not others, I think that the dog has the first claim," said Miss Laura. "He's the friend of man—the oldest and best. Have you ever heard the legend about him and Adam?"

"No," said Mr. Maxwell.

"Well, when Adam was turned out of paradise, all the animals shunned him, and he sat weeping bitterly with his head between his hands, when he felt the soft tongue of some creature gently touching him. He took his hands from his face, and there was a dog that had separated himself from all the other animals, and was trying to comfort him. He became the chosen friend and companion of Adam, and afterward of all men."

"There is another legend," said Mr. Harry, "about our Saviour and a dog. Have you ever heard it?"

"We'll tell you that later," said Mr. Maxwell, "when we know what it is."

Mr. Harry showed his white teeth in an amused smile, and began: "Once upon a time our Lord was going through a town with his disciples. A dead dog lay by the wayside, and every one that passed along flung some offensive epithet at him. Eastern dogs are not like our dogs, and seemingly there was nothing good to be seen in this loathsome creature, but as our Saviour went by, he said, gently, 'Pearls cannot equal the whiteness of his teeth.'"

"What was the name of that old fellow," said Mr. Maxwell abruptly, "who had a beautiful swan that came every day for fifteen years, to bury its head in his bosom and feed from his hand, and would go near no other human being?"

"Saint Hugh, of Lincoln. We heard about him

at the Band of Mercy the other day," said Miss Laura.

"I should think that he would have wanted to have that swan in heaven with him," said Mr. Maxwell. "What a beautiful creature it must have been. Speaking about animals going to heaven, I dare say some of them would object to going, on account of the company they would meet there. Think of the dog kicked to death by his master, the horse driven into his grave, the thousands of cattle starved to death on the plains—will they want to meet their owners in heaven?"

"According to my reckoning, their owners won't be there," said Mr. Harry. "I firmly believe that the Lord will punish every man or woman who ill-treats a dumb creature, just as surely as he will punish those who ill-treat their fellow creatures. If a man's life has been a long series of cruelties to dumb animals, do you suppose that he would enjoy himself in heaven, which will be full of kindness to every one? Not he, he'd rather be in the other place, and there he'll go, I fully believe."

"When you've quite disposed of all your fellow creatures and the dumb creation, Harry, perhaps you will condescend to go out in the orchard and see how your father is getting on with picking the apples," said Mrs. Wood, joining Miss Laura and the two young men, her eyes twinkling and sparkling with amusement.

"The apples will keep, mother," said Mr. Harry, putting his arm around her. "I just came in for a moment to get Laura. Come, Maxwell, we'll all go."

"And not another word about animals," Mrs. Wood called after them. "Laura will go crazy some day, through thinking of their sufferings, if some one doesn't do something to stop her."

Miss Laura turned around suddenly. "Dear Aunt Hattie," she said, "you must not say that. I am a coward, I know, about hearing of animals' pains, but I must get over it. I want to know how they suffer. I ought to know, for when I get to be a woman, I am going to do all I can to help them."

"And I'll join you," said Mr. Maxwell, stretching out his hand to Miss Laura. She did not smile, but looking very earnestly at him, she held it clasped in her own. "You will help me care for them, will you?" she said.

"Yes, I promise," he said gravely. "I'll give myself to the service of dumb animals, if you will."

"And I too," said Mr. Harry, in his deep voice, laying his hand across theirs. Mrs. Wood stood looking at their three fresh, eager young faces, with tears in her eyes. Just as they all stood silently for an instant, the old village clergyman came into the room from the hall. He must have heard what they said, for before they could move he had laid his hands on their three brown heads. "Bless you, my children," he said, "God will lift up the light of His countenance upon you, for you have given yourselves to a noble work. In serving dumb creatures, you are ennobling the human race."

Then he sat down in a chair and looked at them. He was a venerable old man, and had long, white hair, and the Woods thought a great deal of him. He had come to get Mrs. Wood to make some nourishing dishes for a sick woman in the village, and while he was talking to her, Miss Laura and the two young men went out of the house. They hurried across the veranda and over the lawn, talking and laughing, and enjoying themselves as only happy young people can, and with not a trace of their seriousness of a few moments before.

They were going so fast that they ran right into a flock of geese coming up the lane. They were driven by a little boy called Tommy, the son of one of Mr. Wood's farm laborers, and they were chattering and gabbling, and seemed very angry. "What's all this about?" said Mr. Harry, stopping and looking at the boy. "What's the matter with your feathered charges, Tommy, my lad?"

"If it's the geese you mean," said the boy, half crying and looking very much put out, "it's all them nasty potatoes. They won't keep away from them."

"So the potatoes chase the geese, do they?" said Mr. Maxwell teasingly.

"No, no," said the child pettishly, "Mr. Wood, he sets me to watch the geese, and they runs in

among the buckwheat and the potatoes, and I tries
to drive them out, and they doesn't want to come,
and," shamefacedly, "I has to switch their feet,
and I hates to do it, 'cause I'm a Band of Mercy
boy."

"Tommy, my son," said Mr. Maxwell solemnly,
"you will go right to heaven when you die, and
your geese will go with you."

"Hush, hush," said Miss Laura; "don't tease
him"; and putting her arm on the child's shoulder,
she said: "You are a good boy, Tommy, not to
want to hurt the geese. Let me see your switch,
dear."

He showed her a little stick he had in his hand,
and she said: "I don't think you could hurt them
much with that, and if they will be naughty and
steal the potatoes, you have to drive them out.
Take some of my pears and eat them, and you will
forget your trouble."

The child took the fruit, and Miss Laura and
the two young men went on their way, smiling, and
looking over their shoulders at Tommy, who stood
in the middle of the lane, devouring his pears and
keeping one eye on the geese that had gathered a
little in front of him. They were gabbling noisily
and having a kind of indignation meeting, because
they had been driven out of the potato-field.

Tommy's father and mother lived in a little
house down near the road. Mr. Wood never had
his hired men live in his own house. He had two
small houses for them, and they were required

to keep them as neat as Mr. Wood's own house was kept. He said that he didn't see why he should keep a boarding-house, if he was a farmer, nor why his wife should wear herself out waiting on strong, hearty men, that had just as soon take care of themselves. He wished to have his own family about him, and it was better for his men to have some kind of family life for themselves. If one of his men was unmarried, he boarded with the married one, but slept in his own house.

On this October day we found Mr. Wood hard at work under the fruit trees. He had a good many different kinds of apples. Enormous red ones, and long, yellow ones that they called pippins, and little brown ones, and smooth-coated sweet ones, and bright red ones, and others, more than I could mention. Miss Laura often pared one and cut off little bits for me, for I always wanted to eat whatever I saw her eating.

Just a few days after this, Miss Laura and I returned to Fairport, and some of Mr. Wood's apples traveled along with us, for he sent a good many to the Boston market. Mr. and Mrs. Wood came to the station to see us off. Mr. Harry could not come, for he had left Riverdale the day before to go back to his college. Mrs. Wood said that she would be very lonely without her two young people, and she kissed Miss Laura over and over again, and made her promise to come back the next summer.

I was put in a box in the express-car, and Mr.
Wood told the agent that if he knew what was
good for him he would speak to me occasionally,
for I was a very knowing dog, and if he didn't
treat me well, I'd be apt to write him up in the
newspapers. The agent laughed, and quite often
on the way to Fairport he came to my box and
spoke kindly to me. So I did not get so lonely
and frightened as I did on my unhappy journey to
Riverdale.

How glad the Morrises were to see us coming
back. The boys had all arrived home before us,
and such a fuss as they did make over their sister.
They loved her dearly, and never wanted her to
be long away from them. I was rubbed and
stroked, and had to run about offering my paw to
every one. Jim and little Billy licked my face,
and Bella croaked a new sentence they had taught
her: "Glad to see you, Joe. Had a good time?
How's your health?"

We soon settled down for the winter. Miss
Laura began going to school, and came home
every day with a pile of books under her arm.
The summer in the country had done her so much
good that her mother often looked at her fondly,
and said the white-faced child she sent away had
come home a nut-brown maid.

CHAPTER XXX

PERFORMING ANIMALS

A WEEK or two after we got home, I heard the Morris boys talking about an Italian who was coming to Fairport with a troupe of trained animals, and I could see for myself, whenever I went to town, great flaming pictures on the fences, of monkeys sitting at tables, dogs, and ponies, and goats climbing ladders, and rolling balls, and doing various tricks. I wondered very much whether they would be able to do all these extraordinary things, but it turned out that they could.

The Italian's name was Bellini, and one afternoon the whole Morris family went to see him and his animals, and when they came home I heard them talking about it.

"I wish you could have been there, Joe," said Jack, pulling up my paws to rest on his knees. "Now listen, old fellow, and I'll tell you all about it. First of all, there was a perfect jam in the town hall. I sat up in front, with a lot of fellows, and had a splendid view. The old Italian came out dressed in his best suit of clothes—black broadcloth, flower in his buttonhole, and so on. He made a fine bow, and he said he was

269

'pleased to see ze fine audience, and he was going to show zem ze fine animals, ze finest animals in ze world.' Then he held up a little whistle and said he was different from other trainers who used a whip to control their animals. He had only to blow his whistle to show his animals when to begin, end, or change their tricks.

"Some boy yelled, 'Rats! you do whip them sometimes,' and the old man made another bow, and said, 'Sairteenly, he whipped zem just as ze mammas whip ze naughty boys, to make zem keep still when zey was noisy or stubborn.'

"Then everybody laughed at the boy, and the Italian said the performance would begin by a grand procession of all the animals, if some lady would kindly step up to the piano and play a march. Nina Smith—you know Nina, Joe, the girl who has black eyes and wears blue ribbons, and lives around the corner—stepped up to the piano, and banged out a fine loud march. The doors at the side of the platform opened, and out came the animals, two by two, just like Noah's ark. There was a pony with a monkey walking beside it and holding on to its mane, another monkey on a pony's back, two monkeys hand in hand, a dog with a parrot on his back, a goat harnessed to a little carriage, another goat carrying a bird-cage in its mouth with two canaries inside, different kinds of cats, some doves and pigeons, half a dozen white rats with red harness, and dragging a little chariot with a monkey in it, and a common white gander that came in last of all, and did nothing but follow one of the ponies about.

"The Italian spoke of the gander, and said it was a stupid creature, and could learn no tricks, and he kept it only on account of its affection for the pony. He had got them both on a Vermont farm, when he was looking for show animals. The pony's master had made a pet of him, and had taught him to come whenever he whistled. Though the pony was only a scrub of a creature, he had a gentle disposition, and every other animal on the farm liked him. This particular gander had such an admiration for him, that he followed him wherever he went, and if he lost him for an instant, he would mount one of the knolls on the farm and stretch out his neck looking for him. When he caught sight of him he gabbled with delight, and running to him, waddled up and down beside him. Every little while the pony put his nose down, and seemed to be having a conversation with the gander. If the farmer whistled for the pony and he started to run to him, the gander, knowing he could not keep up, would seize the pony's tail in his beak, and flapping his wings, would get along as fast as the pony did, and the pony never kicked him. The Italian saw that this pony would be a good one to train for the stage, so he offered the farmer a large price for him, and took him away.

"Oh, Joe, I forgot to say, that by this time all

the animals had been sent off the stage except the pony and the gander, and they stood looking at the Italian while he talked. I never saw anything so human in dumb animals as that pony's face. He looked as if he understood every word that his master was saying. After this story was over, the Italian told the pony to bow. He nodded his head at the people, and they all laughed. Then the Italian asked him to favor us with a waltz, and the pony got up on his hind legs and danced. You should have seen that gander skirmishing around, so as to be near the pony and yet keep out of the way of his heels. We fellows just roared, and we would have kept him dancing all the afternoon if the Italian hadn't begged 'ze young gentlemen not to make ze noise, but let ze pony do ze rest of his tricks.'

" Pony number two came on the stage, and it was too queer for anything to see the things the two of them did. They helped the Italian on with his coat, they pulled off his rubbers, they took his coat away and brought him a chair, and dragged a table up to it. They brought him letters and papers, and rang bells, and rolled barrels, and swung the Italian in a big swing, and jumped a rope, and walked up and down steps—they just went around that stage as handy with their teeth as two boys would be with their hands, and they seemed to understand every word their master said to them.

" The best trick of all was telling the time and

doing questions in arithmetic. The Italian pulled his watch out of his pocket and showed it to the first pony, whose name was Diamond, and said, 'What time is it?' The pony looked at it, then scratched four times with his forefoot on the platform. The Italian said: 'That's good—four o'clock. But it's a few minutes after four—how many?' The pony scratched again five times. The Italian showed his watch to the audience, and said that it was just five minutes past four. Then he asked the pony how old he was. He scratched four times. That meant four years. He asked him how many days in a week there were, how many months in a year, and he gave him some questions in addition and subtraction, and the pony answered them all correctly. Of course the Italian was giving him some sign, but though we watched him closely we couldn't make out what it was.

"At last, he told the pony that he had been very good, and had done his lessons well; if it would rest him, he might be naughty a little while. All of a sudden a wicked look came into the creature's eyes. He turned around, and kicked up his heels at his master, he pushed over the table and chairs, and knocked down a blackboard where he had been rubbing out figures with a sponge held in his mouth. The Italian pretended to be cross, and said, 'Come, come, this won't do,' and he called the other pony to him, and told him to take that troublesome fellow off the stage. The second one nosed Diamond, and pushed him about,

s

finally bit him by the ear, and led him away, squealing. The gander followed, gabbling as fast as he could, and there was a regular roar of applause.

"After that, there were ladders brought in, Joe, and dogs came on, not well-bred, but curs, something like you. The Italian says he can't teach tricks to pedigree animals as well as to scrubs. Those dogs jumped the ladders, and climbed them, and went through them, and did all kinds of things. The man blew his whistle once, and they began; twice, and they did backward what they had done forward; three times, and they stopped, and every animal—dogs, goats, ponies, and monkeys—after they had finished their tricks, ran up to their master, and he gave them a lump of sugar. They seemed fond of him, and often when they weren't performing, went up to him, and licked his hands or his sleeve.

"There was one boss dog, Joe, with a head like yours. Bob, they called him, and he did all his tricks alone. The Italian went off the stage, and the dog came on and made his bow, and climbed his ladders, and jumped his hurdles, and went off again. The audience howled for an encore, and didn't he come out alone, make another bow, and retire. I saw old Judge Brown wiping the tears from his eyes, he'd laughed so much.

"One of the last tricks was with a goat, and the Italian said it was the best of all, because the goat is such a hard animal to teach. He had a big ball, and the goat got on it and rolled it across the stage without getting off. He looked as nervous as a cat, shaking his old beard, and trying to keep his four hoofs close enough together to keep him on the ball.

"We had a funny little play at the end of the performance. A monkey dressed as a lady, in a white satin frock and a bonnet with a white veil, came on the stage. She was Miss Green and the dog Bob was going to elope with her. He was all rigged out as Mr. Smith, and had on a light suit of clothes, and a tall hat on the side of his head, high collar, long cuffs, and he carried a cane. He was a regular dude. He stepped up to Miss Green on his hind legs, and helped her on to a pony's back. The pony galloped off the stage; then a crowd of monkeys, chattering and wringing their hands, came on. Mr. Smith had run away with their child. They were all dressed up too. There were the father and mother, with gray wigs and black clothes, and the young Greens in bibs and tuckers. They were a queer-looking crowd.

"While they were going on in this way, the pony trotted back on the stage; and they all flew at him and pulled off their daughter from his back, and laughed and chattered, and boxed her ears, and took off her white veil and her satin dress, and put on an old brown thing, and some of them seized the dog, and kicked his hat, and broke his cane, and stripped his clothes off, and threw them in a corner, and bound his legs with cords. A goat came on, harnessed to a little cart, and they threw the dog in it, and wheeled him around the stage a few times. Then they took him out and tied him to a hook in the wall, and the goat ran off the stage, and the monkeys ran to one side, and one of them pulled out a little revolver, pointed it at the dog, pretended to fire, and he dropped down as if he were dead.

" The monkeys stood looking at him, and then there was the most awful hullabaloo you ever heard. Such a barking and yelping, and half a dozen dogs rushed on the stage, and didn't they trundle those monkeys about. They nosed them, and pushed them, and shook them, till they all ran away, all but Miss Green, who sat shivering in a corner. After a while, she crept up to the dead dog, pawed him a little, and didn't he jump up as much alive as any of them? Everybody in the room clapped and shouted, and then the curtain dropped, and the thing was over. I wish he'd give another performance. Early in the morning he has to go to Boston."

Jack pushed my paws from his knees and went outdoors, and I began to think that I should very much like to see those performing animals. It was not yet tea-time, and I should have plenty of time to take a run down to the hotel where they were staying; so I set out. It was a lovely autumn evening. The sun was going down in a haze, and it was quite warm. Earlier in the day

I had heard Mr. Morris say that this was our Indian summer, and that we should soon have cold weather.

Fairport was a pretty little town, and from the principal street one could look out upon the blue water of the bay and see the island opposite, which was quite deserted now, for the summer visitors were gone, and the Island House was closed.

I was running down one of the steep side streets that led to the water when I met a heavily laden cart coming up. It must have been coming from one of the vessels, for it was full of strange-looking boxes and packages. A fine-looking nervous horse was drawing it, and he was straining every nerve to get it up the steep hill. His driver was a burly, hard-faced man, and instead of letting his horse stop a minute to rest he was urging him forward. The poor horse kept looking at his master, his eyes almost starting from his head in terror. He knew that the whip was about to descend on his quivering body; and so it did, and there was no one to interfere. No one but a woman in a ragged shawl who would have no influence with the driver. There was a very good humane society in Fairport, and none of the teamsters dared ill-use their horses if any of the members were near. This was a quiet, out-of-the-way street, with only poor houses on it, and the man probably knew that none of the members of the society would likely be living in them. He whipped his horse, and whipped him, till every lash made my heart

ache, and if I had dared I would have bitten him
severely. Suddenly there was a dull thud in the
street. The horse's heart had given out and he
had fallen down. The driver ran to his head, but
he was quite dead. "Thank God!" said the poorly
dressed woman bitterly; "one more out of this
world of misery." Then she turned and went down
the street. I was glad for the horse. He would
never be frightened or miserable again, and I
went slowly on, thinking that death is the best
thing that can happen to tortured animals.

The Fairport Hotel was built right in the center
of the town, and the shops and houses crowded
quite close about it. It was a high, brick building,
and was called the Fairport House. As I was
running along the sidewalk I heard some one
speak to me, and looking up I saw Charlie Montague. I had heard the Morrises say that his
parents were staying at the hotel for a few weeks,
while their house was being repaired. He had
his Irish setter Brisk with him, and a handsome
dog he was, as he stood waving his silky tail in
the sunlight. Charlie patted me, and then he and
his dog went into the hotel.

I turned into the stable-yard. It was a small,
choked-up place, and as I picked my way under the
cabs and wagons I wondered why the hotel people
didn't buy some of the old houses near-by, and
tear them down, and make a stable-yard worthy of
such a nice hotel. The hotel horses were just
getting rubbed down after their day's work, and

others were coming in. The men were talking and laughing, and there was no sign of strange animals, so I went around to the back of the yard. Here they were, in an empty cow-stable, under a hay-loft. There were two little ponies tied up in a stall, two goats beyond them, and dogs and monkeys in strong traveling cages. I stood in the doorway and stared at them. I was sorry for the dogs to be shut up on such a lovely evening, but I suppose their master was afraid of their getting lost, or being stolen, if he let them loose.

They all seemed very friendly. The ponies turned around and looked at me with their gentle eyes, and then went on munching their hay. I wondered very much where the gander was, and went a little further into the stable. Something white raised itself up out of the brownest pony's crib, and there was the gander close up beside the open mouth of his friend. The monkeys made a jabbering noise, and held on to the bars of their cages with their little black hands, while they looked out at me. The dogs sniffed the air, and wagged their tails, and tried to put their muzzles through the bars of their cages. I liked the dogs best, and I wanted to see the one they called Bob, so I went up quite close to them. There were two little white dogs, something like Billy, two mongrel spaniels, an Irish terrier, and a brown dog asleep in the corner, that I knew must be Bob. He did look a little like me, but he was not quite so ugly, for he had his ears and his tail.

While I was peering through the bars at him,
a man came in the stable. He noticed me the
first thing, but instead of driving me out, he spoke
kindly to me, in a language that I did not understand; so I knew that he was the Italian. How
glad the animals were to see him! The gander
fluttered out of his nest, the ponies pulled at their
halters, the dogs whined and tried to reach his
hands to lick them, and the monkeys chattered
with delight. He laughed, and talked back to
them in queer, soft-sounding words. Then he
took out of a bag on his arm bones for the dogs,
nuts and cakes for the monkeys, nice, juicy carrots for the ponies, some green stuff for the goats,
and corn for the gander.

It was a pretty sight to see the old man feeding
his pets, and it made me feel quite hungry, so I
trotted home. I had a run down-town again that
evening with Mr. Morris, who went to get something from a shop for his wife. He never let his
boys go to town after dark, so if there were
errands to be done, he or Mrs. Morris went. The
town was bright and lively that evening, and a
great many people were walking about and looking
into the shop windows.

When we came home, I went into the kennel
with Jim, and there I slept till the middle of the
night. Then I started up and ran outside. There
was a distant bell ringing, which we often heard
in Fairport, and which always meant fire.

CHAPTER XXXI

A FIRE IN FAIRPORT

 HAD several times run to a fire with the boys and knew that there was always a great noise and excitement. There was a light in the house, so I knew that somebody was getting up. I don't think—indeed I know, for they were good boys—that they ever wanted anybody to lose property, but they did enjoy seeing a blaze, and one of their greatest delights, when there hadn't been a fire for some time, was to build a bonfire in the garden.

Jim and I ran around to the front of the house and waited. In a few minutes, some one came rattling at the front door, and I felt sure it was Jack. However, it was Mr. Morris, and without a word to us, he set off running toward the town. As we hurried after him, other men ran out from the houses along the streets, and either joined him, or dashed ahead. They seemed to have dressed in a hurry, and were thrusting their arms in their coats, and buttoning themselves up as they went. Some of them had hats and some of them had none, and they all had their faces toward the great, red light ahead of us that kept getting brighter and brighter.

"Where's the fire?" they shouted to each other.
"Don't know—afraid it's the hotel, or the town
hall. Hope not. What a blaze! How's the
water supply now? Bad time for a fire."

It was the hotel. We saw that as soon as we
got on the main street. There were people all
about, and a great noise and confusion, and smoke
and blackness, and up above, bright tongues of
flame were leaping against the sky. Jim and I
kept close to Mr. Morris' heels, as he pushed his
way through the crowd. When we got nearer the
burning building, we saw men carrying ladders
and axes, and others were shouting directions, and
rushing out of the hotel, carrying boxes and bundles and furniture in their arms. From the windows above came a steady stream of articles,
thrown among the crowd. A mirror struck Mr.
Morris on the arm, and a whole package of clothes
fell on his head and almost smothered him; but he
brushed them aside and scarcely noticed them.

There was something the matter with Mr. Morris—I knew by the worried sound of his voice
when he spoke to any one. I could not see his
face, though it was as light as day about us, for
we had got jammed in the crowd, and if I had not
kept between his feet, I should have been trodden
to death. Jim, being larger than I was, had got
separated from us.

Presently Mr. Morris raised his voice above the
uproar, and called, "Is every one out of the
hotel?" A voice shouted, "I'm going up to see."

"It's Jim Watson, the fireman," cried some one near. "He's risking his life to go into that pit of flame. Don't go, Watson."

I don't think the brave fireman paid any attention to this warning, for an instant later the same voice said: "He's planting his ladder against the third story. He's bound to go. He'll not get any farther than the second, anyway."

"Where are the Montagues?" shouted Mr. Morris. "Has any one seen the Montagues?"

"Mr. Morris! Mr. Morris!" cried a frightened voice, and young Charles Montague pressed through the people to us. "Where's papa?"

"I don't know. Where did you leave him?" said Mr. Morris, taking his hand and drawing him closer to him. "I was sleeping in his room," said the boy, "and a man knocked at the door, and said, 'Hotel on fire. Five minutes to dress and get out,' and papa told me to put on my clothes and go down-stairs at once, and he ran up to mamma."

"Where was she?" asked Mr. Morris, quickly.

"On the fourth floor. She and her maid Blanche were up there. You know, mamma hasn't been well and couldn't sleep, and our room was so noisy that she moved up-stairs where it was quiet." Mr. Morris gave a kind of groan. "Oh, I'm so hot, and there's such a dreadful noise," said the little boy bursting into tears, "and I want mamma." Mr. Morris soothed him as best he could, and drew him a little to the edge of the crowd.

While he was doing this, there was a piercing
cry. I could not see the person making it, but I
knew it was the Italian's voice. He was screaming in broken English that the fire was spreading
to the stables, and his animals would be burned.
Would no one help him to get them out? There
was a great deal of confused language. Some voices
shouted: "Look after the people first. Let the
animals go." Others said: "For shame. Get the
horses out." But no one seemed to do anything,
for the Italian went on crying for help. I heard
a number of people who were standing near us
say that it had just been found out that several
persons who had been sleeping in the top of the
hotel had not got out. They said that at one of
the attic windows a poor housemaid was shrieking
for help. Here in the street we could see no one
at the upper windows, for smoke was pouring
from them.

The air was very hot and heavy, and I didn't
wonder that Charlie Montague felt ill. He would
have fallen on the ground if Mr. Morris hadn't
taken him in his arms, and carried him out of the
crowd. He put him down on the brick sidewalk,
and unfastened his little shirt, and left me to
watch him, while he held his hands under a leak
in a hose that was fastened to a hydrant near us.
He got enough water to dash on Charlie's face and
chest, and then seeing that the boy was reviving,
he sat down on the curbstone and took him on his
knee. Charlie lay in his arms and moaned   He

was a delicate boy, and he could not stand rough usage as the Morris boys could.

Mr. Morris was terribly uneasy. His face was deathly white, and he shuddered whenever there was a cry from the burning building. "Poor souls—God help them. Oh, this is awful," he said, and then he turned his eyes from the great sheets of flame and strained the little boy to his breast. At last there were wild shrieks that I knew came from no human throats. The fire must have reached the horses. Mr. Morris sprang up, then sank back again. He wanted to go, yet he could be of no use. There were hundreds of men standing about, but the fire had spread so rapidly, and they had so little water to put on it, that there was not much they could do. I wondered whether I could do anything for the poor animals. I was not as much afraid of fire as most dogs, for one of the tricks that the Morris boys had taught me was to put out a blaze with my paws. They would throw a piece of lighted paper on the floor, and I would crush it with my forepaws; and if the blaze was too large for that, I would drag a bit of old carpet over it and jump on it.

I left Mr. Morris, and ran around the corner of the street to the back of the hotel. It was not burned as much here as in the front, and people were spreading out blankets on the roofs of the near-by houses. Some were standing at the windows watching the fire, or packing up their belongings ready to move if it should spread to them

There was a narrow lane running up behind the hotel, and I had just started up this lane, when in front of me I heard such a wailing, piercing noise, that I shuddered and stood still. The Italian's animals were going to be burned up, and they were calling to their master to come and let them out. Their voices sounded like the voices of children in mortal pain. I could not stand it. I was suddenly seized with such an awful horror of the fire, that I turned and ran, feeling so thankful I was not in it. As I got into the street, I stumbled over something. It was a large bird—a parrot, and at first I thought it was Bella. Then I remembered hearing Jack say that the Italian had a parrot. It was not dead, but seemed stupid with the smoke. I seized it in my mouth, and ran and laid it at Mr. Morris' feet. He wrapped it in his handkerchief, and laid it beside him.

I sat and trembled, and did not leave him again. I shall never forget that dreadful night. It seemed as if we were there for hours, but in reality it was only a short time. The hotel soon got to be all red flames, and there was very little smoke. The inside of the building had burned away, and nothing more could be taken out. The firemen and all the people drew back, and there was no noise. Everybody stood gazing silently at the flames. A man stepped quietly up to Mr. Morris, and looking at him, I saw that it was Mr. Montague. He was usually a well-dressed man, with a kind face, and a head of thick, grayish-brown hair. Now his face was black and grimy, his hair was burnt from the front of his head, and his clothes were half torn from his back.

Mr. Morris sprang up when he saw him, and said, "Where is your wife?"

The gentleman did not say a word, but pointed to the burning building.

"Impossible," cried Mr. Morris. "Is there no mistake? Your beautiful young wife, Montague? Can it be so?" Mr. Morris was trembling from head to foot.

"It is true," said Mr. Montague quietly. "Give me the boy." Charlie had fainted again, and his father took him in his arms, and turned away.

"Montague!" cried Mr. Morris, "my heart is sore for you. Can I do nothing?"

"No, thank you," said the gentleman without turning around; but there was more anguish in his voice than in Mr. Morris', and though I am only a dog, I knew that his heart was breaking.

CHAPTER XXXII

BILLY AND THE ITALIAN

MR. MORRIS stayed no longer. He followed Mr. Montague along the sidewalk a little way, and then exchanged a few hurried words with some men who were standing near, and hastened home through streets that seemed dark and dull after the splendor of the fire. Though it was still the middle of the night, Mrs. Morris was up and dressed and waiting for him. She opened the hall door with one hand and held a candle in the other. I felt frightened and miserable, and didn't want to leave Mr. Morris, so I crept in after him.

"Don't make a noise," said Mrs. Morris. "Laura and the boys are sleeping, and I thought it better not to wake them. It has been a terrible fire, hasn't it? Was it the hotel?" Mr. Morris threw himself into a chair and covered his face with his hands.

"Speak to me, William," said Mrs. Morris in a startled tone. "You are not hurt, are you?" and she put her candle on the table, and came and sat down beside him.

He dropped his hands from his face, and tears were running down his cheeks. "Ten lives lost," he said; "among them Mrs. Montague." His words ended in a sob.

Mrs. Morris looked horrified, and gave a little cry, "William, it can't be so!"

It seemed as if Mr. Morris could not sit still. He got up and walked to and fro on the floor. "It was an awful scene, Margaret. I never wish to look upon the like again. Do you remember how I protested against the building of that death-trap? Look at the wide, open spaces around it, and yet they persisted in running it up to the sky, without a single fire escape. God will require an account of those deaths at the hands of the men who put up that building. It is terrible—this disregard of human lives." He threw himself in a chair and buried his face in his hands.

"Where was Mrs. Montague? How did it happen? Was her husband saved, and Charlie?" said Mrs. Morris in a broken voice.

"Yes; Charlie and Mr. Montague are safe. Charlie will recover from it. Montague's life is done. You know his love for his wife. Oh! Margaret! when will men cease to be fools? What does the Lord think of them when they say, 'Am I my brother's keeper?' And the other poor creatures burned to death—their lives are as precious in His sight as Mrs. Montague's."

Mr. Morris looked so weak and ill that Mrs. Morris, like a sensible woman, questioned him no further, but made a fire and got him some hot tea. Then she urged him to lie down on the sofa,

T

and sat by him till daybreak, when she persuaded him to go to bed. I followed her about, and kept touching her dress with my nose. It seemed so good to me to have this pleasant home after all the misery I had seen that night. Once she stopped and took my head between her hands. "Dear old Joe," she said tearfully, "this is a suffering world. It's well there's a better one beyond it."

In the morning the boys went down-town before breakfast and learned all about the fire. It had started in the top story of the hotel, in the room of some fast young men, who were sitting up late playing cards. They had smuggled wine into their room and had been drinking till they were stupid. One of them upset the lamp, and when the flames began to spread so that they could not extinguish them, instead of rousing some one near-by, they rushed down-stairs to get some one there to come up and help them put out the fire. When they returned with some of the hotel people, they found that the flames had spread from their room, which was in an "L" at the back of the house, to the front part, where Mrs. Montague's room was, and where the housemaids belonging to the hotel slept. By this time Mr. Montague had rushed up-stairs; but he found the passageway to his wife's room so full of flames and smoke, that, though he tried again and again to force his way through, he could not. He disappeared for a time, then he came to Mr. Morris and got his boy, and took him to some rooms over his bank, and shut himself up with him.

For some days he would let no one in; then he came out with the look of an old man on his face, and his hair as white as snow, and went out to his beautiful house on the outskirts of the town.

Nearly all the horses belonging to the hotel were burned. A few were rescued by having blankets put over their heads, but most of them were so terrified that they would not stir.

The Morris boys said that they found the old Italian sitting on an empty box, looking at the smoking ruins of the hotel. His head was hanging on his breast, and his eyes were full of tears. His ponies were burned up, he said, and the gander, and the monkeys, and the goats, and his wonderful performing dogs. He had only his birds left, and he was a ruined man. He had toiled all his life to get his troupe of trained animals together, and now they were swept from him. It was cruel and wicked, and he wished he could die. The canaries, and pigeons, and doves the hotel people had allowed him to take to his room, and they were safe. The parrot was lost— an educated parrot that could answer forty questions, and among other things, could take a watch and tell the time of day.

Jack Morris told him they had it safe at home, and that it was very much alive, quarreling furiously with his parrot Bella. The old man's face brightened at this, and then Jack and Carl, finding that he had had no breakfast, went off to a restaurant near-by, and got him some steak and coffee. The Italian was very grateful, and as he ate, Jack said the tears ran into his coffee-cup. He told them how much he loved his animals, and how it " made ze heart bitter to hear zem crying to him to deliver zem from ze raging fire."

The boys came home, and got their breakfast and went to school. Miss Laura did not go out. She sat all day with a very quiet, pained face. She could neither read nor sew, and Mr. and Mrs. Morris were just as unsettled. They talked about the fire in low tones, and I could see that they felt more sad about Mrs. Montague's death than if she had died in an ordinary way. Her dear little canary, Barry, died with her. She would never be separated from him, and he had been taken up to the top of the hotel with her. He probably died an easier death than his poor mistress. Charlie's dog escaped, but was so frightened that he ran to their house, outside the town.

At tea-time, Mr. Morris went down-town to see that the Italian got a comfortable place for the night. When he came back, he said he had found out that he was by no means so old a man as he looked, and that he had talked to him about raising a sum of money for him, till he had become quite cheerful, and said that if Mr. Morris would do that, he would try to gather another troupe of animals together and train them.

" Now, what can we do for this Italian? " asked

Mrs. Morris. "We can't give him much money, but we might let him have one or two of our pets. There's Billy, he's a bright little dog, and not two years old yet. He could teach him anything."

There was a blank silence among the Morris children. Billy was such a gentle, lovable little dog, that he was a favorite with every one in the house. "I suppose we ought to do it," said Miss Laura, at last, "but how can we give him up?"

There was a good deal of discussion, but the end of it was that Billy was given to the Italian. He came up to get him, and was very grateful, and made a great many bows, holding his hat in his hand. Billy took to him at once, and the Italian spoke so kindly to him that we knew he would have a good master. Mr. Morris got quite a large sum of money for the man, and when he handed it to him, the poor fellow was so pleased that he kissed his hand, and promised to send frequent word as to Billy's progress and welfare.

CHAPTER XXXIII

DANDY, THE TRAMP

BOUT a week after Billy left us, the Morris family, much to its surprise, became the owner of a new dog.

He walked into the house one cold, wintry afternoon, and lay calmly down by the fire. He was a brindled bull-terrier, and he had on a silver-plated collar, with "Dandy" engraved on it. He lay all the evening by the fire, and when any of the family spoke to him, he wagged his tail, and looked pleased. I growled a little at him at first, but he never cared a bit, and just dozed off to sleep, so I soon stopped.

He was such a well-bred dog, that the Morrises were afraid some one had lost him. They made some inquiries the next day, and found that he belonged to a New York gentleman who had come to Fairport in the summer in a yacht. This dog did not like the yacht. He came ashore in a boat whenever he got a chance, and if he could not come in a boat, he would swim. He was a tramp, his master said, and he wouldn't stay long in any place. The Morrises were so amused with his impudence that they did not send him away, but said every day, "He will be gone tomorrow."

294

However, Mr. Dandy had gotten into comfortable quarters, and he had no intention of changing them, for a while at least. Then he was very handsome, and had such a pleasant way with him that the family could not help liking him. I never cared for him. He fawned on the Morrises, and pretended he loved them, and afterward turned around and laughed and sneered at them in a way that made me very angry. I used to lecture him sometimes, and growl about him to Jim, but Jim always said: "Let him alone. You can't do him any good. He was born bad. His mother wasn't good. He tells me that she had a bad name among all the dogs in her neighborhood. She was a thief and a runaway." Though he provoked me so often, yet I could not help laughing at some of his stories, they were so funny.

We were lying out in the sun, on the platform at the back of the house one day, and he had been more than usually provoking, so I got up to leave him. He put himself in my way, however, and said coaxingly: "Don't be cross, old fellow. I'll tell you some stories to amuse you. What shall they be about?"

"I think the story of your life would be about as interesting as anything you could make up," I said dryly.

"All right, fact or fiction, whichever you like. Here are some facts, plain and unvarnished. Born and bred in New York. Swell stable. Swell coachman. Swell master. Jeweled fingers of ladies poking at me, first thing I remember. First painful experience—sent to vet. to have ears cut."

"What's a vet.?" I said.

"A veterinary—animal doctor. Vet. didn't cut ears enough. Master sent me back. Cut ears again. Summertime, and flies bad. Ears got sore and festered, and flies very attentive. Coachman set little boy to brush flies off, but he'd run out in yard and leave me. Flies awful. Thought they'd eat me up, or else I'd shake out brains trying to get rid of them. Mother should have stayed home and licked my ears, but was cruising about neighborhood. Finally coachman put me in dark place, powdered ears, and they got well."

"Why didn't they cut your tail too?" I said, looking at his long, slim tail, which was like a sewer rat's.

"'Twasn't the fashion, Mr. Wayback; a bull-terrier's ears are clipped to keep them from getting torn while fighting."

"You're not a fighting dog," I said.

"Not I. Too much trouble. I believe in taking things easy."

"I should think you did," I said scornfully. "You never put yourself out for any one, I notice; but speaking of cropping ears, what do you think of it?"

"Well," he said, with a sly glance at my head, "it isn't a pleasant operation; but one might as well be out of the world as out of fashion. I don't care, now my ears are done."

"But," I said, "think of the poor dogs that will come after you."

"What difference does that make to me?" he said. "I'll be dead and out of the way. Men can cut off their ears, and tails, and legs too, if they want to."

"Dandy," I said angrily, "you're the most selfish dog that I ever saw."

"Don't excite yourself," he said coolly. "Let me get on with my story. When I was a few months old, I began to find the stable-yard narrow and wondered what there was outside of it. I discovered a hole in the garden wall, and used to sneak out at nights. Oh, what fun it was. I got to know a lot of street dogs, and we had gay times, barking under people's windows and making them mad, and getting into back-yards and chasing cats. We used to kill a cat nearly every night. Policemen would chase us, and we would run and run till the water just dripped off our tongues, and we hadn't a bit of breath left. Then I'd go home and sleep all day, and go out again the next night. When I was about a year old, I began to stay out days as well as nights. They couldn't keep me home. Then I ran away for three months. I got with an old lady on Fifth Avenue, who was very fond of dogs. She had four white poodles, and her servants used to wash them, and tie up their hair with blue ribbons, and she used to take them for drives in her phaeton in the park, and they wore gold and silver collars. The biggest poodle wore a ruby in his collar worth five hundred dollars. I went driving too, and sometimes we met my master. He often smiled, and shook his head at me. I heard him tell his coachman one day that I was a little rogue, and he was to let me come and go as I liked."

"If they had whipped you soundly," I said, "it might have made a good dog of you."

"I'm good enough now," said Dandy airily. "The young ladies who drove with my master, used to say that it was priggish and tiresome to be too good. To go on with my story: I stayed with Mrs. Judge Tibbett till I got sick of her fussy ways. She made a simpleton of herself over those poodles. Each one had a high chair at the table and a plate, and they always sat in these chairs and had meals with her, and the servants all called them Master Bijou and Master Tot, and Miss Tiny and Miss Fluff. One day they tried to make me sit in a chair, and I got cross and bit Mrs. Tibbett, and she beat me cruelly, and her servants stoned me away from the house."

"Speaking about fools, Dandy," I said, "if it is polite to call a lady one, I should say that that lady was one. Dogs shouldn't be put out of their place. Why didn't she have some poor children at her table, and in her carriage, and let the dogs run behind?"

"Easy to see you don't know New York," said Dandy with a laugh. "Poor children don't live with rich old ladies. Mrs. Tibbett hated children anyway. Then dogs like poodles would get lost in the mud, or killed in the crowd if they ran behind a carriage. Only knowing dogs like me can make their way about."

I rather doubted this speech, but I said nothing, and he went on patronizingly: "However, Joe, thou hast reason, as the French say. Mrs. Judge Tibbett didn't give her dogs exercise enough. Their claws were as long as Chinamen's nails, and the hair grew over their pads, and they had red eyes and were always sick, and she had to dose them with medicine, and call them her poor, little, 'weeny-teeny, sicky-wicky doggies.' Bah! I got disgusted with her.

"When I left her, I ran away to her niece's, Miss Ball's. She was a sensible young lady, and she used to scold her aunt for the way in which she brought up her dogs. She was almost too sensible, for her pug and I were rubbed and scrubbed within an inch of our lives, and had to go for such long walks that I got thoroughly sick of them. A woman whom the servants called Trotsey, came every morning, and took the pug and me by our chains, and sometimes another dog or two, and took us for long tramps in quiet streets. That was Trotsey's business, to walk dogs, and Miss Ball got a great many fashionable young ladies who could not exercise their dogs, to let Trotsey have them, and they said that it made a great difference in the health and appearance of their pets. Trotsey got fifteen cents an hour for a dog.

Goodness, what appetites those walks gave us, and didn't we make the dog-biscuits disappear? But it was a slow life at Miss Ball's. We saw her for only a little while every day. She slept till noon. After lunch she played with us in the greenhouse, then she was off driving or visiting, and in the evening she always had company, or went to a dance, or to the theater. I soon made up my mind that I'd run away. I jumped out of a window one fine morning, and ran home. I stayed there for a long time. My mother had been run over by a cart and killed, and I wasn't sorry. My master never bothered his head about me, and I could do as I liked.

"One day when I was having a walk, and meeting a lot of dogs that I knew, a little boy came behind me, and before I could tell what he was doing, he had snatched me up, and was running off with me. I couldn't bite him, for he had stuffed some of his rags in my mouth. He took me to a tenement-house, in a part of the city that I had never been in before. He belonged to a very poor family. My word, weren't they badly off—six children, and a mother and father, all living in two tiny rooms. Scarcely a bit of meat did I smell while I was there. I hated their bread and molasses, and the place smelled so badly that I thought I should choke.

"They kept me shut up in their dirty rooms for several days; and the brat of a boy that caught me, slept with his arm around me at night. The weather was hot and sometimes we couldn't sleep, and they had to go up on the roof. After a while, they chained me up in a filthy yard at the back of the house, and there I thought I should go mad. I would have liked to bite them all to death, if I had dared. It's awful to be chained, especially for a dog like me that loves his freedom. The flies worried me, and the noises distracted me, and my flesh would fairly creep from getting no exercise. I was there nearly a month, while they were waiting for a reward to be offered. But none came; and one day, the boy's father, who was a street pedlar, took me by my chain and led me about the streets till he sold me. A gentleman got me for his little boy, but I didn't like the look of him, so I sprang up and bit his hand, and he dropped the chain, and I dodged boys and policemen, and finally reached home more dead than alive, and looking like a skeleton. I had a good time for several weeks, and then I began to get restless and was off again. But I'm getting tired, I want to go to sleep."

"You're not very polite," I said, "to offer to tell a story, and then go to sleep before you finish it."

"Look out for number one, my boy," said Dandy with a yawn; "for if you don't no one else will," and he shut his eyes and was fast asleep in a few minutes.

I sat and looked at him. What a handsome, good-natured, worthless dog he was. A few days later, he told me the rest of his history. After a great many wanderings, he happened home one day just as his master's yacht was going to sail, and they chained him up till they went on board, so that he could be an amusement on the passage to Fairport.

It was in November that Dandy came to us, and he stayed all winter. He made fun of the Morrises all the time, and said they had a dull, poky old house, and he stayed only because Miss Laura was nursing him. He had a little sore on his back that she soon found out was mange. Her father said it was a bad disease for dogs to have, and Dandy had better be shot; but she begged so hard for his life, and said she would cure him in a few weeks, that she was allowed to keep him. Dandy wasn't capable of getting really angry, but he was as disturbed about having this disease as he could be about anything. He said that he had got it from a little, mangy dog that he had played with a few weeks before. He was with the dog only a little while, and didn't think he would take it, but it seemed he knew what an easy thing it was to catch.

Until he got well he was separated from us. Miss Laura kept him up in the loft with the rabbits, where we could not go; and the boys ran him around the garden for exercise. She tried all kinds of cures for him, and I heard her say that though it was a skin disease, his blood must be purified. She gave him some of the pills that she made out of sulphur and butter for Jim, and Billy, and me, to keep our coats silky and smooth. When they didn't cure him, she gave him a few drops of arsenic every day and washed the sore, and indeed his whole body, with tobacco water or carbolic soap. It was the tobacco water that cured him.

Miss Laura always put on gloves when she went near him, and used a brush to wash him, for if a person takes mange from a dog, they may lose their hair and their eyelashes. But if they are careful, no harm comes from nursing a mangy dog, and I have never known of any one taking the disease.

After a time, Dandy's sore healed, and he was set free. He was right glad he said, for he had got heartily sick of the rabbits. He used to bark at them and make them angry, and they would run around the loft, stamping their hind feet at him, in their funny way. I think they disliked him as much as he disliked them. Jim and I did not get the mange. Dandy was not a strong dog, and I think his irregular way of living made him take diseases readily. He would stuff himself when he was hungry, and he always wanted rich food. If he couldn't get what he wanted at the Morrises', he went out and stole, or visited the dumps at the back of the town.

When he did get ill, he was more stupid about doctoring himself than any dog that I have ever seen. He never seemed to know when to eat grass, or herbs, or a little earth, that would have kept him in good condition. A dog should never be without grass. When Dandy got ill, he just suffered till he got well again, and never tried to cure himself. Some dogs even know enough to amputate their limbs. Jim told me a very interesting story of a dog the Morrises once had, called Gyp, whose leg became paralyzed by a kick from a horse. He knew the leg was dead, and gnawed it off nearly to the shoulder, and though he was very ill for a time, yet he got well.

To return to Dandy. I knew he was only waiting for the arrival of spring to leave us, and I was not sorry. The first fine day he was off, and during the rest of the spring and summer we occasionally met him running about the town with a set of fast dogs. One day I stopped and asked him how he contented himself in such a quiet place as Fairport, and he said he was dying to get back to New York, and was hoping that his master's yacht would come and take him away.

Poor Dandy never left Fairport. After all, he was not a really wicked dog. There was nothing vicious about him, and I hate to speak of his end. His master's yacht did not come, and soon the summer was over, and the winter was coming, and no one wanted Dandy, for he had such a bad name. He got hungry and cold, and one day sprang upon a little girl to take away a piece of bread and butter that she was eating. He did not see the large house-dog on the door-sill, and before he could get away the dog had seized him and bitten and shaken him till he was nearly dead. When the dog threw him aside, he crawled back to us, and Miss Laura bandaged his wounds, and made him a bed in the stable.

One Sunday morning, she washed and fed him very tenderly, for she knew he could not live much longer. He was so weak that he could scarcely eat the food that she put in his mouth, so she let him lick some milk from her finger. As she was going to church, I could not go with her, but I ran down the lane and watched her out of sight. When I came back, Dandy was gone. I looked till I found him. He had crawled into the darkest corner of the stable to die, and though he was suffering very much, he never uttered a sound. I sat by him, and thought of his master in New York. If he had brought Dandy up properly he might not now be here in his silent death-agony. A young pup should be trained just as a child is, and punished when he goes wrong. Dandy began badly, and not being checked in his evil ways had come to this. Poor Dandy! Poor, handsome dog of a rich master! He opened his dull eyes, gave me one last glance, then, with a convulsive shudder, his torn limbs were still. He would never suffer any more.

When Miss Laura came home, she cried bitterly to know that he was dead. The boys took him away from her, and made him a grave in the corner of the garden.

U

CHAPTER XXXIV

BLACK JIM

 FEW months after Dandy died we had a new pet—this one, the most amusing and provoking creature that had entered the family, and the one that excited most interest in the town and among our neighbors.

The Morris boys were walking in the pinewood near Fairport one day, and I was trotting ahead of them, when I smelt something alive.

I sniffed about, and there crouching on a heap of pine needles was a featherless young crow.

I barked, and the boys hurried to pick up the poor creature. There were no old crows near-by, so they took it home with them.

It became Jack's pet, and soon it got old enough to follow him about. Jack fed him frogs, mice, worms, beef, and bread and milk, and soon the ugly young bird became a glossy creature with strong wings, a heavy beak, and a voice that used to make me jump when he stole up behind me as I lay sleeping in the sun.

"Our painful pleasure," Miss Laura used to call him, for though she loved him almost as much as her brothers did, he was a great worry to her.

He began by teasing the creatures about the place, especially with regard to their food, until most of them got to understand him so well that they would run if they saw him coming.

The guinea-pig, Jeff, and the rabbits would stick their heads out of the stable-door, and if Black Jim—we had to call him this to distinguish him from Jim the dog—was in the garden, they would go back again. The tame rat always ran to his friend Bella the parrot, for Black Jim was afraid of her saucy tongue.

The pigeons and Willie's bantams hated him, for when they were all out in the garden feeding, he would swoop down among them, and send the pigeons flying and the bantams running with their legs sticking straight out behind them.

Then, with solemn crow satisfaction, he would eat their grain, taking on a pretended air of penitence when Miss Laura scolded him.

One day he played a shabby trick on Mary the cook. She had bought a fine steak, and it lay on a plate in the pantry window.

I saw Black Jim eyeing it from a tree, but before I really knew what was passing through his crow mind, he had swooped down, and had taken it up to the top of the stable.

Mary came into the pantry just in time to see it going, and her gestures and cries were so comical, as she ran out and looked up at Black Jim tearing the family dinner to pieces, that Miss Laura and the boys who had rushed to the windows, just shrieked with laughter.

Sometimes they did not laugh at his tricks. I

saw him one day sneak up to Malta as she sat over her dinner out in the yard. You know cats eat slowly, and the way she mouthed her food, turning her head first on one side and then on the other, seemed to prove to the crow that she had something especially nice.

He made a quick run, nipped her by the tail, bracing himself on his sturdy legs, the way I had seen the Morrises' sailor-boy friend, Henry Smith, brace himself on his ship when he was hauling in a rope.

Malta began spitting and growling, and just as I was rushing to her rescue, she foolishly did what Black Jim wanted her to do—turned on him. He sprang forward, seized a lot of food from the plate and flew off with it.

He got a severe scolding for this from Miss Laura, but he did not care He flew away from her, and went into the house to Mr. Morris' study. He loved that room—there were so many pencils and pens about, and it was such fun to scatter the ink in the big ink-bottle.

I heard Mr. Morris say one day to Miss Laura: "That crow is out of his sphere. Could you not persuade him to join his wild kindred in the woods?"

"He is Jack's pet," she replied, "and though he has taken him to the woods, he always comes back."

"If Jack loves him we must put up with him," said Mr. Morris, and he patiently put all the small articles about the room into drawers.

About the best fun Black Jim had was with the table when it was laid for a meal. He often carried away spoons, knives, forks, and napkin-rings, and hid them under a piece of old carpet in the garden, where Jim the dog and I found them and carried them back to the house.

One day he got a great fright. He was carrying the table-bell in his beak when it rang.

He dropped it as if it had been red-hot, and flying to the top of the stable, said "Caw! Caw!" a great many times.

He not only persecuted Mr. Morris in his study, but in his pulpit. He had a very sociable disposition, and when Sunday came, he wanted to go to church.

As soon as he could fly, he started down the street after the family. I barked warningly, but a crow is wilful, and won't mind any one. He was cunning enough to follow the Morrises at some distance, and when they came home, I heard them talking about his actions.

Just after they were all nicely seated in church, and Mr. Morris was giving out a hymn, the family, to their dismay, heard a friendly "Caw!" and looking up saw Black Jim seated in one of the open windows.

As soon as he discovered their pew he flew to it, as if to say, "How glad you must be to see me!"

They were not glad, and made frantic efforts to catch him, whereupon he scolded them in his harsh voice, flew to Mr. Morris in the pulpit, and perched on his shoulder with an air of, " Here, at least, I shall be welcome."

Mr. Morris seeing his congregation in fits of suppressed laughter, had hard work to keep his composure. Putting his hand in his pocket, he offered Black Jim his gold pencil-case.

Thrown off his guard, the mischievous bird seized it with a grateful " Caw! " and Mr. Morris quickly put his hands over his wings and beckoned to Jack to come and get him.

After that Black Jim was locked up every Sunday morning for a time, but he got so cunning that soon he would not allow himself to be caught. Then Jack used to capture him Saturday evening, until finally, Black Jim became so knowing that he would not let Jack come near him any day toward the end of the week.

Mr. Morris had to put screens in the church windows at his own expense, but when the congregation heard of it, they refunded the money.

Black Jim by this time—we had had him nearly a year—had begun to plague the whole town, but he was so clever that everybody but a few cranky persons forgave him. He did such funny things that he became quite a celebrity, and it is wonderful what human beings will put up with from celebrities.

The housekeepers got to dread Mondays, for he visited the clothes-lines far and near, and stealing the pins for his secret hoard, he let the different washes fly to the four winds of heaven.

One morning he did a very naughty thing, and yet great good came of it. Near the Morrises lived an old gentleman called Daniels who was a passionate lover of flowers. Black Jim often visited him, and would walk around his flower-beds and snip off blossoms here and there.

One would think that Mr. Daniels would hate him, but he did not. He said that birds do good service to man in destroying insect pests, and if Black Jim wished to break off a few flowers, he might. He had plenty, and it would not hurt the plants to be pruned.

I used to call on the old man too, for most dogs love to visit their neighbors, but he never talked to me about his flowers, as he did to Black Jim. Perhaps he thought dogs did not care for them, but I could have assured him that dogs love strong-smelling things.

Well, one day he pointed to a large, beautiful flower in his conservatory, and said that it was a night-blooming cereus, and had come out a few hours earlier. This was early in the morning. He seemed very proud of it, and when he left us to speak to a man, I watched Black Jim anxiously.

He had his head on one side, and he was looking at this large beautiful flower. Unfortunately the conservatory door was open, and before I could utter one bark, he had flown in, broken off the flower, and was carrying it off in his big beak.

I could have bitten him, I was so angry and disturbed about the honor of the family. However,

I was powerless. I can keep cats, and dogs, and chickens in order, but birds are beyond me.

When Mr. Daniels came back, he did not notice that his lovely blossom was gone, and I lay down on a heap of weeds and mourned about the sad conduct of Black Jim.

Then a very strange thing happened. While I lay on the weeds, and Mr. Daniels hoed about some plants, the garden gate opened, and another old man came hurrying up to Mr. Daniels.

Both his hands were stretched out. One held the flower that Black Jim had stolen, the other grasped Mr. Daniels' arm.

"Edward," he said in a choked voice, "will you forgive me?"

Mr. Daniels dropped his hoe, and stared at him in amazement. The other old man extended the flower. "I know how you prize this, Edward— how you have waited for its blossoming—and to bestow on me your choicest bloom—it was noble, considering how I have used you."

Mr. Daniels stared in through the open conservatory door. His flower certainly was missing, but I saw that he could not imagine how it had got into the other old man's hand. However, he was pretty wise, and said nothing, but just shook hands in silence. Then they both acted as if they were ashamed of their emotion, and fell to talking of gardening matters.

I watched them for a while, then I ran home. There was a mystery here I could not fathom, but the explanation came. Before night, a pretty story was flying around town to the effect that a long-drawn-out quarrel between Mr. Daniels and his next door neighbor, Mr. Juniper, had been settled in a delightful way by Mr. Daniels, who had quietly stolen in, and laid on his friend's table the most highly prized flower in his possession.

Mr. Daniels said nothing, and I said nothing, and the rascal Black Jim said nothing, but after a time the true version of the story leaked out. I think some one had seen the crow on his way through the window of Mr. Juniper's house with the flower in his beak.

Anyway it was a great feather in Black Jim's cap, and after that no matter what mischief he did, every one forgave him, for had he not reconciled these two old enemies?

I saw him do a funny thing one day at a baseball game. A man who had some pears in his pocket reached one up to a chubby urchin who sat on the fence above him.

The boy was so young that he could not talk plainly, but he knew what was good to eat, for after one bite he half shut his eyes and said, " It am small, but it am 'lishus."

Black Jim, who attended all the ball games, heard him, and in one swoop he took that " 'lishus " pear from the poor child.

The little urchin's astonishment was so ludicrous, that everybody near burst into roars of laughter, and the man gave him another pear.

Everybody knew Black Jim, and nearly everybody petted him. If Mrs. Morris or Miss Laura went down-town, he often followed them, and when they went into a store he perched near-by, cawing for them to come out.

He never allowed any one to touch him but members of the family. He would let them catch him, and shake him, or tickle him. Often when they were playing with him he would turn on his back, defending himself with his claws and beak, and having as many tricks as a kitten.

He used to go and catch mice for Mrs. Morris' grocer, always getting some dainty in return. The butcher gave him choice morsels of meat, but the dressmaker never liked to see him, for he stole her thimbles and spools.

Nothing frightened him. Once he saw a big dog gnawing a bone. He flew right in his face. I ran up to distract the dog's attention, but there was no need of my interference, for the dog stood, muzzle in air, gazing foolishly at his bone sailing off over the housetops.

We got Black Jim in the spring, and before we had had him a year he became restless. After taking his daily bath, for which he would fairly yell, if Jack forgot to give it to him, he used to fly up to the stable roof, dress his feathers, and stare up into the sky.

One day he espied some wild crows passing overhead, and with a glad " Caw!" he flew up and joined them.

When night came he did not return, and I felt badly, for Jack was seeking his pet all over the neighborhood.

Animals and birds understand each other, but Jack was a human being, and I could not tell him that every drop of wild blood in Jim was calling out for his brother and sister crows.

Jack went to bed in great anxiety, for he feared that some mishap had befallen his pet.

We did not see him for a whole week. Then one day as Jack was standing in the garden, there was a rush of wings, and Jim was on his shoulder, pinching his ear and thrusting his black beak into his young master's face, while he chattered about the joys of wild life.

I never saw Jack so pleased. He could not bear to part from his pet, and all day long he kept him with him, caressing him, and giving him choice bits of food.

Black Jim had a regular carnival of mischief on that visit. I remember for one thing, he called at all his down-town haunts, and court being in session, even got into the judge's private office through an open window.

He upset the judge's inkstand over some valuable legal documents, and flew off with his gold eyeglasses that were never seen again.

Then he disappeared once more. The first crow soaring overhead attracted him, and we did not see him for weeks.

On his second return he was more shy, and would

not allow Jack to catch him. On his third, he sat on the stable roof and talked crow talk very earnestly.

There were several other returns, but he never again flew down into the yard, and finally he became weaned away from us and never came again.

Sometimes the Morrises used to think he was dead, but I knew better. Jim was alive and well, and had a family of his own in the pinewood. He remembered the Morrises, and if any of the family went into the wood, he cawed affectionately, though he did not go near them.

CHAPTER XXXV

THE END OF MY STORY

I HAVE now come to the last chapter of my story. I thought when I began to write, that I would put down the events of each year of my life, but I fear that would make my story too long, and neither Miss Laura nor any boys and girls would care to read it. So I will stop just here, though I would gladly go on, for I have enjoyed so much talking over old times, that I am very sorry to leave off.

Every year I have been at the Morrises' something pleasant has happened to me, but I cannot put all these things down, nor can I tell how Miss Laura and the boys grew and changed, year by year, till now they are quite grown up. I shall just bring my tale down to the present time, and then I shall stop talking, and go lie down in my basket, for I am an old dog now, and get tired very easily.

I was a year old when I went to the Morris family, and I have been with them for twelve years. I am not living in the same house with Mr. and Mrs. Morris now, but I am with my dear Miss Laura, who is Miss Laura no longer, but Mrs. Gray. She married Mr. Harry four years ago, and

317

lives with him and Mr. and Mrs. Wood, on Dingley Farm. Mr. and Mrs. Morris live in a cottage
near-by. Mr. Morris is not very strong, and can
preach no longer. The boys are all scattered.
Jack married pretty Miss Bessie Drury, and lives
on a large farm near here. Miss Bessie says that
she hates to be a farmer's wife, but she always
looks very happy and contented, so I think that
she must be mistaken. Carl is a merchant in New
York, Ned is a clerk in a bank, and Willie is
studying at a place called Harvard. He says that
after he finishes his studies, he is going to live
with his father and mother.

Mr. and Mrs. Morris' old friends often come to
see them. Mrs. Drury passes through Riverdale
every summer on her way to Newport, and Mr.
Montague and Charlie come every other summer.
Charlie always brings with him his old dog Brisk,
who is getting feeble like myself. We lie on the
veranda in the sunshine, and listen to the Morris
family talking about old days, and sometimes it
makes us feel quite young again. In addition to
Brisk we have a Scotch collie. He is very handsome, and is a constant attendant of Miss Laura's.
We are great friends, he and I, but he can get
about much better than I can.

When the Morris boys are all here in the summer we have gay times. All through the winter
we look forward to their coming, for they make
the old farmhouse so lively. Mr. Maxwell never
misses a summer in coming to Riverdale. He has

such a following of dumb animals now, that he
says he can't move them any farther away from
Boston than this, and he doesn't know what he
will do with them, unless he sets up a menagerie.
He asked Miss Laura the other day if she thought
that the old Italian would take him into partner-
ship. He did not know what had happened to
poor Bellini, so Miss Laura told him.

A few years ago the Italian came to Riverdale
to exhibit his new stock of performing animals.
They were almost as good as the old ones, but he
had not quite so many as he had before. All the
Morris family and a great many of their friends
went to his performance, and Miss Laura said
afterward, that when cunning little Billy came on
the stage, and made his bow, and went through his
antics of jumping through hoops and catching
balls, she almost had hysterics. The Italian had
made a special pet of him, and treated him more
like a human being than a dog. Billy rather put
on airs when he came up to the farm to see us,
but he was such a dear little dog, in spite of being
almost spoiled by his master, that Jim and I could
not get angry with him. In a few days they went
away, and we heard nothing but good news from
them, till last winter. Then a letter came to Miss
Laura from a nurse in a New York hospital.
She said that the Italian was very near his end,
and he wanted her to write to Mrs. Gray to tell
her that he had sold all his animals but the little
dog that her family had so kindly given him. He

was sending him back to her, and with his last breath he would pray for heaven's blessing on the kind lady and her family that had befriended him when he was in trouble.

The next day Billy arrived, a thin white scarecrow of a dog. He was sick and unhappy, and would eat nothing, and started up at the slightest sound. He was listening for the Italian's footsteps, but he never came, and one day Mr. Harry looked up from his newspaper and said, "Laura, Bellini is dead." Miss Laura's eyes filled with tears, and Billy, who had jumped up when he heard his master's name, fell back again. He knew what they were talking about, and from that instant he ceased listening for footsteps, and lay quite still till he died. Miss Laura had him put in a little wooden box, and buried him in a corner of the garden, and when she is working among her flowers, she often speaks regretfully of him, and of poor Dandy, who lies in the garden at Fairport.

Bella the parrot lives with Mrs. Morris, and is as smart as ever. I have heard that parrots live to a very great age. Some of them even get to be a hundred years old. If that is the case, Bella will outlive all of us. She notices that I am getting blind and feeble, and when I go down to see Mrs. Morris, she calls out to me: "Keep a stiff upper lip, Beautiful Joe. Never say die, Beautiful Joe. Keep the game a-going, Beautiful Joe."

Mrs. Morris says that she doesn't know where Bella picks up her slang words. I think it is Mr.

Ned who teaches her, for when he comes home in the summer he often says with a sly twinkle in his eyes, "Come out into the garden, Bella," and he lies in a hammock under the trees, and Bella perches on a branch near him, and he talks to her by the hour. Anyway, it is in the autumn after he leaves Riverdale that Bella always shocks Mrs. Morris with her slang talk.

I am glad that I am to end my days in Riverdale. Fairport was a very nice place, but it was not open and free like this farm. I take a walk every morning that the sun shines. I go out among the horses and cows, and stop to watch the hens pecking at their food. This is a happy place, and I hope my dear Miss Laura will live to enjoy it many years after I am gone.

I have very few worries. The pigs bother me a little in the spring, by rooting up the bones that I bury in the fields in the fall, but that is a small matter, and I try not to mind it. I get a great many bones here, and I should be glad if I had some poor city dogs to help me eat them. I don't think bones are good for pigs.

Then there is Mr. Harry's tame squirrel out in one of the barns that teases me considerably. He knows that I can't chase him, now that my legs are so stiff with rheumatism, and he takes delight in showing me how spry he can be, darting around me and whisking his tail almost in my face, and trying to get me to run after him, so that he can laugh at me. I don't think that he is a

v

very thoughtful squirrel, but I try not to notice him.

The sailor-boy who gave Bella to the Morris children has grown to be a large, stout man, and is the first mate of a vessel. He sometimes comes here, and when he does, he always brings presents of foreign fruits and curiosities of different kinds to his old friends.

Malta the cat is still living, and is with Mrs. Morris. Davy the rat is gone, so is poor old Jim. He went away one day last summer, and no one ever knew what became of him. Mr. Morris searched everywhere for him, and offered a large reward to any one who would find him, but he never came back. I think that he felt he was going to die, and went into some out-of-the-way place. He remembered how badly Miss Laura felt when Dandy died, and he wanted to spare her the greater sorrow of his death. He was always such a thoughtful dog, and so anxious not to give trouble. I am more selfish. I could not go away from Miss Laura, even to die. When my last hour comes, I want to see her gentle face bending over me, and then I shall not mind how much I suffer.

She is just as tender-hearted as ever, but she tries not to feel too badly about the sorrow and suffering in the world, because she says that would weaken her, and she wants all her strength to try to put a stop to some of it. She does a great deal of good in Riverdale, and I do not think that there is any one in all the country around who is as much beloved as she is.

She has never forgotten the resolve she made some years ago, that she would do all she could to protect dumb creatures. Mr. Harry and Mr. Maxwell have helped her nobly. Mr. Maxwell's work is largely done in Boston, and Miss Laura and Mr. Harry have to do most of theirs by writing, for Riverdale has got to be a model village in respect of the treatment of all kinds of animals.

It is a model village not only in that respect, but in others. It has seemed as if all other improvements went hand in hand with the humane treatment of animals. Thoughtfulness toward lower creatures has made the people more and more thoughtful toward each other, and this little town is getting to have quite a name through the State for its good schools, good society, and good business and religious standing. Many people are moving into it, to educate their children. The Riverdale people are very particular about what sort of strangers come to live among them.

A man who came here two years ago and opened a shop, was seen kicking a small kitten out of his house. The next day a committee of Riverdale citizens waited on him and said they had had a great deal of trouble to root out cruelty from their village, and they didn't want any one to come there and introduce it again, and they thought he had better move on to some other place. The man was utterly astonished, and said he'd never

heard of such particular people. He had had no
thought of being cruel. He didn't think that the
kitten cared; but now when he turned the thing
over in his mind, he didn't suppose cats liked being
kicked about any more than he would like it himself, and he would promise to be kind to them
in future. He said too, that if they had no ob-
jection, he would stay on, for if the people there
treated dumb animals with such consideration, they
would certainly treat human beings better, and
he thought it would be a good place to bring up
his children. Of course they let him stay, and
he is now a man who is celebrated for his kindness
to every living thing; and he never refuses to help
Miss Laura when she goes to him for money to
carry out any of her humane schemes.

There is one most important saying of Miss
Laura's that comes out of her years of service
for dumb animals that I must put in before I close,
and it is this: She says that cruel and vicious
owners of animals should be punished; but to
merely thoughtless people one should say simply:
" Be kind. Make a study of your animals' wants,
and see that they are satisfied. You should know
better than any one else, how to treat your animal,
for you are with it all the time, and know its
disposition, and just how much work it can stand,
and how much rest and food it needs, and just
how it is different from every other animal. If
it is sick or unhappy, you are the one to take care
of it; for nearly every animal loves its own master.

better than a stranger, and will get well more quickly under his care."

Miss Laura says that if men and women are kind in every respect to their dumb servants, they will be astonished to find how much happiness they will bring into their lives, and how faithful and grateful their animals will be to them.

Now I must really close my story. Good-by to the boys and girls who may read it; and if it is not wrong for a dog to say it, I should like to add, "God bless you all." If in my feeble way I have been able to impress you with the fact that dogs and many other animals love their masters and mistresses, and live only to please them, my little story will not have been written in vain. My last words are: "Boys and girls, be kind to dumb animals, not only because you will lose nothing by it, but because you ought to; for they were placed on the earth by the same Kind Hand that made all living creatures."